Porridge
The inside story

Paul Ableman is a novelist, playwright and critic and lives in London with his second wife, Sheila. He has a son by his first marriage. Amongst his novels are: *I Hear Voices*, *Vac* and most recently *Tornado Pratt*. He reviews regularly for the *Spectator* and *Books and Bookmen*. He has also written television and radio plays and short stories.

Dick Clement and Ian La Frenais have been collaborators since their first television series, *The Likely Lads*. They now live in California where, through their own production company, Witzend, they write, produce and direct for television, the cinema and theatre.

Paul Ableman
Porridge

The inside story

based on the screenplay by
Dick Clement and Ian La Frenais

Pan Original
Pan Books London and Sydney

A Witzend publication for Pan Books
First published 1979 by Pan Books Ltd,
Cavaye Place, London SW10 9PG
© Witzend Productions Ltd 1979
ISBN 0 330 25923 7
Printed and bound in Great Britain by
Richard Clay (The Chaucer Press) Ltd, Bungay, Suffolk

to Sheila

1 New arrivals

Hello. It's me, Norman Stanley Fletcher. Remember me? I'm the bloke with the funny diet. I only eat porridge. 'Course, that's not true. Anyone who knows about the humane reforms that have transformed the British prison service in recent years will laugh like a cockroach at the notion that the cuisine we now enjoy in those palaces of recreation and culture known as Her Majesty's Penal Correction Establishments, or something like that, is limited. And limited to porridge? 'Course not. That went out with the treadmills. Now, we get very nutritive goo of different colours that comes out of big hygienic drums. And, just to make it more enjoyable, the Home Office has devised a list of attractive names for these tasty comestibles. Some of it is called MEAT. Other offerings are called FRUIT or VEGETABLES. It all tastes the same, except when Lennie burns it or adds salt instead of sugar, but it's packed with vitamins and builds up our muscles for the tread— no, of course, they went out, didn't they?

Where was I? Where indeed? Where have I been most of my life? In the nick. Rubbish! That's not true. It can't be true. Otherwise, how could I have fathered three lovely kids and turned over half the small shops in North London? I must have spent some time on the outside. It just *seems* that I've spent my whole life doing bird.

Lovely expression, that, don't you think? Doing bird – winging over hill or dale, free as the air. Oh, for the wings of a condor – big South American bird, that is, that flies sideways in case it's being tailed by the law. If I had the wings of a condor, over these prison walls I would fly! Which prison walls? The ones that are presently incarcerating me and six hundred other poor sods on the bleak Cumberland moors. Right in one. I refer to the grim, grey, granite walls of Slade Prison.

Still, it won't be long now. I can see it, in front of me as I write, my home-made calendar on which I tick off the days. Very popular hobby that is, in the nick, ticking off the days. Takes a lot of practice to get it right. In the first place, you have to be literate, which eliminates a fair proportion of lags at a blow. You should see Bunny Warren trying to tick off the days.

'Is that a six, Fletch?' he asks me pleadingly, his unsharpened pencil poised at the crude calendar I have prepared for him in return for quarter an ounce of snout.

'No, that's a four, Bunny, you dyslexic goon,' I correct him gently. 'This one's a six. It's a circle with a whisker on top.'

Bunny nods happily and poises his pencil but then the pathetic helpless look comes into his eyes again.

'Fletch, how do you write a tick?'

I knew a bloke in Parkhurst who ticked off the days two at a time and then had a nervous breakdown when he found he'd only done half his bird. Funny expression that – bird – don't you think? Must be Cockney rhyming slang. Bird on the rick – nick? Bird in the ale – gaol? Though, Gawd knows how the bird got into the ale. I'll ask a Cockney the next time I happen to meet one. Some poor nurk from Muswell Hill persecuted by biased judges and prejudiced juries. Someone just like me. Who might suggest that the reference is to a bird *cage*. That's us, unhappy winged creatures beating pathetically at the bars of our cage in our longing to escape into the great wide beautiful world out there.

Which brings me to the subject of this book. At least, I hope it's going to be a book. Something I've been considering doing ever since my first term. I mean, a lot of cons make quite a killing out of literature. They spend months planning a big job, pull it off, go into hiding for a month, get nabbed in the end, lose all the money to dishonest colleagues who squander it on fat living instead of investing it for them, serve seven years out of their twelve, come out, write a bleeding book about it and make more lolly than they nicked in the first place. Admittedly this usually happens with your class thieves, the ones that stop big expresses thundering through the night and extract fifty billion in used one-pound notes which they can't find a warehouse big enough to store it in, or the smooth operators who oil into Heathrow posing as government inspectors and calmly drive off with a pantechnicon loaded with high-grade bullion supposedly for laboratory analysis to see if it's made of painted pewter or something. That's really the kind of crime your reading public laps up, the big glamour crimes. I realize that few readers, browsing through your railway bookstall before embarking on a business trip to Glasgow, would be grabbed by the memoirs of a petty thief like me. I mean, rifling the money-box of the Hoxton Shoppers' and Mutual Aid Guild or breaking into a closed dry cleaners is not the kind of caper that keeps the fans on the edge of their seats.

Well, I have to admit it – I have never been in the TOP league. No one has ever seen Norman Stanley Fletcher with his hand-picked team of nine international felons boring his way with a laser into the impregnable foundations of the Japan and Arab Investment Trust. When a helicopter descends on a luxury liner two days out of Southampton and three laughing villains get out to relieve cruising millionnaires of all their worldly possessions, I have always been somewhere else, usually arguing with a constable that it was another they saw emerging from the back window of a terraced house in Highgate. So what I have to offer is not a pulse-racing account of life on the upper slopes of banditry. And yet, I do have a tale to tell. You see, there is one story connected with villainy that is even more unputdownable to your straight citizen than that of impossible crimes and unbelievable pickings. I refer, of course, to your first-hand, heart-stopping, suspense-packed account of a gaol-break.

But, I hear you object, only I don't hear you object because you are out there engulfing vast tankards of best bitter and I am alone in my dreary cell, but I can still imagine what you would object to if you was here peering over my shoulder which is the height of bad manners inside or outside. So just pull your nose back before I twist it off if you want me to go on.

Right, where was I? Oh, yes, now I remember, you was about to object that it's been done before. So it has, but does it ever fail to grip? I mean, the sudden perception that a bulge in the floor of one corner of the lavatory is really a cemented-over duct leading to a vent that connects with a conduit that runs parallel to an air-shaft that drops to a cellar which is adjacent to a disused cess-pit which adjoins an old torture chamber which is immediately underneath the inner-perimeter wall. Then you get the weeks of planning and recruiting a trustworthy team, followed by the months of back-breaking work which none of us would do on the outside for quadruple time and princely bonuses. You have to solve complicated problems like how to get out the spoil. This is finally achieved by scooping it out with paper cups and conveying it in the bowls of pipes to the recreation yard where some members of the team build a tasteful rockery. Then there's the making of ropes out of old jock-straps, the fashioning of grappling irons in the metalwork shop and so on. Finally, eighteen months after the bulge was spotted, and just a week before the ringleader is due for parole, the break is on. Five determined men slither through the bowels of the prison for seven hours, sometimes separated by no more than a shoe-sole from sneering guards, until they dash gloriously for freedom. One trips and sprains his ankle. Two fall off the wall. One gets as far as the canal and drowns. The fifth, who was due for parole, gets clean away and enjoys six months of freedom before he is spotted by a meter-reader and returned to nick with three years added to his sentence. Never fails to glue the eyeballs to the page, that kind of stuff. But our break – Lennie's and mine – was nothing like that. Then why am I wasting your precious time that could be spent nodding over 'Match of the Day' and gulping lager while your trouble and strife prepares the nosh? I'll tell you why. Because our break was unique in the annals of Slade Prison and perhaps in the whole history of the British penal service. Lennie and I broke *into* prison.

No, no, my mother did *not* come from Ireland. There was a reason for it, as you will find out and now that I've aroused your curiosity you will just have to hang about and find out what it was, won't you? You see, I'm counting on the sales from this masterpiece to keep the family in beans and beer when I get out, which won't be long now, because I am never, never, never – and that's straight up even if you have heard it all before, you sceptical nurk – never going to do no more porridge!

It all started— I like that. Very classy beginning to any book, don't you think?

It all started when three new arrivals arrived in Slade Nick. Now, of course, that's not uncommon. One of the things that gives prison life its special flavour, apart from the primitive sanitary arrangements, is the way your little community keeps changing. The same thing happens on the outside too, of course, but more slowly. There you have time to adjust. But in the nick, new cons are always arriving and those who've done their bird are leaving. It makes for very unsettling social relationships and I knew one long-server, in Maidstone it was, who was called Everard and who could hammer a nail into a plank with his forehead. Why did I say that? That's not what I meant to say. Now I remember – the relevant thing about Everard was that he always asked new arrivals how long they had to serve and if it was under eighteen months, he wouldn't pass the time with them. He said it wasn't worth forming a friendship with someone who was here today and gone tomorrow but he was a very obliging bloke and if any new arrival wanted to see him do it, he was prepared to hammer a nail into a plank with his forehead. He had a deep dimple in his forehead from years of hammering but it never seemed to bother him. Come to think of it, he was called Dimple Everard. But I must resume my thread.

My thread when I last left it was about three new arrivals that September. I was quite chuffed at the time because Christmas was getting near. Now Christmas in the nick is not such a heart-warming experience as it is on the outside. No childish voices are at the door singing carols – no, just the usual bawling of the screws which is like sound-effects for one of the Tarzan films. True, the fare is better than what you get the rest of the year and they give you a kind of congealed pink goo from a tin marked TURKEY and a gritty brown goo called CHRISTMAS PUDDING. In addition, the Governor sometimes smiles and mutters 'Merry Christmas' through clenched teeth. But these delights do not rival the glowing hearth, the piled-up presents and the joyous shouts of the little ones as the old lady waddles in with the flaming pudding which you get at home. Not by a long chalk. So why was I so chuffed at the approach of this particular Christmas? Because it was my last big landmark or should I say nick-mark before release. I was due to go out in a year and once Christmas was passed it was just a matter of sweating it out through the bleak winter months and then I would be practically on my way south to good old Muswell Hill and the bosom of my family.

So, like I said, there was nothing at the time about these three new arrivals – two cons and a screw – to make me sit up and take notice. But in view of subsequent events – I will describe to you exactly the scene when they arrived. Ah but, I hear you protest, in my imagination, of course – how do you, Norman Stanley Fletcher, know exactly what the scene was like when they arrived? I mean, was you there? No, I was not there, and I was not there when a lot of the things that I will write about in this book happened. But I know about them because I have made it my business to know about them. I have done what we authors call 'research', which means nosey-parkering about and asking everyone to fill me in. So now I know the complete facts surrounding the hair-raising events that led to The Great Break-In.

It started at a clapped-out old railway station situated on the barren moors. An antiquated three-coach train of the kind which is usually only seen in television serials set in the olden days pulled up and five men got out. Four of them were together and two of those four were very much together, in fact handcuffed together, although this circumstance was concealed from the curious gaze of the sheep who were grazing all about by a mac slung discreetly over their fetters. The other two men in the group were, of course, the escorting screws. One of these was Mr Barrowclough, Slade's favourite screw, who has a mild disposition and the appearance of a cow. The other was a hard young screw called Miller. Drawn up in the station yard was a dark, blue minibus with the words 'H.M. Prison Slade' stencilled on the side.

These four men started to move off the platform towards the minibus when they were approached by the only other passenger mad enough to get off at that forbidding spot. This was a tall man with short cropped hair, neatly but not fashionably dressed and spottable to any con at a hundred yards in a heavy groundmist as yet another screw.

'Can I cadge a lift?' he asked Mr Barrowclough, who shied faintly in alarm. The new screw hastily produced his ID card and flashed it. He went on, 'My name's Beale. I've just been posted here.'

Barrowclough sighed in relief, having feared he might be dealing with some heavy sent up from London to spring his charges.

'Oh, I see, a brother officer. Of course.'

Miller climbed in the front of the minibus and Barrowclough

and Beale got in the back with the two new cons. These were very different specimens. One was a sturdy self-contained man in his forties, name of Oakes. Oakes looked as if he knew his way around, both inside and outside. The other one was a boy of nineteen with a pinched face and that forlorn manner of the first-timer who is close to tears but is much too tough to show it. His name was Rudge. Beale made a gesture at the youngster and asked Barrowclough:

'What's laddo in for?'

'Better not to ask, you know. In my experience, I find if you know what a man's done, it may prejudice you against him. Best to start clean. Benefit of the doubt. Find out what he is, not what he was.'

Beale nodded appreciatively and then turned to Rudge and barked:

'What you in for, son?'

Rudge started but then his lips set and he muttered sullenly:

'Two years.'

Beale shook his head wearily.

'Didn't mean time. I meant offence.'

Oakes smiled faintly and answered for Rudge.

'None taken.'

Beale immediately turned and favoured Oakes with a hard stare which Oakes bore with fortitude. Beale confided to Barrowclough:

'Know his sort, don't we? See if he's still smiling next week.'

And with such pleasantries bouncing about inside it, the little bus hummed on across the great bleak moors.

And now I suppose I will have to do something I have been trying to avoid: describe it to you. What? The dungeon, the hole, the horrible gloomy sordid mass of steel and stone called Slade Prison. I have heard how public-school boys at Eton and such kindergartens have a terrible time. When they first get there, all the big boys tar and feather them and make them stand on the roof all night. Then for the first year they get beaten on their backsides if they so much as sneeze. The bullying is chronic and in addition they have to learn Latin. They sleep on special carved blocks of ice in refrigerated rooms and get fed on ship's biscuit and beans. But no sooner do they leave but nostalgia comes down on them like the Sweeney on a bank mob and they spend the rest of their life flocking back to their old torture chambers for reunions and gatherings with other victims of the old school from all over the world. Then again, take your regimental loonies. They may have passed their army time together up to their necks in mud and blood, billeted with cobras and scorpions, sweating with malaria and blackwater fever, but put them into striped pants and return them to The Smoke and they brood wistfully on the paradise they have lost. There is no horrible environment or set of torments that can be inflicted on men which doesn't later present itself to them as having been a tremendous lark. Except the nick. I never heard of any Old Lag's dinners. No one ever sent me a card inviting me to a Wormwood Scrubs reunion party. There are no sentimental moments when your released con wipes away a tear recalling some great rag after lights out, or murmurs to himself: those were the days. All you want to do when you get out is forget. Forget that such hell-holes exist and that you were ever locked up in them.

If I had the choice, what I'd like to describe for you is how the sun sinks behind the palms of Teneriffe, even though I never been there. Or I could paint a very exciting picture of Saturday night in the Hound and Hare in Muswell Hill, where I have been, many times. But no. I have set myself a task. I have assumed the responsibilities of an author and I have a duty to tell you, just what kind of place Slade Nick is.

I'll make it quick. Slade Prison is a great pile of rotting Victorian stone set on the most dreary, barren part of the Cumberland moors. Inside, it's all bars and catwalks, landings and locked doors. It's not a high security nick and there are no heavies, other than our own beloved Godfather, Grouty, there. The cells in each block are ranged in tiers around a central well at the bottom of which is an empty space optimistically called the recreation area. That's where, until the evening's good telly starts which is when we are locked up, we are allowed to sit and gaze at the 'Magic Roundabout' and suchlike or divert ourselves with ping-pong and other games. Matter of fact, this term I have interested myself in the game of kings, or is it the king of games? Anyhow, I am referring to chess which I regularly play with an intelligent old con called Hedley and, if I do say so myself, I can push a handy pawn by now. One thing no one's ever short of inside is time and time is what is needed to play chess well. It's surprising how many good chess players emerge from the nick and one day Bobby Fisher is going to be mated at the post by some old lag.

Slade has got the usual workshops cleverly designed to break a man's spirit without producing anything of real value to the world. There, dispirited men sew mailbags or weave fishing nets by the hour. Of course, they get paid for this work. Very scrupulous the authorities are about that. If you saved all the money you earned in say a five-year sentence, at the end of it you could probably buy yourself a very fine second-hand bicycle to pedal home on. Of course, the lads don't save it but squander it all on riotous living. They think nothing of lashing out twice a week on a whole half ounce of tobacco, known as snout to the inmates, as well as a KitKat bar. Snout, incidentally, is what we use for currency inside, and anything that changes hands – and it is surprising how brisk is the hum of commerce – does so for a specific amount of snout. A soft toilet roll might be worth three roll-ups. A tube of toothpaste and a razor blade might fetch a quarter of an ounce.

The prison also shelters a tiny hospital which is far from providing the fabulous comforts of the Harley Street Clinic but is still regarded as the next best thing to Butlin's by the lads. All over the nick cons are dreaming up schemes for busting a finger or a toe so that they can get into the infirmary for a week or two. Harry Grout's minders sometimes help them out there.

There is a library of dog-eared books, most of them with missing pages which have been used for roll-ups in emergencies. I used to be the librarian, which is a very plum job inside. Of course, everyone has to work and there is keen competition for the more bearable jobs, like being a clerk in the office. At the time I am writing about, I was working on the prison farm. This is considered to be one of the better jobs since at least you get outside the walls – the inner walls that is – for a period every day and you're more or less your own boss.

I was, in fact, standing by the pig pen when I first met young Rudge. He was slouching along behind Mr Barrowclough, pointedly not taking an interest in his surroundings.

'Afternoon, Mr Barrowclough,' I called politely.

Barrowclough noted that I was not, at that precise moment, engaged in shovelling pig dung or anything unsavoury of that kind. Of course, if it had been Mackay approaching – oh, I haven't mentioned Mackay yet? Well, you'll get to know him. He has a Scotch accent and a military manner that he picked up serving with some highland regiment and he regards himself as the hammer of the criminal classes. Now, if it had been Mackay leading young Rudge towards me, I *would* have been shovelling pig dung but no one takes much trouble about old Barrowclough.

'Busy, Fletcher?' asked the soft-hearted screw, with what was intended to be cutting sarcasm but sounded more like the moo of an anxious milker who's temporarily lost sight of its calf.

'More than ever, sir,' I returned breezily. 'Still, as you are well aware, I'm not one to complain.'

Barrowclough glanced about and tried to turn up the severity level in his voice.

'I can't actually see what it is you're supposed to be doing.'

I nodded towards the reeking midden just over the fence where a line of greedy porkers were jostling at the trough.

'The pigs, sir,' I explained. 'They won't eat without my reassuring presence. Very highly strung – your average pig.'

I turned and contemplated the young felon with him. Rudge was not a bad-looking lad but there was nothing special about his appearance. I'd seen hundreds like him in a dozen nicks, kids from the slums and the tower blocks who'd graduated from nicking toys in Woolworth's to real capers. Being inexperienced, and usually none too bright, they almost all get caught the first few times. And get sent to Thieves College, ie the nick, to get proper training for their destined career. I reckoned he was probably doing eighteen months for house-breaking (which turned out to be three months out) and that by the time he was my age he'd have done the best part of twenty years behind bars, like I had. I'd been like him once.

'Who's this, then?' I asked Barrowclough.

'Rudge. Newly assigned to the farm.'

I nodded.

'Well, Gawd knows we need all the help we can get.'

I reached for the distasteful implement behind me and handed the shovel to Rudge.

'Here,' I said.

The boy made no attempt to take it but eyed me without warmth.

'What?' he asked.

'Shovel it,' I urged.

'Shovel what?'

I nodded towards the enclosure full of squealing pigs that also contained a good deal of what pigs naturally produce and I don't mean bacon.

'Shovel that.'

I could see that he was a lad who would learn fast. He had a natural talent for evading orders, which is useful for survival inside.

'Shovel it where?'

I pointed, and explained patiently.

'Shovel it from there to there.'

Rudge licked his lips slightly. He was running out of tactics.

'Why?'

I smiled pityingly.

'Ah, why? If we knew that, son – but, we don't do we? Ours is not to reason why, ours is just to clean the sty.'

And I held the shovel closer to him. Reluctantly, he put a hand on it but looked hopefully towards the screw.

'You'd better do as Fletcher says,' Mr Barrowclough confirmed.

Rudge sighed and muttered something, doubtless insolent but inaudible, under his breath. Then he moved away towards the pen. When he was out of earshot, I asked:

'How did he work this, then?'

Like I said, there is very great competition inside for the more tolerable jobs and working on the farm was one of them. I continued,

'First day inside – the farm? What is he, Governor's nephew?'

Barrowclough coughed in faint reproof at my scandalous suggestion and then explained.

'He's a first offender and very young. Admin. thought it best.'

I shrugged.

'Well, I hope he pulls his weight and knuckles down. Still, ain't fair, is it? But then when was life ever fair?'

A cloud settled on poor Barra's features and he sighed deeply.

'That's very true, Fletcher. Very true indeed . . .'

I don't exactly detest old Barrowclough but it was less to cheer him up than because I thought there might be some amusement in it that I asked:

'You seem a bit down in the mouth. What's the matter?'

The forlorn screw shook his head dismally.

'Oh, nothing new. Same old story.'

I twigged at once. Poor Barra is afflicted with an old woman who has a very loving nature. There's nothing she won't do for any man on earth, with the exception of her husband. I said mischievously,

'Oh dear. Has Mrs Barrowclough left you, then?'

'Unhappily – no, Fletcher.'

While I was shooting the somewhat tainted breeze beside the pigsty with old Barrowclough, in another part of the nick Mr Mackay was taking the new recruit, Beale, on a tour of the prison.

Very smart in his new jackboots and prison officer's jacket, Beale strode beside Mackay, already discovering that his senior was a man after his own heart. Beale decided to model himself on the Scotch Führer.

Together they entered the workshop where a lot of cowed men were weaving fishing nets. Mackay's vengeful eye roved over them and his lip twisted into its habitual sneer from which his high-pitched Hibernian whine emerged.

'As you can see, Mr Beale, these men are gainfully employed in the manufacture of fishing nets.'

Tommy Armstrong, a large con with a sense of humour, stood up, hand clasped to his heart and exclaimed piously:

'For those in peril on the sea.'

'That will do, Armstrong,' Mackay silenced him. Then the Big Brother of Slade Nick continued, 'Other output includes the inevitable mailbags. Prisoners are also employed in our electrical shop, maintenance shop, laundry and the prison farm.'

A frown replaced the cocky smirk on his features and he approached a lilac con called Whittaker. We use the word 'lilac' inside to designate those inmates who, if their minds and not their bodies governed such matters, would be serving their time in Holloway, which is, of course, as everyone knows, a women's nick.

'Are you wearing make-up again, Whittaker?' Mackay asked the gorgeous felon.

Whittaker tossed his head slightly and – some people never learn – attempted to soothe The Beast with a winsome smile.

'Only a touch of rouge, Mr Mackay,' he purred.

'Take it off!' snarled Mackay.

Whittaker pouted girlishly and glanced about the room.

'Anyone got any cleansing cream?'

As the two iron men in uniform strode out of the workshop, a number of the cons there were fumbling in their pockets to see if they had.

As they crossed the prison yard together, Beale asked sombrely:

'Get a lot of that, sir?'

'Insubordination?'

'Poofery.'

Mackay grimaced.

'Inevitable, Mr Beale. We find it best to put them all together in G Wing or, as we term it, "married quarters".'

They marched in silence for a little way, Beale brooding on the revolting attributes of crooks.

'Don't understand it myself,' he confessed at last. 'Never did.'

Mackay bestowed on him some good advice, bred from years of experience.

'Don't let that show, Mr Beale. My attitude is, whatever his bent, each man in here is as despicable as the next.'

Beale glanced at his superior with added respect.

'That's very fair minded, sir.'

Their next port of call was the farm where, as I've explained, Rudge, Barrowclough and myself were socializing with the pigs. Naturally, when I saw Mackay's furious form appear on the horizon I began to bustle about and look busy. But it was poor Rudge, unloading a wheelbarrow full of dung, who had the first encounter with the Gestapo.

'Name?' snarled Mackay, glaring at the lad.

'Rudge.'

Beale immediately prompted:

'Sir.'

Mackay then delivered his set piece to green cons.

'Prison officers will be addressed as "Sir" or as "Mister" followed by the last name which in my case is Mackay. Clear?'

Rudge nodded slowly.

'Yes—'

Mackay's neck jerked ominously but Rudge was cool. He continued at the same pace, just this side of insubordination.

'—Mr Mackay.'

Mackay gave him a long hard look before turning on his heel with:

'Carry on.'

The two screws moved a little closer to where I was uncoiling a hose. Mr Barrowclough had ambled off a few yards. I heard Mackay explaining:

'The farm produces sixty per cent of what the prison eats, Mr Beale. We have a little livestock, as you see. Pigs, poultry. Also a few allotments for the older lags.'

Mr Barrowclough at this point edged deferentially towards them.

'Afternoon, Mr Mackay.'

Mackay favoured his somewhat despised subordinate with a tight smile.

'Mr Barrowclough. Have you met, Mr Beale?'

'Oh yes, I had that pleasure on the bus.'

Mackay confided to Beale:

'Mr Barrowclough here has a somewhat different attitude than mine towards the prisoners.' And then to the bovine presence, 'You see yourself as a humanitarian, don't you, Frank?'

Barrowclough cleared his throat huskily, as if a few sharp stalks of hay were tickling it, and admitted:

'I think our role is to help the prisoners, not punish them. To encourage them in a programme of self-improvement and rehabilitation. So that they're prepared to re-enter society.'

Beale greeted these mushy sentiments with a snort of contempt and, glancing at his boss for approval, said firmly:

'I'd've thought our role was to make sure the scum stay locked up!'

I noticed that even Mackay raised an eyebrow at the word

'scum' while Barra drew back as if from a bumblebee that was about to settle on his nose. He swallowed and said:

'Yes, well, I'd best be getting on—'

And he ambled off towards the main building. I knew my turn was coming up. Sure enough, when I next heard Mackay's voice, as I fastened my hose to a tap, it was immediately behind me and its tone was the jolly one he uses for jeering at the inmates and which sounds a bit like ice grating along the side of an ice-breaker in the Weddell Sea, if that's the sea I mean.

'No guided tour of Slade Prison, Mr Beale, would be complete without meeting Fletcher, Norman Stanley.'

I straightened myself up slowly and, chewing gum ostentatiously, grunted:

'Afternoon, Mr Mackay.'

As I'd anticipated, the monster from the black lagoon ignored my civil greeting and merely made the rasping sound he imagines to be a chuckle before continuing:

'Typical recidivist. Been doing porridge most of his life. Knows it all. Should be watched, not believed.'

I smiled without using my eyes.

'You know me, sir. Turn the other cheek, keep my nose clean. Bides my time. No bother.'

Beale, feeling something was expected from him, asked:

'Long to do?'

I nodded.

'Long enough.'

'What you in for?'

I shook my head sadly, like a man bowed with guilt.

'I got caught.'

With which, I turned my back on them both and pretended to be busy with my hose. Behind me, I heard Mackay grate:

'Got the picture?'

Followed by a grunt of assent from his new disciple. Then the two of them moved away towards the allotments and as soon as they were out of sight I called Rudge and we set off towards the palatial three-star restaurant very few people beside Egon Ronay knows is concealed within the walls of Slade Prison for dinner.

After a superb meal of khaki goo, green goo and white goo followed by some very attractive mixed blue and yellow goo, I retired to my cosy maisonette for a few minutes peace and a brush-up before the afternoon shift. I managed the brush up all right but the peace was denied me. Bunny Warren, a childish, dyslexic felon who looks harmless so long as he's not brandishing a deadly weapon, arrived with a letter in his hand.

Finding conversation with Bunny unrewarding, I made a dive for the door but he barred my way. He held out his letter, pathetic appeal in his eye.

'Got this letter from the wife, Fletch. Will you read it for me?'

I sighed.

'If you can't read, Warren, how d'you know it's from the wife?'

The nurk raised the sheet of scrawled Woolworth's notepaper he'd extracted from the envelope to his nose and twitched it, his nose not the letter, reverently.

'That's Betty's scent,' he cooed.

I took the sheet from him and raised it gingerly to my own nose. It reminded me of Portsmouth harbour.

'Work in a tarpaulin factory, does she?' I asked.

But Warren was too keyed up with tender emotion to take offence.

'Go on, read it,' he begged.

I shook my head firmly.

'Haven't time, Bunny, but I'll pick out the highlights for you.'

I ran my practised eyes rapidly across the round, illiterate scrawl.

'Betty says: *Dearest Bunny, blah blah blah blah blah blah*. Now the next page. Oh yes, *blah blah blah blah—*'

'Hang on!' cried Bunny indignantly. '*Blah blah* what?'

I shook my head decisively.

'It's only trivia, Bunny. Weather's rotten, her mother's got catarrh. She's retiled the lav . . . the canary's got haemorrhoids. She's met a welder down the Fiesta Club and she's thinking of moving in with him. Dull stuff like that – and now I must be off, Bunny.'

As I passed him, I noted the glazed look in his eyes which always signifies that Bunny is exerting his mental powers to the limit, which is about that of a sheepdog. And as I disappeared down the catwalk, I heard him say in a puzzled voice:

'We haven't got a canary.'

Later, as I approached the pig pen, I noted with approval that Rudge was back before me. I breezed up to him, nodded at the wheelbarrow and said crisply:

'C'mon.'

Rudge made no move. He asked:

'Where we going?'

I gestured towards a cluster of farm buildings.

'Over there.'

Rudge still made no move to comply. This irritated me since I was, for the present, his superior officer.

'Then what?' he asked.

I sighed.

'We come back.'

Rudge glanced suspiciously towards the destination I had proposed.

'What's the point in that?' he asked.

'None.'

'I don't get it.'

I approached him. The lad had to start learning some time.

'The point is, to keep on the move, son. Look as if we're doing something. Otherwise, they'll give us something to do. Which will be worse than what we would be doing if we were doing what we were supposed to be doing.'

Rudge swallowed. I could see I'd blinded him with science. He changed the subject.

'What's it like, this nick?'

I shrugged.

'Bird's bird, son. They're all the same. We're in and we can't get out.'

He didn't say anything but he turned slightly and gazed off across the fields. I knew exactly what was in his mind.

'Some do,' he said.

I came back sharply.

'Leave it off.'

'What's it to you?' he asked irritably.

'I'll tell you what,' I said, and there was steel in my voice. 'If you do a bunk, it comes down on me. I don't want that because it took me a long time to get the screws to give me this job.'

Rudge stared at me for a moment in silence and I suddenly

knew that he was going to have a hard life. But when he finally spoke it was quite softly.

'Whose side are you on, anyway?'

It was time for him to learn the big lesson.

'Mine,' I said, also softly. 'Not yours. Not theirs. Mine!'

2 Passing the time

'Course, if you think about it that's a very silly title for this chapter. You don't pass the time in the nick the way you pass it on the outside. On the outside you always have pastimes with which to pass the time. If it's Saturday night, you might go down to the Black Lion and pass the time with some of the old lags – or lads. Bit of a sing-song and a dozen light-and-bitters and the time passes very sweetly. But no penal reformer has yet had the bright idea of equipping British gaols with attractive bars. For the cons that is. The screws usually have a boozing corner of sorts and the one at Slade will loom quite large in my tale.

For your free man, there is a whole range of hobbies and leisure activities, ranging from luxury cruises and call girls for the privileged classes to pigeon racing and do-it-yourself handicrafts, as well as regular boozing, for the likes of us. Of course, the likes of us sometimes call girls, especially after regular boozing and when the old woman happens to be visiting a sick relative in Rhyl or someplace. But the girls you call on such occasions are not strictly speaking call girls and do not always respond to your call. Still, they sometimes add a dimension of interest to life which is lacking in the average cell block, unless you happen to be a poof, which I'm not, and even then conducting an amour in the latrines is not like a scented night at the Hilton for your stockbroker out on the tiles, is it? Hang on, I'm losing the thread. Time, time – plenty of that about but – oh yes, pastimes. We have those, of course. The governors and senior screws are very keen on providing pastimes for their charges because they prefer to have them taking a course in elementary geology, say, or running up a model of the *Ark Royal* out of matchsticks for a nephew in the hobby shop to standing on the roof of the nick throwing slates down on all and sundry which is the work that the devil makes for idle cons. So there's great pressure inside for us to pass the time creatively. But that's just it, the time inside is not like the time outside and so no matter how you fill it, it never gets filled but remains just the same kind of empty time. You see, what I should have called this chapter is 'Marking time'. Then why didn't I? Because I happen to have been a serving soldier who done more than his bit in Malaya defeating the savage terrorists and, as a result of the arduous training I underwent to equip me for my heroic military career, I know exactly what is meant by marking time. It means standing on some bit of sandy gravel thumping up and down with your feet but – and this is the vital point – not progressing one inch. 'Left, right! Left right!' bawls the sergeant, and up and down pound the old plates of meat but no advance takes place. 'Left, right, left right!' on and on and on, 'Left, right, left, right, left, right, left, right.' See what I mean? That's the whole story, not just of this chapter but, in a way, of this whole book. But would your traveller setting out for Edinburgh shell out a couple of quid to read two hundred pages of left, right, left, right, left, right? I very much doubt it, much as I regret it since it would simplify my task very considerably if that's all I needed to write.

So what I'm really proposing to tell you about just now is less about how we pass the time while doing time than how we push it around a bit, or dab a few spots of paint on it, usually filched from the paint store, to give it a little more texture and interest than it would have if it just passed drearily on its own.

When I got back to the flowery (remember? flowery dell = cell, which is a typical and fascinating example of the rich poetic irony that your uneducated Cockney has instinctively put into his rhyming slang which is why scholars from all over the world and especially Pakistan, flock to the East End to study it) – when I got back to my cell that evening, after labouring in the pigsty, I was tickled to find Lennie translating Bunny's letter for him.

'*Oh well*,' Lennie was reading to a rapt Bunny, '*that's all I have time for now. There's the ironing to be done before "Starsky and Hutch". Needless to say, I love you and miss your loving* – er – *arms*, would it be?'

Bunny gulped, turned pink and said hastily.

'That's right – arms.'

Lennie continued:

'Then, there's lots of kisses and hugs. Nice letter.'

Warren frowned in perplexity.

'So there's nothing in there about a welder or a canary?'

Lennie shook his head positively.

'No. Couldn't have missed either of those.'

I fear a faint chuckle escaped me at this point, alerting Bunny who turned and pointed an accusing finger in my direction.

'So much for your reading, Fletch. There's no welder and no canary and I never thought there was neither.'

At which Bunny turned haughtily and scampered out of the flowery.

'What did he mean?' asked Lennie.

I shrugged and began to remove my pungent outer garments, while Lennie prudently retreated to the opposite corner of our apartment.

'Search me. Stir crazy, perhaps.'

Lennie sniffed delicately.

'That new kid, Rudge. How did he wangle the farm?'

I shrugged again.

'Charm, I expect.'

Lennie looked thoughtful.

'He's been sitting in his cell since chow. Just staring at the wall.'

I grinned.

'Well, he's just had his first experience of your cottage pie, hasn't he? It's best not to move around too much.'

Lennie works in the kitchen. He's not really a bad cook but what can you do if the ingredients is all made from the same plastic and just dyed different colours? He said thoughtfully:

'He's only a lad.'

'Oh, listen to him!' I said ironically, but Lennie ignored my irony as he often does. He went on:

'I just remember my first night inside, that's all. When that door bangs shut—'

I remembered it too. And I remembered my own first night, all those years ago. That was when the walls came to life and said 'gotcha!' That was when the real time stopped and the marking time began.

'Why don't you go and have a word with him?' suggested Lennie.

I sighed.

'Why?'

'You're very good at it. You perked me up when I first come inside.'

I poured water into my bowl.

'I broke you in, Godber, 'cause you was forced upon *my* cell. So it was in my interest not to have a manic depressive in the bottom bunk.'

'Suit yourself,' said Lennie huffily.

'I will.'

Gawd, what did he want? What could I do for the kid that his mum and dad, welfare officers, probation officers, judges and juries and the whole bleeding official lot of them had failed to do? Uncle Norman, the cons' councillor? A few well-chosen words from Fletcher, the felons' friend, and young Rudge would go forth and win the Duke of Edinburgh's award for scaling Ben Nevis on stilts and be made Minister of Sport. Was that it? But if I had the knack, why was I a four-time loser whose most conspicuous triumph in life was winning the Amateur Night cup in the old Pig and Whistle with my rendering of the 'Desert Song'?

Later that night, I was playing chess with Hedley. After a while I rose to my feet, said 'scuse me' and headed for the latrines. Contrary to what you're probably thinking, my sudden departure was not dictated by the desire to avoid losing yet again to the old scroat, who makes such stupid moves he confuses you, but because I had seen someone else moving in the same direction.

In the loo, I eased up beside Rudge and went through the motions as if for an ordinary Jimmy Riddle.

'Evening,' I said pleasantly.

He uttered a vague sound, which might have meant anything, but I ignored his lack of cordiality.

'Listen,' I began earnestly, 'I know it's bad. Prison's like life

27

really. You have to have something to believe in. Something to hang on to, to stop you going under. It's harder here, of course, 'cause the screws hold all the cards. You can't buck the system – mad to try. But now and again, you can lift the heart with the occasional little victory.'

I paused and waited. It was quite a long wait and I was beginning to think: So much for my trouble; but then Grudge said rudgingly – no the other way round:

'Like what?'

'Tiny things,' I said quickly, wanting to keep his attention now I'd got it. 'Getting pills from the M.O. for an illness you ain't got. Lifting a tin of peaches from the kitchen. Stashing snout where they can't find it. Anything as long as you feel you've put one over on them. As Shakespeare said: don't let the bastards grind you down.'

There was a faint grunt from the lad, which again could have meant anything. I sighed. I'd done my best.

'Well, nice talking to you, Rudge.'

I turned to leave. Then it struck me he was spending an extraordinary long time divesting himself of surplus liquid. I didn't really think it signified anything but nervousness. Still, I turned back and offered one last gem of wisdom.

'Wouldn't hang around the lav too long if I was you. Not a safe place in the nick. Get 'em all in here: transvestites, homosexuals, drug addicts. I tell you, when someone comes in for a shit, it's like a breath of fresh air!'

I sailed back to the old dell with that virtuous feeling which has sustained missionaries up the Congo even when the ungrateful savages have preferred to ignore their advice and use them for javelin practice. Before I reached our little sanctuary I became aware of a sharp pain in my right heel but glancing down found that there was no spear sticking out of it. Then I recalled my right sock was largely hole and consequently my heel had got rubbed something rotten. I took off my boot and hobbled into home-base. Lennie was providentially darning.

'Where have you been?' he asked.

'Playing chess,' I explained, preferring to hide my light under a bushel, which is an expression I have never properly understood. I mean, does it have to be a bushel? And what is a bushel?

'Listen, young Godber, you owe me some darning wool.'

'Already gave you some.'

'That was in exchange for the orange,' I reminded him patiently.

'Tangerine,' corrected Lennie. 'And about the size of a walnut. Anyhow, that was to pay me for the stamp.'

'What stamp?' I asked irritably, sitting down beside him and massaging my sore heel.

'For your pools.'

The trouble with Godber is that he can never keep the record straight.

'I paid you for the stamp,' I pointed out. 'With a squeeze of my toothpaste.'

'That was for the darning wool.'

'This haggling is undignified. Have you got any wool or haven't you?'

'Yes.'

'Will you give me some?'

'Yes.'

'What?'

'I said yes.'

Why? I mean why did he say yes? It was normal to say 'naff off' or 'up yours' or some other pleasantry. There was a code which governed these transactions and Lennie knew it by now. Feeling a bit of a nana, I asked:

'Just like that? Free, gratis and for nothing?'

'Yes,' said Lennie firmly.

What can you do with amateurs?

'Oh, buttocks!' I exclaimed.

So Lennie and I sat side by side like two old wives and darned socks. At first, we gossiped about prison life. Was it true that Jackson over in B Wing had had a fit and bitten the screw Collinson in the leg? And that Collinson had been rushed to London on the night express from Carlisle for special anti-rabies injections? Lennie said it couldn't be true because he'd seen Collinson bullying Ives just before grub-time. What a pity. Was it a fact that they were going to build a high-security wing on to Slade? Lennie said McLaren had been told this by Banyard, the unfrocked dentist, who'd overheard Miller discussing it with

Mackay. Not very likely, we agreed. But, by degrees, we fell silent, each of us alone with his thoughts. And my thoughts, whenever I was alone and awake, usually turned to my family.

Three kids, born at five-year intervals between sentences: two fine girls and a fine boy. Ingrid was a young woman now, a condition she'd achieved with very little help from her old man. On her last visit she'd told me Raymond was doing very well at school. And my old woman, who'd stuck by me all these years – naffing hell, that was life! Raising kids, looking after your old woman, being head of a family. And this was— I cut myself off. This was just the kind of thinking prisoners must *not* indulge in. It drives you crazy with frustration, makes you want to crash out at any cost and get back to your loved ones. There's only one way to do your porridge, day by day and hour by hour and minutes by minute. Anything else is a passport to madness. When you're doing time, you've got to mark time: left, right, left, right, left—

'Fletcher, can I speak to you for a moment?'

'Yes, sergeant,' I said automatically.

'I beg your pardon?'

'What? Oh—'

I glanced up and saw a long pink object pointed straight at me. Some way behind it I perceived Banyard's face and that made me realize that the first thing I'd seen had been his nose. Banyard is a very high-class felon, with a BBC accent, who was a flourishing dentist on the outside. But then he developed a habit, whenever he was treating a pretty female patient, of sending his nurse out to buy coffee and dispensing laughing gas like Vodka at a Russian wedding. Some of the patients made allegations as to what transpired while they were convulsed, and Banyard wound up in Slade. I told him he should sue his brief for gross incompetence because all anyone had to do was to measure his nose and then affirm that it would have been physically impossible for him to have done what he was charged with. He couldn't have got close enough.

'What is it, Banyard?' I asked, snapping out of my reverie.

'Fletcher, I'm getting up a petition about the food.'

'What's wrong with the food?' asked Lennie, bristling.

'Oh, it's not your fault, Godber,' said Banyard soothingly. 'You do the best you can with the ingredients. But there's absolutely no food value in what they give us.'

'Yes, now that you mention it, your nose is a little shrunk,' I said, eyeing his amazing trunk critically.

'Will you sign, Fletcher?'

'Won't do no good.'

'What other course is there open to us?'

'Well, you could go on hunger strike.'

Banyard, in spite of his accent, is not really a front runner in the intelligence stakes.

'Do you think that might improve the fare?'

'Only if you starved to death.'

Banyard nodded thoughtfully, just brushing my ear with his hooter.

'I'll give it some thought. You won't sign my petition?'

'You know my rule, Banyard, don't stir things up unless you can be sure of upsetting the stir. This one's a loser.'

'Who's for Monopoly?' asked McLaren, slouching into the dell. 'Not you, Banyard. You keep knocking the hotels off the board with your nose.'

Banyard has a pugnacious streak and I wondered if he would retaliate. It's not difficult with McLaren since, although he was born in Glasgow and is pure Hibernian in speech, one of his parents came from the West Indies and he's as black as the ace of clubs, which is a more appropriate card for his activities outside the nick than the one more commonly used. But Banyard was apparently too concerned about his emaciated beak to take offence. He held out a sheet of paper containing a sprinkling of names and pleaded:

'Won't you sign this petition, McLaren?'

'Is it for girls to be brought in?'

'Don't be absurd. It's about the appalling food.'

'What's appalling about it? The steak and kidney pudding we had for tea was super.'

'Er . . .' said Lennie hesitantly, 'it was cauliflower cheese but some cinnamon got into the cheese mix.'

'So what? It was delicious,' enthused McLaren. Then he sneered at Banyard, 'I suppose you think you're entitled to something better, because you went to public school, is that it?'

Banyard shook his head haughtily.

'On the contrary. I'm well used to this type of food. I went to Harrow.'

I tried to pour oil on these troubled waters.

'See, he had a golden start in life. It's worse for him inside than most of us because he's had further to drop. Professional man – dentist – tragic.'

McLaren snorted.

'It was no laughing matter for the poor women he had under the laughing gas, was it?'

Banyard sighed deeply.

'There's no need for that, McLaren. We don't have to keep unearthing each other's pasts. I'm paying for my peccadillos.'

In spite of his dwarfed brain, Banyard does know a lot of words from going to Harrow and university. This one was new to me but I didn't let on.

'Oh well,' I exclaimed breezily, 'if you're paying, I'll have a large one.'

But Black Jock had no inhibitions about revealing his ignorance.

'What's a peccadillo?' he asked.

'A peccadillo,' I informed him, maintaining the jovial tone, 'is a South African bird that flies backwards to keep the sand out of its eyes.'

'Anyway,' exclaimed the ebony haggis-eater, 'I'm off to play Monopoly.'

'I'll come with you,' I offered. 'Not for Monopoly but because I just have to straighten out Hedley about the Queen's Pawn Gambit accepted.'

'What's that?' asked McLaren, as we departed, 'a present from Whittaker?'

Hedley was waiting for me impatiently, as I'd expected, in that charming and well appointed area known affectionately to everyone as Funland. It consists of the open space at the bottom of the cell block, where each evening a television set tuned to some Martian station that only transmits jagged lines and dots is set up as well as a rickety old ping-pong table and several ordinary trestle tables with benches. There we carefree playboys are at liberty to disport ourselves in all manner of joyous pursuits or just to relax and exchange views on important topics of the day, such as whether Mackay really was sired by a werewolf.

I produced my half of our precious chessboard. Hedley produced his and soon we were locked in titanic mental conflict.

About twenty minutes later, as I saw out of the corner of my eye, Mackay and Beale stamped noisily along the landing just above our heads. Hedley looked up at them and I took the opportunity to nudge his king into the square it should have been in if he hadn't been playing such wilfully stupid, and thus confusing, chess.

Hedley looked down again and leaned towards me.

'I don't like the look of that new one, Fletch. What's his name, Beale? And what have you been doing to my king?'

'What,' I asked indignantly, 'are you incinerating, Hedley?'

Hedley pointed to the board.

'It were there and now it's there.'

'Course, that's really all Hedley has to offer at chess, a good memory, which enables him to think four or five moves in advance, and thus gives him an unfair advantage because he doesn't do what you expect him to do. I shook my head irritably.

'Was it? Well, maybe I jogged the table. I don't know. Put it back. Put it where you like, if winning's that important to you.'

'I will, Fletch.'

And he moved his king back to its original position, knowing full well it meant that he would have mate in three moves. He went on:

'I don't mind losing if it's fair and square.'

I gazed glumly at the board. My position was hopeless.

'Show me a man who laughs at defeat,' I said bravely, 'and I'll show you a chiropodist with a sense of humour.'

'What?' asked Hedley puzzled.

'De feet, get it? De feet.'

'Oh,' said Hedley, who has the fun-loving qualities of a moose. Then he moved his knight and said, 'Checkmate.'

I sighed and pushed the board away.

'Dead boring game,' I exclaimed.

'That's five-hundred and ninety-seven pints you owe me,' said Hedley gravely, marking it in his dog-eared pocket diary.

'I know, I know. When do you get out, Hedley?'

The old villain smiled faintly.

'Around 1985 – if I get parole.'

'Well, with inflation continuing I'll send you round a six pack of Long Life. That should just about cover it.'

Then I started setting up the pieces again.

'Time for one more before lock-up. Double or nothing.'

We had three more games before lock-up, mainly because Hedley played such weird chess that my well thought out plans had no chance to mature and none of the games lasted more than about five minutes. When the screws bawled 'Into your cells,' I owed Hedley enough beer to float the *Ark Royal*. But that wasn't what was bothering me. I couldn't work out why a dim old screwsman like him kept beating me at chess. I had ten times the nous he had. It was proved, if nothing else, by his police record. Hedley was fifty-eight and he had spent twenty-seven of those years behind bars. He was such a rotten thief that he'd done one term for picking the pocket of a CID sergeant. He was drawn like a magnet towards burglar alarms and every time he went out of the nick the whole district was soon ringing like a scrubber's doorbell. But he kept beating me at chess. Why?

As we packed up our things, Mackay and Beale returned along the landing and paused above us to survey the scene. I heard Mackay say:

'Almost lock-up. Then I'll buy you a jar, Mr Beale.'

'Wouldn't say no to that, sir,' returned his junior deferentially.

'The prison officers have formed a club. It's known as The Prison Officers' Club. It was formerly the coke store before we converted to gas. It's a little basic perhaps, but it's remarkable what you can do with a pot of paint, a few horse brasses and little imagination. GET WEAVING, YOU MEN!'

Hedley and I, each with his half of the board, said goodnight and headed for our respective cells. As I undressed for kip, Lennie said:

'What's up with you then?'

'Nothing.'

'Haven't said a word since you got in. Hedley beat you again, did he?'

'Some of the games, yes.'

'How many?'

'Five, if you must know.'

'And how many did you play?'

'Less than six and I don't want no cheap sneers from you, Godber. You have no concept of the intellectual challenge of chess, or any other games for that matter.'

'Beat you at pontoon, didn't I?'

'Just the turn of the card, that is. Pure luck. The only kind of game you understand.'

'Played all kind of games at school.'

'Oh yes? Then why did I have to explain to you that backgammon is not rashers from a pig's bottom? Anyway, if you don't mind, Godber, I've had a very harrowing day. I'd like to get some kip.'

Right on cue, the lights went out and I pulled the blankets snugly up around my chin and prepared to forget my woes in healing slumber. One thing I've always been grateful for is I'm a very sound sleeper. That's an important thing for a prisoner. Means one third of your sentence is taken care of. And you wake up in the morning refreshed and ready to throw back in their faces the slings and arrow that the screws hurl at you. But for some reason, I found it difficult to drift off on that particular night. It was not that the nick was any noisier than usual, just the customary clanging of the guard's boots along the landing and the odd groan from some junkie who'd managed to nick a load of pills from the dispensary and was now discovering they were a powerful laxative. The trouble was my mind would not calm down. I kept playing over and over again the games I'd had with Hedley. It wasn't that I was thinking of brilliant moves with which I could have clobbered him. It was just that the pawns and bishops and knights and the rest kept sliding and hopping across a great chess-board in my mind. But very gradually sleep began to come. Only it was not sound, deep refreshing sleep but a series of short dozes, filled with weird dreams, from which I kept snapping awake again with a gasp.

First off I dreamt that Hedley and I were no longer cons but had changed into two screws. We both had prison officers' uniforms on but instead of hats on our heads we had crowns. I was the king and he was the queen. We were walking through the nick and I said to him:

'Perhaps you'd care to join me in the coke cellar and we can settle accounts?'

'Wouldn't say no to that, Fletch.'

'Here we are then.'

And I opened a door which led into a kind of nightclub, only where the dance-floor should have been there was just a great pile of coke about three storeys high and right at the top of it was the bar. We scrambled with great difficulty up the coke pile and I heard Hedley gasping and panting and thought: He'll never make it. But he did. When we got to the top, there was Lennie behind the bar, looking very sad, which is not like Lennie at all. I said:

'I'll have a pint of best bitter and two million pints for the queen here.'

'Very good, Fletcher,' said Lennie in the fruity voice of Banyard. I peered hard at Lennie's nose but it seemed the right shape. Lennie set the drinks on the table and with one gulp Hedley drank his two million pints and I thought: Stupid this. I'd have done better hijacking a Guinness tanker or something.

Then suddenly I was aware that Hedley's face was very close to mine and he was wearing lipstick and rouge. He said:

'You still owe me millions and millions of pints, Fletch.'

I drew back a bit and said:

'I know. You'll get it.'

'I don't mind scrubbing it, Fletch. If you're nice to me. Know what I mean, Fletch? Know what I mean?'

I began retreating towards a door that I knew was behind me and saying:

'This isn't like you, Hedley. This isn't like you.'

I was horrified, especially because Hedley was now a horrible skinny old woman, still with the crown on his head but now dressed in a low cut evening dress which also somehow showed his thin hairy legs. I reached behind me and opened the door, shouting:

'You'll get your beer, Hedley, but that's all you'll get. That's all you'll get.'

Then I backed quickly through the door and slammed it in his face. When I turned round there was a tremendous chess-board stretching away to the horizon and there, right in the distance, was my own terraced house in Muswell Hill and at the windows were my old woman and the kids waving at me and beckoning me. I started towards them joyously but I knew that I had to make knight moves because they is the bent ones. Then, as I started leaping in strange angles towards them, I saw the chess-board was also full of screws and judges and police cars and other pieces of the law which were trying to trap me. Some came zooming at me diagonally like bishops and others rushed straight ahead like rooks and some just stomped forwards, like pawns or coppers on a search, forming a solid wall that I would never get through. And now I could hear my old woman calling: 'Come on, love, you can do it! The kids is longing to see you. I've got a few million tins of beer in and we'll have a lovely evening round the telly. Come on, love. Come on, my old dear Fletch.' And I hopped madly towards them, gasping with effort, as the screws got closer and thicker and then I gave a shout of despair – and woke up.

It wasn't until the first grey light of morning began to seep through the bars that I got any peaceful sleep. For this reason I woke up feeling thick and dull and even after I'd sluiced my face I still felt under the weather. I was dressing slowly, scowling at the thought of the foul breakfast Lennie would be even then perpetrating in the kitchen, when Stapley, a blackmailer and lay preacher, peered into the dell.

'Coming to breakfast, Fletch?'

'In good time. In good time.'

'Did you hear that horrible scream in the night?'

'Which one?'

'It was that poor fellow Atkinson. He's been having these nightmares for ages now. He told the shrink but he only gave him an aspirin. You have to feel compassion for him, don't you, Fletch? A human soul like that in such torment?'

'What about all the souls you sold, Stapley?'

'I know that I've sinned, Fletch. And I'm paying. The Lord exacts a heavy penalty.'

'Oh yes? What do you do, leave it in a sealed envelope under a pew?'

Stapley smiled sweetly, and remarked:

' "Every idle word that men shall speak, they shall give account thereof in the day of judgment." Matthew, twelve, thirty-six.'

I picked up my boot and made as if to hurl it at him.

'Every hypocrite that pesters Fletcher of a morning shall get lump on head. Fletcher, seven, thirty.'

With very gratifying speed, Stapley's head disappeared from

the doorway and, feeling distinctly more chuffed, I finished dressing and set off towards the chow hall.

As I ambled along the landing, I noticed young Rudge belting along on the opposite side. He was going too fast, always a sign of a first-timer. A nick is like a minefield. You pick your way about slowly and cautiously for fear of stepping on trouble. And that's just what happened to Rudge. Except he didn't step on a mine. He ran full tilt into it. Only it wasn't a mine but something much worse. It was the Czar of Slade Prison himself, Harry Grout.

I'd seen it coming a second before it happened. Grouty had been ascending the stairs at a stately pace, accompanied by his two minders, and Rudge had swung off the landing into the stairwell and – pow! I'd had no time to shout a warning. Now I froze and watched events. The first thing that became clear was that Rudge had no idea whom he'd collided with and I cursed myself for not having clued him up about Grouty. There was no damage done. Grouty, in spite of his bulk, has the necessary quick instincts of his calling and, the instant Rudge's flying form had confronted him, he'd put out an arm and deflected the lad into the railings. Grouty was smiling that deep endearing smile of his which begins just below the eyes and ends at the tip of his second chin.

'What's the rush, son?' he asked mildly. 'You should watch where you're going.'

Rudge straightened himself up, rubbing the elbow he'd bumped, and snapped back.

'You should watch where *you're* going.'

I felt a slight shiver ripple down the back of my neck. I looked at Grouty's two strong-arms, one squat and bald and the other tall, broad and with long black greasy hair which gave him a deceptively girlish appearance. They made a slight involuntary movement towards Rudge but, trained to perfect obedience by Grouty, took no further action without his signal. I saw that Grouty's eyes, normally neatly folded into a menacing slit, had widened slightly, a very nasty sign, but he still spoke softly.

'What's your name, son?'

Surely, I thought, Rudge will get the message now. I mean, wherever he's done his street-corner apprenticeship in crime there must be some local heavy a bit like Grouty. Surely, he'll recognize the signs. But no. Young Rudge snapped back cheekily.

'What's it to you?'

Grouty's semaphore was very subtle. I just saw his right elbow twitch and the next moment Samson had twisted the kid like a rubber doll into a half-nelson. Rudge let out a scream of pain and then, with a sigh of relief, I saw something. Belting along the landing, from his little office, came a screw called Lassiter. But the power of the barons is mighty in the nick. As soon as Lassiter had sussed out the actors in the little drama he came to an uncertain halt. Grouty looked up at him non-chalantly and said clearly:

'There's no problem here, Mr Lassiter.'

I actually saw Lassiter's larynx bob slightly as he gulped and then the cowardly screw nodded, turned and retreated back to his office.

'Your name, son?' Grouty prompted the kid again.

The youngster, his face contorted with agony, managed to gasp:

'Name – name's Rudge. Ahhh!'

Grouty nodded, and returned the favour.

'My name's Harry Grout. Don't think we've had the pleasure. These are my friends, Samson and Delilah. Samson got his nickname because of the muscles and she got her's because of her striking resemblance to Hedy Lamarr.'

All this while Samson was twisting the boy's arm behind his back with those iron biceps of his and Rudge, although he'd got control of himself and was not making any more sound, was turning white with pain. Something had to be done or I'd have to muck out the pigs myself later on. I hurried towards the group, affecting not to notice the drama in progress.

'Here, Grouty!' I called, as I drew near.

Grouty glanced in my direction. I've done him one or two turns in the past, mainly because he asked me and no one ever refuses a favour to Grouty when he asks for one, and he nodded affably.

'Good morning, Fletch.'

Keeping my eyes firmly away from Rudge and Samson I launched into an improvised yarn.

'I just hear this one, Grouty. You know that dipstick what

works in the laundry, Robbie Patton? Well, apparently his old lady wants a divorce. So she sees a solicitor. He says, you got to have grounds – "Now there's insanity, but your old man's not bonkers, is he?" She shakes her head. "Then there's desertion – but since he's in the nick, he ain't going nowhere, is he?" She shakes her head again. "Then, there's cruelty – how about that?" "Oh no," the dumb female lisps, "my Robbie wouldn't hurt a fly." "I'm afraid," says the brief, "that only leaves adultery." "What's that?" she asks. So the lawyer explains to her the concept of adultery. Her face brightens. "Well, we've got him there," she says, "he's not the father of my child." Ha ha – good one, eh, Grouty?'

He nodded but I was sorry to notice that his smile failed to include his eyes.

'Very amusing, Fletch.'

'I don't get it,' grunted Delilah.

But my intervention seemed to have done the trick. Grouty made another signal, a very slight nod this time, to Samson and the bruiser released Rudge's arm. Rudge could not restrain a slight moan as he began to massage his wrenched shoulder. Grouty said to the lad:

'Pleased to have met you, Rudge,' and then the terrible trio continued on their way.

'Who was he?' gasped Rudge.

'Harry Grout,' I explained. 'He runs this nick.'

'Thought that was the Governor's job,' groaned the kid, reasonably.

'Only officially. Next time you run into Grouty – and he'll be watching you now – bow, curtsy or lick his boots if that's what he wants.'

And I set off once more towards my breakfast goo. But I had only taken a step when a word from Rudge halted me. It was an unexpected word and it completed the job of lifting my spirits which my encounter with Stapley had begun.

'Thanks.'

As luck would have it, I found myself sitting at breakfast next to the other new arrival, Oakes. Only later it occurred to me that it hadn't been luck but that Oakes had rigged it for his own purposes. Oakes started the conversation.

'Saw that,' he grunted between mouthfuls of porridge. (Yes, we do really get a fair amount of porridge in the diet, specially in winter.)

'What?' I asked innocently.

'What you did for the kid.'

'Oh, that? Well, he's my assistant, isn't he? Wouldn't be no use to me with articulated arms.'

We slurped porridge in silence for a time. I was trying to remember something; where I'd heard the name Oakes before. I'd never done time with him. I was certain of that. And I didn't think I'd ever heard him mentioned by one of the lads. But there was something—

'He's the man around here, is he?' Oakes asked.

'What? Who?'

'What's his name – Grout? London heavy, isn't he?'

There was something in the way Oakes talked which made me uneasy. Most people just sensed Grouty's authority and once they'd sensed it they didn't discuss him in such a free and easy way. That was it, there was no fear and respect in Oakes' voice, and fear and respect are the two things Grouty always inspires in people. Mind you, there was no disrespect in Oakes' tone either, just interest, as if he was talking about an equal. I said:

'Yuh well – Grouty has a certain amount of influence, although it's not true, as some believe, that the Governor simply passes on his orders.'

Oakes smiled pleasantly and we slurped some more.

'Pal of his, are you?' he asked next.

Pal? Of Grouty's? It was like asking the tea lady at the House of Commons if she hobnobbed with the Prime Minister.

'We've been acquainted for some time,' I said, trying to suppress a shudder at one or two memories.

'Just here – inside? Or did you know him outside as well?'

'Just here,' I said quickly. 'Just here.'

Oakes smiled again and then I recognized the smile. Sydney Oakes – Manchester top heavy. Of course, his face had smiled out from the *Sun* after his last big job – and it had been a *big* job! He'd been nabbed in the end but they'd never found the loot. Yeah but – that was years ago. Then I had it. He wasn't starting his sentence here. He'd been transferred from some other nick.

41

And he wasn't the typical Slade customer either. He was in a different league from anyone else – anyone else, that is, except Grouty. So now there were two top villains on the premises.

I gulped down the last of my porridge and rose to leave.

'Nice to have met you,' said Oakes.

'Yeah – you too—' I muttered.

But I wasn't too happy. Two big men in a small nick could lead to anything and something told me I was going to be around when 'anything' happened. How right I was!

3 Fill the flowing bowl

'Well, Mr Beale,' said Mr Mackay jovially, after lock-up, 'I think we've earned a dram. What do you say?'

'It's a long drive into Workington, isn't it, sir?'

'Come, come, Mr Beale, you're forgetting. The Prison Officers' Club – I've been looking forward to introducing you to it.'

'Ah – yes, sir.'

Mr Mackay suppressed a slight pulse of irritation. Why was it no one showed any enthusiasm for his baby? He considered that it had been very imaginative and bold of himself to see the potential of the old coke store when the prison had gone over to gas for its heating. He'd approached the Governor and explained his plan and the Governor had graciously given permission for the club. Then he, Mackay, had rooted around in the second-hand shops in Workington and, out of his own pocket, purchased some very classy horse brasses with which to decorate the place. He'd supervised the construction of the bar – by us cons, needless to say – and the installation of the furniture. And now the ruddy club was open for business. But somehow it didn't get very much. Why was it? Surely the other officers should regard it, as he did, as a place for rest and recreation and where professional matters could be chewed over in an unofficial setting. Damn it, he was proud of his club but this newcomer, Beale, who hadn't even seen it yet, seemed somehow to have contracted the prevailing attitude of scepticism about its attractions. Mackay jerked his neck sharply to one side to try and dislodge the irritation, and said:

'Come along, Mr Beale. I guarantee you'll like the atmosphere.'

And the two screws stumped off to the dingy wooden door in the massive wall which led to the former coke cellar. Mackay flung open – well, heaved open – the creaking old door and stood back.

'There we are!' he announced proudly. 'Welcome to the Slade Prison, Prison Officers' Club. What do you think of it, Mr Beale?'

The new screw peered in dubiously. The sight that met his eyes was not one of bright lights and inviting furniture. He perceived no tables covered with shining white cloths and laid with gleaming knives and forks. No satin-smooth dance-floor invited his booted feet to glide into a delightful tango. There were no elegantly dressed revellers laughing merrily as they gulched champagne from shining goblets. The thrilling strains of a first-rate orchestra did not enchant his ear holes. No, it has to be admitted that the facilities were not such as one might expect to find in The Talk of the Town or other tony London clubs. They did not even begin to compare with the simpler allurements – such as a juke box, bar stools and a one-armed bandit – offered by my own much-beloved Rainbow Club in Muswell Hill where I have whiled away many an afternoon reminiscing over old crimes.

What Mr Beale clapped eyes on was a cold bare room of whitewashed brick in which a grotty lamp made from one of those Chianti bottles with straw bottoms was practically the only cheerful facet. No, that is not quite true. Some tatty curtains had been pulled across the barred windows thus hiding their true nature about as well as a couple of scatter cushions would camouflage an electric chair. Then there were the horse brasses hung on nails and a poster showing a bull fighter persecuting a bull. There was, of course, a simple functional bar equipped with the usual range of intoxicating spirits and beer-pumps and behind the bar a door leading to the store room in which the precious fluids were safely locked away from anyone who might care to lay hands on them – which is what I'm leading up to really. There was also a notice board hung on the wall which gave particulars of the treats available to off-duty screws like a trip to Morecambe and an away match with the darts team.

'Well, Mr Beale, what do you think of it?'

Mr Beale thought it looked like a coke store with a bar in it but he did not feel it would be tactful to admit this feeling.

'Quite snug, don't you think?' prompted Mackay, a trifle pointedly.

'Very nice, sir,' gulped poor Beale.

And the two screws marched up to the bar.

'Evening all,' sang Mackay cheerfully.

'All' consisted of three screws, Barrowclough, Cox and Miller, standing shivering with their half pints. They all dutifully called back a greeting to their chief. Then a sixth person made his presence felt. Chalky, the barman, who had been fixing a new keg on to the tap, rose up from beneath the bar.

'Ah, Chalky—' began Mackay, but Beale nipped in swiftly.

'What will you have, sir?' he asked in a toadying way.

But Mackay, as lordly as a highland laird displaying the facilities of his estate to a couple of visiting oil sheiks prepared to pay ten thousand quid for a salmon and twice that for a grouse (which we have daily for free in the nick, ha ha) said:

'No, no – it's my shout.' And he turned to the trembling figure of poor frozen Barrowclough who looked as pathetic as a heifer in a snow drift. 'What will you have, Frank?'

'Oh no, I'd better not,' returned Barrowclough. 'I must be off in a minute.'

Mackay was again aware of that spurt of irritation. Why were they always so keen to get out of his ravishing club? But he again twitched his turkey neck and recovered his poise.

'Nonsense, man,' he pronounced firmly. And then to Chalky: 'Same again here. Mr Beale and I will have a pint of your finest, and I will have a wee dram on the side. Purely medicinal.'

Chalky drew the beers and dispensed Mackay's nip and, while this was going on, silence fell on the little company, which allowed them to hear the cruel wind whistling across the moor. Even Mackay felt a treacherous stir of doubt as to whether his club was really as cosy as it should be. But, after he'd downed his fire-water at a gulp, the warm glow in his belly brought back his confidence. He turned to his disciple Beale.

'Of course,' he said earnestly, 'there's always room for improvement. If you can think of any way in which the club can be made more comfortable just let the committee know. I happen to be the chairman.'

'I'll do that, yes,' said Beale, then added with the sickening insincerity of the boot-licker, 'but I can't imagine any way it could be improved, sir.'

'Oh, I don't know,' beamed Mackay. 'The great thing about a club like this is it gives us prison officers a chance to unwind at the end of the day and have a few laughs. Need a few, after dealing with that rabble inside. Isn't that true, Frank?'

Barrowclough gulped hard because he has always – and I give him full marks for that – regarded us inmates as human beings and not just rabble. But he didn't dare contradict Mackay directly. So he said miserably:

'Oh, yes, it's invaluable in that respect.'

Mackay nodded with satisfaction. Then he remembered that Beale was new to the game and still needed to be knocked into the proper vicious shape for being a Grade A screw.

'You haven't entered a glamour profession, Mr Beale,' he commenced earnestly. 'We're underpaid, understaffed and over-looked. Even though every time we walk those landings, we put our lives on the line. The public never hears of us, of course. Except adversely. When some namby-pamby politician takes up the case of a psychopath who claims that we've abused him.'

'What do the politicians know?' asked Beale tactfully.

Mackay grunted assent and continued:

'That's why you'll find we're a pretty tight bunch. Unified, if you like, in the face of criminal hostility and public indifference. That's why this place – this Prison Officers' Club – is of such tremendous importance to us and why we treasure it.'

He glanced around to receive the approving looks he was sure that this speech would win from his brother officers. But they all appeared to have had urgent business elsewhere. Beale and him were the only ones left.

'Where the hell is everybody!' roared Mackay, his neck jerking like a belly dancer's belly.

Mackay was not the only one in the nick who spent a good deal of time thinking about the Prison Officers' Club that September. There was one other person for whom it was becoming something of an obsession. Who? Norman Stanley Fletcher. And why? Why did I find my thoughts repeatedly returning to it as, for example, I stood and watched the pigs snuffling at their trough? No, that wasn't the only reason. It was also because it was the one place in the whole bleeding nick where there was a good supply of booze. Now, don't get the wrong idea. I have never been a lush or a wino. On the outside, I have no difficulty waiting until morning opening time before downing my first pint. If you was to open the fridge in our kitchen – the neat little one I nicked from that cut-rate warehouse – you would find it contained no more than a dozen or so of lagers. I am just your common or garden sociable drinker who recognizes that alcohol is an agreeable staff to help you pick your way along life's stony path. But *when* is that path most stony? Right in one. When you're doing time. When is the need for a stout stick with which to ease the strain on your aching feet greatest? When the biased judge intones: You will go to prison for five bleeding years. And then for the five bleeding years after he says it, or three if you're lucky and get parole. And that is just when the fiendish State, which thinks of nothing but crushing men and has always failed to perceive that the spirit of daring and enterprise which is so much part of the criminal's make-up is really, properly looked at, a priceless national asset, declares: thou shalt not booze! What a balm and a blessing it would be for your hapless felon, during the long nights of his incarceration, if he could keep a half bottle of scotch in his locker or amble down the landing to a well appointed bar to commune with his fellow unfortunates.

For a lot of cons, the enforced deprivation of nature's great gift is the worst hardship they have to face. And for that reason a great deal of ingenuity is spent inside most of Her Majesty's penal establishments in trying to get a drink. Now one approach, which I have never favoured, is simply to gulp down anything not actually marked POISON in dirty great red letters with a skull and crossbones menacingly drawn beside it that you can lay your hands on. I remember one dipsomaniac, assigned, because he'd been a mechanic on the outside, to looking after the prison vehicles, who drank about a gallon of petrol a day for several weeks until they found him writhing underneath a pick-up truck. He'd blown his mind completely and had to be carted off to some bin. Others swallow rubbing alcohol, cleaning fluid and even the contents of fire extinguishers. But there is considerable risk and certain discomfort attached to these practices and I have always shunned them. The other approach, which I have myself enthusiastically practised, is what might be called the 'poteen' method, ie to brew, ferment, distil or otherwise manufacture some kind of home-brew that actually contains alcohol. It's not all that difficult since the Lord in His wisdom has decreed that almost all vegetable matter, suitably treated, will begin to turn into alcohol; and I have, in the past, produced some quite acceptable beverages out of materials as varied as orange pips, potato peelings, dried apricots and once from some armfuls of dandelions picked while we was doing ditching out on the moors and smuggled back into our cells in our underpants. However, nine times out of ten, the screws find this stuff no matter how ingeniously you store it and then again, and with the best will in the world, its quality never really equals that of even the grottiest merchandise on sale in your local off-licence.

Christmas, as I have mentioned before, was approaching and that is the time when the absence of intoxicating beverages is most keenly felt by all cons. And this Christmas I had left it too late to produce anything much in the way of home-brew. I knew that it was likely that somewhere in the nick a secret still was steaming and that, come the joyful holiday, I might acquire a few thimblefuls of stimulating refreshment. But I couldn't get that Prison Officers' Club out of my mind. In there, there was booze galore. Whisky, gin, beer, everything to delight the felon's heart. If only there was some way to lay hands on it—

'What are you thinking of, Fletcher?' rasped Mackay, coming up behind me unexpectedly as I watched the pigs devouring their mash (which, it had already occurred to me, might easily provide the basis for some kind of intoxicant).

'Booze,' I murmured absently, before I'd realized who it was that had accosted me.

'Booze, is it?' chuckled the Monster. 'You're in luck, Fletcher.'

I blinked and straightened up.

'How do you mean, Mr Mackay?' I asked, bewildered.

'It so happens our barman, Chalky, is down with carbuncles. I need a replacement for a week or two.'

'Barman? Me?' I asked, dazed. 'What are you saying, Mr Mackay?'

'Make a change from pigs, won't it, Fletcher?'

Not really, I thought, but naturally kept it to myself.

'Come along, Fletcher, I'm going to show you your new duties.'

It was like a dream, only a good one this time. Mr Mackay, my old tormentor, leading me to an ocean of booze. In a daze, I gave Rudge detailed instructions as to the continued well-being of our swine, and then followed the swaggering screw to the Prison Officers' Club.

Can you imagine how I felt? For years the nearest thing I'd seen to a drink was a bottle-cap full of murky fluid, smelling like ammonia and tasting like prussic acid. And now Mr Mackay was ushering me into an aladdin's cave of refreshment. Upside down, behind the bar, gleamed row after row of ravishing bottles full of shining, transparent delight: whisky, gin, vodka, rum. Neatly ranked beneath the bar was a line of stout barrels, each chock-full of succulent beer. I felt my heart fluttering like that of a miser being shown round the mint. Already I could see little caches of booze sprouting in secret corners of the nick where Lennie and I could dart in for a refreshing gulp during our normal rounds, and as for Christmas—

'Is that understood, Fletcher?' asked Mackay.

He'd been explaining my duties to me – me, who'd been barman in the sergeants' mess in Kuala Lumpur and could draw a pint of beer and roll a fag at the same time.

'No problem, Mr Mackay,' I said earnestly, 'and I want you to know, sir, that I shall not abuse the trust you have placed in me.'

Mackay cackled like a witch about to jab the crucial pin into her wax doll.

'Trust doesn't come into it, Fletcher.'

I was a bit taken aback. Mackay knew as well as I did what booze means to a con, but I couldn't see it was in my interests to dot the *i*s. So I just gulped and said meekly:

'Of course not, sir.'

'Ah, but do you know why trust doesn't come into it, Fletcher?'

I had a feeling that what he *didn't* mean was that he'd had a change of heart and had arranged this treat for me because of a sudden overwhelming feeling of affection.

'Why is that, sir?' I asked.

'Because, Fletcher,' he chuckled evilly, 'you would find it easier to steal the Governor's shirt than to make off with one single drop of intoxicating fluid from this bar.'

He then outlined the anti-theft precautions that he'd devised and I had to admit they seemed thorough. In the first place, I would be searched entering and leaving, then I was never, under any circumstances, to be in the place alone. At opening time, I would wait until a screw arrived with the key and he would precede me in. At closing time, I would precede the last screw out. If the place cleared, I would have to leave before the last customer and wait outside until a new one arrived. Any time I had to get new stock from the store room I would be accompanied by a screw. And all this was only the beginning. Every drop of booze had to match exactly with the monetary receipts or I would be out on my ear. But the unkindest cut of all was there would be no leavings or dregs which, of course, no con would despise and which I had been counting on to gradually build up a little private cellar. Mackay pointed dramatically to a bin and announced that it was a third full of Jeyes fluid.

'All prison officers,' he continued meaningfully, 'have been instructed that all remnants and slops are to be emptied into that bin. There will be nothing, repeat nothing, left in glasses to find its way into criminal stomachs. Is that clear, Fletcher?'

'Very clear, Mr Mackay, which is more than can be said for what's going to be in that bin.'

'I think we understand each other, Fletcher.'

Too true. I understood it now very clearly. It wasn't Santa Mackay that had brought me to this beautiful cave of plenty. It was the same old sadistic fiend he'd always been. I mean, what's worse than craving something with all your heart? Having that something in front of your eyes and not being able to get at it. Take your hermit who goes into the desert to escape the pangs of the flesh – as long as he's sitting up there on his pole all alone with nothing to look at but sand and the odd camel ambling past, he can stay the course. But take your same hermit and set him up on the stage of a Soho strip joint and it just wouldn't be on. Isn't there some story about a king who was planted by an evil wizard up to his neck in a lake and then made mad with thirst? Every time he bent over for a swig of that pure tempting water, the lake sank down and he couldn't get at it. Then when he straightened up again the water rose to his neck once more. Diabolical. But nothing compared to the hideous fate Mackay had devised for me. I was also going to be up to my neck in a lake but not one of boring old water. Mackay had planted me up to my neck in a lake of booze and the intention was that I wasn't to get a drop. And he'd be watching me, I knew that, waiting for me to break and when I did, which was perhaps the whole point of the operation, he'd haul me before the Governor and I'd probably get solitary and loss of remission. Yes, it was a scheme worthy of his black heart. But, at first, I was not unduly dismayed. One thing at a time – at least I was close to the booze. Now it was down to me to find some way of outsmarting Mackay and making off with my fair share.

But by the end of the first week of my new job, I was beginning to wonder if I was going to make it. Mackay's precautions were proving nearly foolproof. Goes without saying I'd managed to get a taste of the stuff now and then, mainly by dipping my finger in customers' drinks and then sucking it and once I managed to mop up quite a large pool of spilled Gordon's and, when no eye was upon me, squeeze it into a glass and get a very satisfying gulp. But this was really just increasing the frustration. There I was spending half my waking life in a drinking den and never once managing to get a real lift. It was torment. My sufferings were increased by the pressure that my fellow inmates, knowing of my activities, were beginning to put on me.

'What the heel are you messing about with, Fletch?' asked Black Jock indignantly, at the fourth committee meeting. It was a committee we'd got together, composed of myself, Lennie, McLaren and Bunny Warren, to promote the removal of our fair share of liquor from the club. We called it PIST, short for Prisoners' Intrigue for Stealing Tipple, but so far all we'd come up with was impractical Heath Robinson-type schemes for piping the stuff out through tunnels and suchlike.

'It's not that easy,' I said wearily. 'Mackay's thought of everything.'

'Not like you, Fletch,' grumbled Bunny. 'You sure you and Godber aren't stashing it away?'

'I resent that, Warren,' I returned bitterly. 'Much worse for me – water, water everywhere and not a drop to drink, as the poet said.'

'We don't want poetry. We want booze!' said McLaren, with an unpleasant note of menace in his voice.

'Then think of some practical scheme for obtaining it,' I urged him for the tenth time.

Bunny's eyes assumed the glazed look which always heralds the production of some daft idea. Sure enough, in a moment he exclaimed:

'Think I've got it. You empty the slop bin down the drain outside the club – isn't that right, Fletch?'

'Right.'

'So all we've got to do is put a big plastic bag in the drain and we're laughing.'

I nodded enthusiastically.

'You mean we can all have a final binge on Jeyes fluid before we dies in horrible agony?'

' 'Course not. That would be suicide. We treat it with chemicals first. I heard a programme on the radio about how you can separate things with chemicals. So that's what we do and then we can drink the booze.'

'And where do we find the master chemist and the fully equipped laboratory to perform these wonders, you stupid nurk? Bunny, we'd proceed much faster if you would limit your contribution to total silence.'

'Well, at least I get ideas,' he sulked.

'And that's what you'd better do, Fletch,' said Jock nastily, rising to his feet, 'before the next committee meeting tomorrow night. I'll tell you quite frankly – I'm getting a wee bit impatient.'

'But—'

But it was too late. McLaren, looking like a thundercloud, something he does well, stalked out of the dell. Lennie and I looked at each other and sighed.

The next day, I ran out of gin during lunchtime opening hours and had to get a screw to accompany me into the store room for more. There were two customers in the place, Miller and Barrowclough, and I drew Miller. We went through into the real aladdin's cave at the rear and once more I felt my brain reel as I contemplated its case after case of fine spirits, enough to keep the entire convict population of Slade blissfully drunk for the whole holiday period and all destined to vanish down the throats of the detested screws. Once more, as I extracted the replacement bottle of Gordon's, I snatched glances all about, trying to come up with some scheme for appropriating a bottle or two. Above my head was a wooden hatch which I'd figured out must have been how coke was once delivered. But I could tell that the hatch was outside the inner wall and so there would be no way, even if there was any method of removing a bottle without it being missed, which there wasn't, that it could be collected even if poked up through the hatch.

'Hurry up, Fletcher,' grunted Miller.

I extracted the fresh bottle, sighed, and we returned to the bar. Miller drained his light ale and headed towards the door. Before he got there, he paused and then turned and looked at old Barrowclough with what, if he hadn't been a screw, I might have mistaken for a concerned expression.

'Everything all right, Frank?' he asked.

Mr Barrowclough raised his head slowly, like a cow contemplating a train chugging past the bottom of its field.

'Hm? Oh yes, thank you, Mishter Shmiller,' he replied with a distinct slur. And that did it! Certainly I've read about that Italian bloke that jumped out of his bath because the idea for the loofah or whatever had come to him in a flash. I wasn't the first one to get a great discovery like a bolt of lightning. But it was so clear, so perfect, so fully formed that I could hardly refrain from shouting, just like that Italian, 'You stinker!' or something. That night, when the committee assembled, and before Black Jock could even growl threateningly, I held up my hand and announced:

'Gentlemen, I have the solution to our little problem. We is all as good as smashed already. I think I can promise you that this Christmas will be a merry one.'

They gazed at me like they must have gazed at Einstein when

he proclaimed the Theory of Relativity, which concerns how to deal with your mother-in-law, and you could have heard a tonsil drop. Then Lennie said:

'How do you mean, Fletch?'

'I mean that we've been thinking like mutton-heads, me included, making everything complicated. Like they say in chess: simple moves is the best. Now what is the simplest way of obtaining booze?'

'Nip down to the off-licence and buy it,' rasped Jock with what I could tell he thought of as devastating irony.

'Exactly! And that's just what we is going to do. Except we will purchase it from the local equivalent of the off-licence which happens to be the Prison Officers' Club.'

Again there was silence. I saw that Lennie was looking at me in a slightly pitying way as if he thought that the ordeal I'd been going through had finally blown my thinking equipment. But I wasn't worried. I went on:

'Bunny, you can answer this one: what is it you require before you can purchase booze in a shop?'

Bunny wrinkled up his brow. It was possibly an unfair challenge to his rudimentary brains but then his eye brightened and he suggested:

'Money?'

'Right in one. So hand over every penny you own – and I know about the two quid you got stashed away from flogging those spectacles you whipped from the Parole Board lady. You too, Jock. We have to pool all our resources and, to prove my own full cooperation, I'll just get the one pound, seventy-nine pence which represents all my earthly treasure from the hole in the mattress.'

'Hang on,' exclaimed Jock wearily, holding up his hand. 'I want to get this straight: you're telling us you're just going to walk in this evening and buy a bottle of hooch?'

'No, I'm not. I'm telling you that the one thing I can smuggle into the club is money because although they search me they never make me take off my shoes.'

'So,' continued Jock, trying to keep up with me, 'you smuggle money in. Then what?'

'Then, as you suggest, I buy hooch, only in quarter bottles,

53

and I put it down in the off-sales book to Mr Barrowclough.'

Lennie looked puzzled.

'Sounds to me, Fletch, as if you're proposing we buy Barra some booze.'

'Right. Only he doesn't know about it.'

Jock began to look thoughtful, as if some glimmering of my stupendous scheme was beginning to dawn on him.

'All right. I'm with you that far, Fletch. On paper you then own a quarter bottle of Scotch. But then what? They search you when you leave. How do you get it out?'

I permitted myself a little triumphant chuckle.

'I don't. Barrowclough does.'

'What?'

They gazed at me in doubt and wonder.

'Barrowclough?' exclaimed Jock doubtfully. 'He's the best of that bunch but he'd never do a thing like that.'

' 'Course he wouldn't – if he *knew* he was doing it.'

Then I stopped mucking about and told them the plan in all its beauty. Mind you, it wasn't that simple. It would take a lot of the different skills we all possessed. It was based on the sad fact, which I'd ascertained in sympathetic conversation that afternoon, that Barra's wife was having a tender relationship with a local shepherd. As a result of this humiliation, Barra was hitting the bottle and was now my most regular customer, guaranteed to be mopping it up during opening hours.

The next day Jock 'accidentally' cut his hand and, while being treated in the medical room, managed to snaffle a few mogadon pills. With one of these, and the exact amount of money for a quarter bottle of Haig in my left sock, I reported for duty at lunchtime. Miller let me in, frisked me and ordered a lager. Mackay came in for a half and a nip and, sure enough, before long, long-faced Barrowclough arrived and settled down on his own with a large Scotch. I noticed that Mackay and Miller glanced at him from time to time but then Beale arrived and he and Mackay discussed the vile qualities of prisoners with relish. An hour later, only Barrowclough was left. By then, I'd succeeded in extracting the money and pills from my sock and, the next time Barrowclough ordered a Scotch, it reached him enriched with powdered mogadon. As soon as I saw that he was getting a bit dopey, I wrote him down for a quarter bottle of whisky and put the money from PIST in the off-sales tin. Then, the next time I served Barrowclough a drink, I slipped the quarter bottle into his pocket. He never noticed. In fact, the state he was in, he wouldn't have registered if I'd tucked a small python into his pocket. At closing time, very unsteady by now, he departed. By then, Beale had returned and it was him that saw me off the premises. The only thing that bothered me was, I thought perhaps I'd overdone it with the mogadon. Barrowclough was making himself senseless enough without any help from me, and it wouldn't do if he passed out or collapsed before – but it worked like a charm. As Barrowclough reeled through the prison on his normal rounds, Bunny, darting round the corner without paying due attention, as he is prone to do, crashed head-long into the dazed Barrowclough, nearly knocking the bovine screw down. Bunny, of course, apologized profusely and then hurried on. Now, of course, Bunny's one indisputable talent is as a dip. He has some of the nimblest and most sensitive fingers ever to pass through Slade Prison and, when he left the blinking Barrowclough, the quarter bottle of Scotch had miraculously jumped into Bunny's own pocket. Not that it stayed there long. Bunny scampered on to the kitchen where Lennie, without attracting attention, had already succeeded in draining a tin of tomato juice through a pin-sized hole and now, by some magic of his own, managed to replace the insipid red juice with the fiery brown stuff that Bunny brought him. Lennie then sealed the tin and placed it at the back of a special shelf in the stores and – the deed was done. PIST had succeeded in transferring a quarter bottle of Scotch from the Prison Officers' Club to its own private cellar without leaving a trail that anyone could follow. What a triumph!

That night, PIST held a very jovial meeting in Lennie's and my cell.

'You're a wonder, Fletch,' conceded Black Jock admiringly.

'Yuh well,' I lowered my eyes modestly.

'As far as I can see,' said Lennie thoughtfully, 'there's no reason why we shouldn't nick a quarter bottle a day more or less indefinitely.'

We were all silent, contemplating this giddy prospect.

'We'd run out of money,' objected Bunny.

'Still, we've got enough for quite a few more, haven't we, Fletch?' asked McLaren hopefully.

'Six anyway, and then we can all flog our valuables. No, what I'm more afraid of is that Mrs Barrowclough will get bored with her current swain. Our drinking future is solely dependent on her love life.'

It was a sobering thought but Bunny cheered us up by recalling:

'When she was going with the meter reader, she kept it up for two months.'

'So, presumably, did the meter reader,' I added humorously. 'A shepherd should have at least as much staying power.'

Then we settled down to make detailed plans for the next day.

For the next four days, the operation went as smooth as a bent brief's plea and on the evening of the fourth day, PIST held a very special meeting.

'Fellow members,' I announced, 'we are gathered together this evening to commemorate, and celebrate, the conclusion of our first week of successful trading. Len?'

I turned to my flat-mate expectantly. Bunny, minding at the door, gave the all-clear and Lennie dipped his hand swiftly into the mattress and produced what looked like an unlabelled tin. This is exactly what it was but, after Lennie had pierced it in two places, what gushed out, into our eagerly waiting mugs, was not prison goo but a glorious stream of Haig's finest. For the next half hour, rapture was the keynote but, of course, a quarter of a quarter bottle does not go all that far and all too soon the tin was empty.

'Pity the stores are closed,' sighed Black Jock, 'or I'd table the motion that we open another tin.'

'Yeah,' I grunted, 'we deserve it. Should have thought of it before.'

'I did,' murmured Lennie modestly and, reaching into the mattress, produced another gleaming tin.

Naturally, we bestowed a vote of thanks on our colleague for his foresight and then proceeded to get lightly, but very satisfyingly, smashed.

'I suppose your foresight didn't run to a third tin?' asked McLaren hopefully but Lennie shook his head.

'Wouldn't be safe. Can't have Bunny turning cartwheels at lock-up. They'd notice.'

This was indisputably true. Bunny was already showing a tendency towards rolling eyes and loose limbs.

'Besides,' I said, 'our real aim is a festive Festive Season. We've only three tins stashed now and our luck could run out any time.'

Little did I know that my words were to prove prophetic. The very next day, as I went to slip the usual quarter bottle into the somnolent Barrowclough's pocket, the door suddenly flew open and Beale strode in like a whirlwind, well, like a whirlwind in boots. At that instant, my hand, holding the delectable bottle, was about six inches from Barra's pocket. Naturally, I was not caught napping, although I was undoubtedly caught. But, with the smooth transition only a life of crime equips a man with, I continued moving my hand up to the table, where I deposited the bottle in front of the dozing screw, announcing in a cheerful voice:

'There's your quarter bottle of Haig, Mr Barrowclough, I marked it off on the off-sales.'

Had it worked? Beale's eyes narrowed and he looked suspiciously from me to the bottle.

'What are you up to, Fletcher?' he asked nastily.

'Doing my job, sir,' I returned earnestly, 'as willingly and efficiently as I can.'

'What's that bottle of whisky there?'

'For Mr Barrowclough, sir. He often takes a quarter with him.'

'Does he?'

Beale strode over to us. He reached down and shook Barra's shoulder.

'Frank? Did you order this whisky?'

'Hm? Wha— wazzamatter?' blinked the cuckold.

'Fletcher alleges you ordered this quarter bottle of whisky.'

'You remember, sir,' I urged helpfully, 'you said you needed it to keep you going.'

'Did I?' gasped Barrowclough. 'Very probably I did, Mr Beale. My life is not an easy one at present.'

'Harrmph,' commented Beale but, to my dismay, he then strode to the bar and seized the off-sales book. He turned through it, and then turned back to Barra.

'You've been doing this regularly, Frank.'

'That's right,' I piped up. 'All week, because his missus – that is – surely we should have a little compassion for another's marital misfortunes, Mr Beale?'

'Shut up, Fletcher. Frank, have you been taking a quarter of a bottle with you every lunchtime?'

Barrowclough shook his head wearily but, to my immense relief, contradicted the gesture by murmuring:

'Quite possibly. Quite possibly.'

'I see,' grunted Beale sourly. 'Well then, I suggest you tuck it away in your pocket, Frank, before Fletcher gets any naughty ideas.'

I chuckled disarmingly as if the suggestion was a ludicrous one. But my heart was in my mouth as I watched Barra reach over limply and take the bottle. Would he stash it in the right pocket? Or the wrong one? It turned out, to my immense relief at the time and great dismay later, to be the right one only that turned out to be the wrong one if you see what I mean which you probably don't but will when I've explained what followed. What followed, of course, was the normal continuation of our, by now, smooth-running operation. Barra finally reeled off into the prison proper and had his usual violent encounter with Bunny. Bunny pattered swiftly on to the kitchen and transferred the joy juice to Lennie. Lennie coaxed it into the customary prepared tin and stashed the tin in the customary place. And it was then that Beale pounced. He'd guessed, it turned out, that something was up the moment he'd laid eyes on me and the bottle in the club. But he was now showing the kind of demon's stuff that was in him. He'd monitored the whole of our operation after that because he knew that if he didn't track the stuff to its source, he wouldn't get his hands on what he shrewdly suspected we'd already nicked. So you see what I meant when I said Barra put it in the right pocket which proved to be the wrong one? If he'd put it in the wrong pocket then, when he'd had his prearranged meeting with Bunny, the nimble felon would have failed to cop the merchandise and Beale would never have brought off his big stroke what sent Bunny, me and Lennie to the solitary wing for three sordid days. Black Jock got off Scot free, ha ha – get it, *Scot* free? because no one knew he was a member of PIST and indeed the secret of PIST was never revealed to the screws and to this day remains one of the most colourful chapters in the history of Slade Prison.

When we came out of solitary, PIST met for the last time. There were no recriminations. Everyone agreed that it had been a sweet caper and that the half bottle of hooch we'd shared had made it the finest evening any of us could remember. We were also cheered when word reached us that Mackay had been reprimanded by the Governor for putting temptation in my path and that was also the reason why I got my job on the farm back. We all agreed that henceforth we would keep a very sharp eye out for some opportunity to pay Beale back for what he'd done to us. Later in this book I hope to tell you how we did it.

4 Big deals and little deals

A certain amount of nicking goes on in the nick which is not all that surprising when you consider that six hundred thieves are locked up there. What *is* surprising is how *little* thieving actually takes place. The most important reason for this, in my opinion, is that thieving in the nick goes against the instincts of the thief. What do I mean by that? I mean that the method of operation followed by almost any professional grab artist is to make a nice haul somewhere and then to remove himself, and the loot, as far as he possibly can from the scene of the crime. Now this is of course very difficult – why mince words? – impossible, in the nick. You are trapped on the scene of the crime which also happens to be the scene of your punishment for previous crimes. This produces a very uncomfortable situation for the criminal. At any moment, his victim may bear down upon him, demanding to search his possessions in order to recover his watch/razor/snout or whatever. Also, the victim bearing down on him is not some meek and polite bloke who wouldn't say boo to a bee but another thief, and quite likely a burly one serving time for grievous bodily harm. Grievous bodily harm is something that is practised by some thieves – although I've never had no part in it myself – but which all thieves dislike having practised on themselves. So you have to be very careful who you nick from if you're on the nick in the nick. Of course, that leaves the screws, and nicking from them, as from any casual visitor, is a time-honoured practice although the pickings are usually slim. Another reason which restrains thieves from thieving in the nick is a kind of thieves' honour. It is all very well for thieves to thieve from honest citizens but there is a code which says: do not thieve from your own kind. There are reptilian specimens like Ives who ignore this code but all it usually gets them is having their shins dented by Grouty's heavies when they get caught thieving, which they almost always do in the end.

So what is the result of this situation? There is a great deal of trading in the nick. This is ironical if you think about it. You lock up six hundred thieves together and straight away they all turn into small businessmen. Now, of course, the quality and quantity of merchandise swopped in the nick is not anything that would send a ripple of excitement through the world's commodity markets. Your Clores and Rothschilds would be unlikely to hold top-level conferences, briefing expensive silks and taking the advice of technical experts, in order to participate in a deal involving the exchange of three hand-rolled snouts for a fruit and nut bar. They would consider it beneath their dignity to negotiate the transfer of a soft toilet roll, purloined from the Governor's private loo, in exchange for eight safety pins and half a tube of toothpaste. There is no doubt that businessmen on the outside, no matter how small, would regard most of the transactions that occur behind bars as somewhat pathetic. And so they are. But it is amazing how much they can mean to a convicted felon. I have myself felt nearly as much satisfaction and sense of ruthless business enterprise from obtaining a razor-blade on credit as your free tycoon feels when he snaffles up a steel mill.

So in this chapter I propose to acquaint you with some of the commerce that goes on inside. Now in spite of what I said above, all of it is not petty and I will start with a truly big deal. I only learned about it much later, when its results began to manifest themselves in a way that particularly affected me and Lennie. But all will be revealed in due course.

It started when Barrowclough strolled past the open door of Grouty's cell one morning. And here I had better pause to describe to you in greater detail than I have already done our own beloved Harry Grout and also his fairytale flowery dell, the only one in the whole of Slade Nick which quite often really is flowery because Grouty somehow manages to lay his hands on bunches of fresh flowers.

Harry Grout is a class villain from The Smoke. He's a London man with the grey face of the East End which is where his name is one to be reckoned with. Over the past decade or so Grout's firm has always been one of the three or four top outfits there and Grouty commands respect in any nick in the land. He's about fifty with a sharp-featured face and a soft-featured body, soft from too many years behind bars since he came unstuck and was brought back from Alassio in Italy, manacled to Scotcher of the Yard. But Grouty has resources denied to most cons and he uses these to buy both luxuries and servants. The luxuries fill his dell, where he has a stereo system, lovebirds in a cage, curtains and a pretty bed-cover. It's more like a cosy holiday bungalow than a prison cell. But, you may ask if you do not know how these things are fixed inside, why do the screws and Governor permit this departure from prison rules? It's something I've often asked myself and the only answer I've ever been able to give myself that makes sense is the old one: money talks. Yes, it even talks to the minions of the law in a language they understand.

Now, as to servants, Grouty's are not the kind that the Duke of Clarence, if there is still a Duke of Clarence in the land, would favour standing behind him dolled up in knee-breeches and powdered wigs. If Grouty's servants was to appear in 'Upstairs Downstairs' the producer, and probably even the camera crew, would be unable to perform their tasks for shuddering. Grouty's servants are always better known for brawn than brain and for obedience than beauty. They are, in a word, mindless heavies but their devotion is absolute. I heard that Grouty, for some deal he was planning, once needed an item from the prison hospital. Without hesitation, one of his servants smashed his own arm with a hammer and so got himself into the infirmary. If they will do that to themselves, imagine what they will do to you if Grouty instructs them? Better not imagine it. It keeps you from getting the sleep you so desperately need if you are to get through your term and stay sane.

So this was the customer, past whose cell the timid screw Barrowclough was strolling on the morning of which I write.

Grouty was, at that precise moment, shaving with a battery-powered electric shaver and peering at his own joyless countenance in a small magnifying mirror. In this mirror, he also now perceived Barra peering at him. He turned, causing Slade's favourite screw to shy faintly like a cow being milked by cold hands.

'Oh – Grout—' stuttered Barrowclough.

Grouty smiled his terrible smile.

'Yes?'

Barrowclough deeply regretted having initiated the encounter but now he was stuck with it.

'Er – shouldn't you – well – be at your place of work by now?'

Grouty hardly ever raises his voice. It is normally little louder than a snake's hiss and he returned softly:

'Of course I would be, Mr Barrowclough, but I'm going to see the M.O.'

Mr Barrowclough shook his long head like a Friesian troubled by bluebottles.

'Oh,' he mooed, in a concerned way, 'I hope it's nothing serious?'

Grouty smiled.

'Never felt better,' he announced.

He then switched off his razor and blew the hairs from its head. Mr Barrowclough winced like a roped shorthorn as some of them wafted into his eye. Then, feeling he'd asserted prison discipline, Barrowclough ambled off.

A few minutes later, Grouty waddled into the waiting room outside the clinic. Like all rooms in the nick, it was bare of everything but essentials which, in this case, meant a few chairs for the hopeful patients to wilt on. When the great man entered, about six cons, tastefully ornamented with various bandages and plasters, were attending the doctor's call. They formed a rough queue with Ives at its head and Banyard and Oakes further down the line. Ives, as soon as he clapped eyes on the new arrival, immediately exclaimed:

'D'you want to go next, Mr Grout? I'm in no rush.'

Grout shook his head amiably.

'I'm afraid,' he remarked, in his nasal Cockney drawl, 'you'll all have to clear off. I need this room for a meeting.'

This announcement caused a good deal of consternation. In the normal course of things, naturally, the slightest hint of a request from Grouty would be enough to send half the nick flying to do his bidding. But in this situation there was another, and almost equally powerful, urge at work. Health is a matter of far greater concern in the nick than outside and not because your average con is a hypochondriac. No, the reason is because various favours are, however reluctantly, dispensed by the doctor. He can get a man off duty or on to light duty. He can hand out tasty pills and medicine which, if the recipient does not choose to indulge in them himself, can usually be exchanged for other goodies. Best of all, the medical officer can, if he is sufficiently impressed by the seriousness of the prisoner's condition, order the man into hospital which is as good as a holiday on the Costa Brava to your incarcerated felon. So the line of cons hopefully waiting for their turn to hoodwink the M.O. was not specially chuffed at being ordered off by Grouty. Then again, one or two of them really were ailing and genuinely required medical attention. Grouty beamed at them all and, raising his voice a shade, or perhaps it would be more accurate to say, lowering the temperature of his voice a shade, urged:

'On your way, lads.'

At this a general break for the door began. But one stout felon, the unfrocked dentist Banyard, stood his ground. Sighting down his nose at the Czar of Slade Nick, he proclaimed boldly.

'Look, I don't know what this is about, but I require urgent treatment. My boil needs lancing.'

'Really?' said Grouty sympathetically. 'Well, I might be able to arrange for one of my lads to do it – if you don't clear off, that is.'

Banyard gulped and then, deciding that prudence was better than being a mug, allowed the others to sweep him out with them. But when the door had closed behind the mob one con remained. It was Oakes and he didn't seem in the least intimidated by having disobeyed the great man's instruction. The fact is, it was to have a pow-wow with Oakes that Grouty had cleared the room. Oakes started the ball rolling by smiling and remarking:

'We haven't met.'

He held out his hand. A hint of a frown crossed Grouty's brow but then evaporated. Grout held out his own hand and the two strong men shook.

'I'm Harry Grout.'

'Everybody knows that,' Oakes complimented him. 'I'm Sydney Oakes.'

Grouty nodded.

'I know your form, Oaksey,' he returned the compliment. 'You're no second-rater. You was moved here from Wakefield where you obviously kept your nose clean. Halfway through a twelve-stretch for armed robbery, isn't it?'

'That's right.'

Grouty nodded reflectively.

'Big tickle, that last job of yours. I hope the money's safely tucked away.'

Oakes smiled pleasantly.

'Someone's been investing it for me.'

'Safe as prefabs then,' joked the Grout.

It was clear that these two spoke the same language. And now the real subject of their little meeting came out. Oakes said.

'That's why I want out. I want to unfreeze my assets and piss off to the sun.'

'I can see how you would,' sympathized Grouty.

'Obviously, there'd be the appropriate recompense to your good self.'

Grouty smiled faintly.

'I like the word "recompense".'

It was time for bargaining. Oaksey kicked off with:

'I was thinking in the region of—'

But Grouty was not one to lose the initiative. He cut in quickly:

'No, let me tell you my thinking. Five thousand – three before, two after. It's only fair the lion's share should come up front. Once people take off to the sun, they're often careless about tidying up their affairs.'

Oakes considered this in silence for a moment. It was more than he'd intended offering. On the other hand, he was well aware that he wasn't going nowhere unless it was by the grace of Grouty. He nodded.

'Where d'you want it put?'

'The Hastings and Thanet building society. Bexhill branch.'

It was a businesslike answer and Oakes had expected no less from Grouty.

'When will you do it?'

Grouty considered for a moment.

'You'll have to give me up to three months.'

'And supposing you don't spring me?'

Grouty shrugged.

'You get your money back, Oaksey. Mind you I keep the interest. Eight and three quarter per cent at the moment.'

The two understood each other perfectly. Oakes felt his heart beat a little faster. He had faith in the other. It might be a few months yet but – he was on his way. Just then, the inner door flew open and the M.O. popped his head out.

'Next—' he began and then saw that only two healthy-looking cons remained in his waiting room. 'Where have they all gone?' he asked, surprised.

Grouty smiled his silky smile.

'They all got better, doc,' he explained.

So it was fixed. Big events were in the offing at Slade Nick but it was a long time until I got wind of them even though Grouty probably already had me in mind to play a part in the operation. 'Course, thinking back on it, I sensed something was up quite early on but there's many occasions inside when it's best not to admit to yourself what you're beginning to guess because knowledge can be a very uncomfortable thing for a con to have.

So while Grouty was busy laying the foundations for his big deal I was just mooching around as usual, waiting for a little deal or two to turn up and, as so often happens, when the next one did turn up it was pretty much by chance. In the end, it got slightly mixed up with Grouty's own big schemes, mainly because it confirmed to him once again that I was as fly as anyone walking the landings and just the lad he needed for his purposes.

Now the most appreciative customers of Lennie's productions in the kitchen were not any of the inmates. They were the pigs who daily dived into the remains with as much enthusiasm as Arabs and Americans display for the rich eatables dished up by the Savoy Grill when they is dining there and making deals to buy up the Houses of Parliament and ship them to the Arizona desert or wherever. Part of the duties of Rudge and myself was to collect these revolting slops daily and feed them to the porkers. This job had its good and its bad side. Its bad side was having to watch the disgusting beasts rooting around in the mess which made it even harder for us to consume the stuff when it was dished up in the dining room. The good side was that it made a break in the day and gave us a little trip to the kitchen where something interesting might be going on. On the whole, the good side outweighed the bad and so I always felt quite cheerful as we pushed our cart towards the kitchen yard. At the gates leading into the yard there was an extra treat. A screw who could have made a fortune in a massage parlour gave us a going over to make sure we were not smuggling pitchforks or anything forbidden into the nick. As his hands roved over me, with soft insinuating touch, I wriggled happily and sang:

'*When they begin the beguine. It brings me back a night of tropical splendour* – couldn't you get some baby oil to improve the service, Mr Miller?'

'Less lip, Fletcher. All right, you're clear.'

I waited while my young companion submitted to the indecent attentions and then we both pushed on into the yard with our reeking cart.

As we approached the loading bays outside the kitchen, a figure in the familiar uniform wobbled towards us from the opposite direction. It was Prison Officer Beale on his new prison issue bicycle. Dismounting, he leaned the bike against the kitchen wall and stooped down, thus presenting a very seductive target which it would almost have been worth a week in solitary to aim a boot at. Then he began to remove his bicycle clips.

'Morning, Mr Beale,' I said affably as we drew near.

He straightened up and darted me a look not exactly slopping over with the milk of human kindness.

'Where are you going with that?' he snapped, pointing an accusing finger at the cart.

I looked him straight in the eye and said clearly:

'Pig swill.'

He started back in amazement at what he took to be an unspeakable insult.

'What?'

'Picking up the swill for the pigs, Mr Beale,' I explained earnestly. 'You know – pig swill.'

His eyes narrowed with suspicion but he couldn't be sure that I wasn't innocent of insolence. I nodded towards his bicycle.

'I wouldn't leave that there if I was you, Mr Beale.'

He placed his hands on his hips.

'When I want your advice I'll ask for it.'

I shrugged.

'Suit yourself, sir. Lot of thieves in here, though. Come on, Rudgie.'

And we heaved our cart up to the kitchen doors. As we started through them, I found it hard to restrain a chuckle. Out of the corner of my eye I saw Beale glance about in a slightly shamefaced way and then seize the handlebars of his bike and begin to wheel it after us.

Once inside the huge steaming kitchen, I perceived Lennie and his Neanderthal assistant Donovan peering into the simmering depths of an enormous cauldron. From the odours which arose from it – a blend between Southend estuary mud and the downwind tang of a municipal rubbish dump – I realized that Lennie was preparing to delight us all again with his rich soup. Even as I watched, the Fanny Craddock of Slade Nick lowered a massive ladle into the depths and withdrew about a pint of murky brown liquid. He raised this to his lips and sipped delicately producing the sound of a fond goodnight kiss between two hottentots. He nodded but his discriminating palate was not fully satisfied.

'It lacks something, Donovan,' he pronounced.

Donovan gazed impassively at the bubbling surface, ready to do the chef's bidding. Lennie continued thoughtfully:

'Now with this soup, Elizabeth David recommends some coriander, bay leaves and a dash of black pepper. We haven't got any coriander or bay leaves but fetch the pepper would you, Donovan?'

'Right,' growled the massive commis and stalked ponderously over to the table on which rested a giant drum of the hot powder.

' 'lo, Len,' I greeted my cellie and, as he turned to acknowledge the cheery word, Donovan emptied the whole drum into the cauldron. Lennie turned back to his creation just as the last of the black cloud disappeared into the soup. He shook his head in mild reproof and remarked:

'I said a dash, Donovan.'

'Uh?'

Now you will be wondering why I had earlier been so concerned about Mr Beale's bike. I mean, as you will have gathered, after the episode of the tinned hooch, his welfare was not a matter particularly dear to my heart. If his wife had left him, his kids been sold into slavery and if he himself had developed a plague of boils and lost his life savings in the crash of a small building society, run by a bloke I knew in Parkhurst who specialized in small bent building societies, I would not have been the first to shed a tear. Nor the last. My eye would have remained dry. Then why did I apparently take pains to ensure that no harm came to his bike which, if it had happened, would have given him a black mark and earned him a reprimand from the Governor? There was a reason for it. In fact, such is the lightning reflex for putting one over on the screws which is generated in all cons, the very instant I had seen him arrive on his two wheels, a plan had formed in my mind. And for that plan, it was essential that the machine be got *inside*. And that is what I had achieved.

Now, as if consumed by thirst from my arduous pig-keeping activities, I went over to the sink, which was near where Lennie was working, and drew myself a mug of cool refreshing water. As I sipped it I whispered softly, in that special voice which indicates to a brother-felon that something is afoot, 'Len.' He glanced at me cautiously and I nodded my head towards the bicycle. And then – oh, it was a treat! There's nothing like it. No one who's not done time in one of Her Majesty's Holiday

Camps for Criminals has any real conception of what is meant by the word 'teamwork'. I mean, you may think your Red Arrows aerobatic team, whizzing towards each other at eight times the speed of light or whatever, and passing close enough to flick paint off the wingtips, have got cooperation. So they have, but it's nothing to cons sensing a caper. I mean, you watch Liverpool spiriting the ball down the field, flicking it to an empty space which when it arrives there is magically filled by a striker and you think: that's teamwork. So it is, but it's like clumsy fumbling compared to felons teaming up to put one over.

Len caught on instantly and raised an eyebrow in acknowledgement. Passing the prospective victim, Beale, who was snooping around the saucepans as if hot on the trail of contraband, he carried the empty drum of pepper – which did not figure in the plan but just made it look as if he was going about his business – towards the garbage pails. His course took him close to McLaren, who was operating the potato peeler. As he passed, he breathed: 'Jock.' The dusky clansman instantly picked up the vibration. He glanced at Lennie out of the corner of his eye and Lennie nodded slightly in the direction of the bike. Had Beale been gazing directly into McLaren's face at point-blank range he might just have picked up the infinitely subtle smile which briefly creased the dusky Hibernian's features. I was meanwhile loading my cart with potato peelings. Rudge was helping me. Naturally, I made no attempt to include him in the ploy. He was too green to have the instinct for it and besides he was probably too innocent still to see the point of it. McLaren gave me the ghost of a wink and then turned and offered the same item to Taff, who was working the bacon slicer. Taff, who had already been alerted by some slight tingle in the atmosphere, duly noted the flicker of Jock's eyelid and the delicate tilt of his head. And now the operation was under way. Jock and I began to move casually towards Beale's two-wheeled transport and, right on cue, a hideous scream rang out from Taffy.

Beale immediately span round towards the pig carver who was leaping and twitching like a decapitated hen, his right hand buried in his left armpit.

'Oh, Gawd in 'eaven,' bellowed Taff. 'I've taken off my finger, I have!!'

Beale hurried over to the apparently afflicted man, exclaiming: 'What's this? What's this?'

And McLaren and I bore down on the magnetic bicycle. But, as some poet has already remarked, the best laid capers of mice and men often get screwed up at the last moment. Luckily for us, as it turned out, the moment was not too late or we might have been nabbed red handed. As it was, we had nearly reached the bike when a familiar rasp smote our earholes.

'What's going on, here?'

Mackay was amongst us. Jock and I needed no signals. Wheeling gracefully, we swung back towards our appointed places. I just had scope to murmur:

'Shame,' as we separated.

'Aye,' returned McLaren.

Meanwhile, Boss Mackay had joined his colleague who was peering at the hopping Taff. I felt sorry for Taff because he was now going to have to carry the can. But he was a shrewd con and I suspected he'd talk his way out of it.

'This man's had an accident, Mr Mackay,' explained Beale.

'Really?' asked Mackay, with a distinctly sceptical note in his voice. 'Let me see, Llewellyn. As for the rest of you, carry on with your duties.'

As I resumed wheeling my pig-swill wagon about the kitchen, I watched with interest to see how Taff would extricate himself.

Very gingerly, as if afraid of staining the kitchen floor with his life-blood, he withdrew his right hand from under his armpit. Then he gazed at it in well simulated amazement.

'But – but—' he stammered. 'I could've sworn – I felt the hot, burning sensation as the knife – Mr Mackay, do you think my finger's gone and I'm just imagining it's still there?'

Mackay reached forward brusquely, seized the digit and twisted it sharply, causing Taff to squeal in genuine pain.

'No, I think we can assume it's still in place.'

Now, of course, Mackay was not Beale. Mackay had moved amongst cons for a good many years and he knew most of our little ways. He turned and gazed hard about the kitchen. It did not take long for his glance to alight on the object of the exercise.

'Is that your bicycle, Mr Beale?' he asked sharply.

'Yes, sir,' admitted Mr Beale. Then, thinking to show his fore-sight, he added, 'I took the precaution of bringing it indoors.'

Mackay shook his head and his face twisted into a hideous grimace which he intended as a pitying smile.

'Into this thieves' kitchen? Ask yourself a question, Mr Beale – was that wise?'

'Well—'

Beale gazed about, and some of the hard won wisdom of his superior seemed to reach him. He shook his head, sighed and asked:

'What would they want with it, sir?'

'God only knows. Their motto is "Rob now, think later".'

And leaving his now wiser subordinate to ponder on what he'd learned, Mackay strode over to Lennie who was once more doing his Casper of the Hilton act.

'What's on the menu today, Godber?' he rasped.

'Crème Dubarry, sir,' lied Lennie. 'Followed by curry.'

Mackay peered dubiously into the second great bubbling cauldron.

'Curried what?'

'Curried – er – meat, sir.'

'What meat, Godber?'

Lennie shrugged.

'Dunno, sir, doesn't say. Could be kangaroo meat, I s'pose. Just says tinned meat on the tin, sir.'

Mackay reached out a hand, like a surgeon requiring a new instrument at a particularly delicate stage of a transplant operation, and snapped:

'Ladle.'

Lennie nodded to Donovan and, when the message had had the necessary second and a half that was required before it reached the massive felon's rudimentary brain, Donovan handed Mackay a ladle.

While the screw was sampling the fare, I whispered to Rudge:

'Sees himself as an expert on curry, he does. On account of where he was in the army.'

'Where was he stationed,' asked Rudge, 'India?'

'Bradford,' I returned.

I noticed that Beale had now rejoined his governor and was

standing respectfully a few places behind. Mackay tasted the concoction and smacked his lips appreciatively.

'Fair, Godber, fair,' he conceded. 'P'raps a dash more curry powder.'

As he said the words, a kind of electric spark jumped from con to con as we all realized the possibilities. Perhaps something could be salvaged after all from the previous fiasco. With the ghost of a smile, Lennie beckoned Donovan and then pointed towards an enormous drum of curry powder on the nearby table. There was the necessary brief delay and then Donovan extended a tremendous arm like the boom of a crane, seized the curry powder and in one great sweeping movement emptied the whole thing in the cauldron.

It was spectacular! It was superb. The important thing to remember about these classic moves against the enemy is that they are not just for today but for all time. The appreciative audience is not restricted to the lucky handful of inmates who happen to be present when they occur but, by word of mouth, the glad tidings are spread far afield and in a matter of days, even on the other side of the country, little groups of prisoners congregate to hear the story repeated and to fall about in delight and mirth.

As the great yellow cloud of curry powder engulfed Mackay, and even before the first explosive sneeze had been wrenched from his black innards, I noted Jock sidling purposefully towards the bicycle. On the other side of the kitchen Wilton, a normally meek felon doing time for petty fraud, engaged in carrying a stack of plates to the store cupboard, was so electrified by the occasion that he distinctly murmured 'hurrah' and hurled his plates into the air, which action was naturally soon followed by a most satisfying crash. Finding myself strategically placed beside the potato peeling machine, an old antagonist of mine which I knew well, I hastily pushed several levers and in a trice a cascade of potatoes was bounding and thumping all over the kitchen. Beale nearly went potty. He rushed around roaring incoherent orders while Mackay heaved and shook like a statue of a tyrant being finally pulled down in a people's rebellion. Finally he managed to scream coherently:

'My eyes! My eyes! Don't just stand there, Beale, you blasted idiot! Fetch the M.O!'

Beale said:

'At once, sir. At once.'

And went pounding across the kitchen to his machine. Black Jock had by then completed his adjustments to it and I promptly stationed myself by the window. Beale wheeled his bike outside, mounted and rode off towards the medical room. I waited. Five feet – ten – and then both wheels fell off causing the rider to collapse in a heap. I doubled up in uncontrollable mirth. It was, all in all, the best time any of us could remember since the prison bus broke down on the way home from a darts match and five screws had to walk ten miles home to the nick through a blizzard, arriving half-frozen to death.

But, you might well be thinking, surely reprisals would soon follow? That was not the least delightful aspect of the whole caper. There were no reprisals. No one could be charged with anything provable. Mackay had demanded the curry powder himself. There were several witnesses to the fact that, before his arrival, Donovan had emptied a whole drum of pepper into the soup and anyhow Donovan's mental weakness was well known to all. No one had seen anyone tampering with Mr Beale's bike. But the main reason is, the screws do not like to admit that they've been had. Of course, the whole of the nick knows about it almost as soon as it happens but men of dignity, as Mackay had been before he inhaled the curry powder, are always reluctant for tidings of their little mishaps to reach the Governor. So there was no kick-back.

That night, I was lying on my bunk reading the *Sun*, or rather alternately reading the *Sun* and pausing to recall with pleasure the events of the morning, when Lennie, still decked out in his chef's gear, arrived. The long day was over, but what a day it had been.

' 'lo, Len,' I greeted him pleasantly. Then I put my hand down at my side and made some movements with my fingers. There was a tinkling sound in the dell reminiscent of a bicycle bell, which was understandable since that's just what it was.

'Is that what you got – a bell?' asked Lennie.

I raised the little treasure and displayed it to him. It was shiny and immaculate.

'Never been used,' I announced proudly.

'What are *you* going to use it for?' asked Lennie curiously.

I shook my head vaguely.

'Dunno—'

'Why'd you nick it then?'

'Course, Lennie's not as green as Rudge but he hasn't got that wealth of prison experience which tells a man that if there's anything official to be nicked it should be nicked.

'Because it was there,' I explained patiently.

'I can't understand why Mackay hasn't come down on us like a ton of bricks,' said Lennie thoughtfully.

'Lot of reasons,' I said, and I outlined to him the ones I've just told you up above. Then I heaved myself off my bunk and went to the door and gazed about. There was no screw in sight. I turned back to Lennie.

'Besides, there's another reason. Mackay lost something in the kitchen today.'

'Pride? Is that what you mean?' Lennie asked, peeling off his battlestained apron and filling the washbowl.

'Something else. Before you get wet, have a look.'

Lennie turned from the basin.

'Look where?'

'In your mattress.'

Lennie seemed none too chuffed at this.

'So if there's a search, I'd get the blame?'

I nodded complacently.

'You would, yes.'

Lennie shook his head reproachfully.

'You think of everything, you do.'

I smiled modestly.

'I try to. Go on, have a quick shufty.'

Lennie went to the door and had the customary glance about. While he was doing so, I reached inside Lennie's mattress, through the cunningly concealed flap which is not standard prison design but which, nonetheless, most of the mattresses in the nick have. I withdrew an object which did not appear very exciting. Nor was it very exciting being a plain box-shaped plastic soap dish. I replaced the flap in the mattress and then handed the dish to Lennie. He looked mystified.

'You nicked a soap dish?' he asked.

' 'Course not. I found the soap dish – remember? – last week in the showers.'

'Then—'

'Just open it.'

Lennie carefully removed the plastic cover and his eyes widened.

'Ugh!' he exclaimed distastefully.

I chuckled, reached over and grabbed the full set of menacing looking false teeth from the dish. Clacking them like a castanet, I remarked:

'Jaws three.'

'They're hideous, they are,' said Lennie truthfully. 'Where'd you get them?'

'Mackay sneezed them into the pig bin.'

And I took the soap dish back from him and began to replace the lot in the mattress. But Lennie protested indignantly.

'Here, I'm not sleeping on them.'

'It's all right,' I chuckled, 'they won't bite.'

'They could burn though. They're red hot, they are. Mackay'll turn the nick upside down looking for them.'

I shook my head confidently.

'He'll negotiate first.'

'Big risk,' said Lennie doubtfully.

I couldn't resist it.

'Nothing dentured, nothing gained.'

Of course, it was true, what he'd said, there *was* a slight risk of Mackay doing a big turnover operation but I was pretty sure he wouldn't. Those teeth must be very precious to him. He would put feelers out and we'd be likely to make a few quid on the deal. So I started to undress for bed feeling very content with the day's operations. But a moment later, my sense of well-being was rudely terminated. Slimey Ives put his head round the door and announced:

'Fletch, Grouty wants to see you.'

5 Keeping fit

Generally speaking, there is a great deal of enthusiasm in the nick for body-building and physical fitness. It makes me laugh to see some con who has spent the week perhaps building a new garage for the Governor or carrying sacks of chicken feed from lorries to the barn devote his precious rest hours at the weekend to more back-breaking toil. Of course, when this poor nurk goes pounding round the cinder track surrounding our pathetic football field or bashing some equally hollow-headed felon with boxing gloves in the gym, he does not regard what he is doing as back-breaking toil. No, he thinks of it as keeping fit. But for me, sweat is sweat and no one's armpits smell sweeter because they has acquired their pong as a result of exercises than as a result of what the screws call work. In other words, my idea of relaxation at the weekend is a mug of tea, a snout and a snooze on my bunk, with perhaps a peep or two at *Girls of the World* if I've been lucky enough to acquire a second-hand copy of that valuable and instructive publication.

Now, it has to be admitted that bodily well-being and muscular development *do* have a very real part to play in the average criminal's career. It is no use hurling a brick through a jeweller's window (which, in itself, argues certain reserves of energy) and then plucking out the glittering fruit if, just when you hear the klaxon of the first approaching police car, your leg muscles seize up and you can't hobble an inch. It must also be admitted that certain specialized villains require bodily agility and brute power which would ornament an Olympic athlete. I mean, consider your cat-burglar making his way up a sheer ten-storey apartment block because he knows there's a drawerful of gems awaiting him. He certainly has to be fit. Mick the Monkey, a nimble little fellow I shared a cell with in Sheffield and who was hobbling at the time because he'd fallen off a roof in Pimlico, told me he devoted three hours a day to climbing practice. Then again, your strong-arm has a definite professional requirement for bulging biceps. No use setting off to put the frighteners on a bent fence if you haven't got the equipment to lay out a kitten. Such blokes is regularly found in prison gyms pounding bags of sand and being photographed by the screws for future reference. But – and this is the point I have been leading up to – most criminal capers don't require more muscle, or much more muscle, than an office job in the city. What they really require – and what all the top villains have got – is brains! But has this elementary truth gained any headway in the average nick? Do you see many cons swatting over the encyclopedia or taking degrees in advanced computer technology? 'Course you don't. The silly nurks haven't enough brains to realize that what they need is brains. And now, if you'll excuse me, I'll just get back to the *Sun* and ... ha ha, get it? I was making a joke at my own expense because the truth is I have not done all that much to cultivate my own intelligence inside. I reckon if I'd got down to serious study by now I would have the most massive intellect the world's ever known and could get a top job with any government constructing a big enough bomb to blow up the whole solar system. Still, at least I recognize that brains is better than brawn and I also recognize that the main reason Norman Stanley Fletcher has never been more than a small-time crook is because he never did his studies properly. But at least I can see through the physical fitness con. That kind of physical fitness anyhow.

But the fact is that the title of this chapter, 'Keeping fit', is not meant to refer to that kind of physical fitness. Now when Ives the Virus buzzed into my cell at the end of the last chapter and transmitted a summons from King Grout, my thoughts immediately ran to physical fitness. But it was not the kind connected with gaining more health. It was just the kind connected with keeping what health I'd already got. That's the effect any mention of Grouty and his designs has on most cons. You begin to think of splints and sticking plaster, of arm-slings and bandaged heads.

'What was that, Ives?' I asked, striving to keep any unseemly tremor from my voice.

'You heard me, Fletch. Grouty wants to see you – now!'

And the deadly germ whizzed off. Lennie and I looked at each other. Then, with one accord, we both looked at Lennie's mattress. He was the first to express what was in both our thoughts.

'Mackay's teeth!'

It was obvious. Grouty had got wind of the top screw's disappearing dentures and now was claiming his rights. Only why *was* it his rights? An unexpected feeling of manly rebellion rose up in my breast similar to what some downtrodden peasant sometimes feels when he sees the baron's men raping his old woman and driving off his couple of head of boney cattle. Those teeth were my cattle and I could not see why I should let Grouty rape them. I would find it too painful. He would too, if you come to think of it. No, what I mean is, Grouty had everything: the tobacco concession, the pill concession, a share of all the profitable action that took place in the nick. Those teeth, which, successfully negotiated, might be worth a couple of quid in real currency, were a windfall – or at least a curry-fall – that had come to me. I squared my shoulders.

'I ain't giving them up, Len,' I said with determination.

'Don't blame you, Fletch. Is it true you can get crutches on the national health?'

His question somehow immediately had the effect of dampening my resolution. In fact, my resolution quickly got so wet that I was about to get the teeth and set off for Grouty's with them. But then Len said:

'Does he know you've got them?'

I shook my head.

'Couldn't do. Didn't know myself until I fed the pigs and one of them jerked back squealing from the trough.'

'And you haven't told anyone else?'

'Not likely to pin the news on the notice board, was I?'

Lennie thought hard for a minute or two.

'Then all you've got to do is disclaim any knowledge of the matter and we stash the teeth.'

'They're already stashed,' I pointed out.

'I mean – somewhere where no one can find them.'

I sighed deeply. There was no such place. It's the old, old problem in the nick. In a building overcrowded with hundreds of criminals, and guards trained to sniff out a pinch of hidden tobacco, how can you set about hiding something? Of course, everyone tries it and wonderful is the ingenuity used but the truth is there just is no safe stash inside.

'Like in Mr Mackay's mouth?' I suggested humorously.

'I know a place,' said Len firmly.

I looked at him.

'You sure?'

'Trust me.'

And so, of course, I did. Nevertheless, I could feel a distinct tendency of my heart to flutter when I set off for Grouty's mansion.

Never fails to amaze me. I mean, you walk past rows of miserable stone boxes, practically identical except perhaps for a picture of a loved one on the wall. Or, if there's no nude torn from the *Sun*, there'll just be a radio here or a bit of grimy carpet there, some pathetic touch which just makes it possible to distinguish one cage from the next. And then you come to Grouty's ... Grouty's what? It would be both insulting and inaccurate to describe such a sumptuous dwelling, bijou certainly but offering many of the attractions of some Arab's mansion flat in Mayfair, as a cell.

As I entered I glanced about at the expensive fittings, the caged love-birds, the hi fi set, the curtains and carpets and bedspread and I thought: yes, you could get through your stretch in this place without too much hassle. But then, another thought surprised me. I suddenly perceived that it was still a cell, that no matter what you did to it, the essential truth remained. You lived as an incarcerated man. And it suddenly seemed to me that Grouty was not making it easier for himself but harder with all these perpetual reminders of the outside world. Still, I can't say I wouldn't have swopped if I'd had the chance.

Now when you enter your regular cell, you're most likely to find its inmate lying on his bunk reading or just staring at the wall. This, of course, was not the case in Grouty's palace. The great man had the hi fi on and was obviously getting keen enjoyment from 'Desert Island Discs' since he was waving his hand in approximate time to the music. He was not relaxing in his comfortable little armchair for this treat and the reason he was not doing so was that Tinker, the prison tailor, was engaged in measuring him for a new uniform. The garment, streaked with chalk marks and held together with pins, was being made to prison design but there all resemblance to the rough rags the rest of us have to wear ended. It was smooth and sleek and looked like something Hardy Amies might have dreamed up as leisure wear for the Duke of Edinburgh. Nor was Tinker the only servant in attendance upon his lordship. The girlish but powerful Delilah was occupied in feeding millet to the love-birds.

In time to the music, Grouty beckoned me towards him. With a smile and a polite nod for Delilah, I obeyed the summons and entered. Grouty made a slight movement towards Delilah who immediately abandoned the birds and scarpered. Then Grouty switched off his radio and favoured me with his attention. Naturally, he did not ask me to sit down and nor did he offer me one of the delicious looking After Eight mints I perceived on his bedside table.

' "Desert Island Discs",' he said buoyantly. 'Always been an ambition of mine to be on that programme. I was on the old "Late Night Line-Up" twice but I think there's something about radio which give a man social cachet. What do you think, Fletch?'

'I'd be happy to do either if the cashay was right, Grouty. But they don't pay nothing for amateur nights at the Pig and Whistle which I confess is the closest I ever got to media exposure.'

'How does the outfit strike you?'

'Very nice threads, Grouty.'

He extended a fashionable arm.

'Feel that – one hundred per cent cashmere.'

I dutifully felt. Good quality shmutta alright. Grouty resumed:

'He's doing me one in barathea too – for when the weather gets warmer.'

'Which it hardly ever does up here.'

There was a pause while Tinker finished pinning the left leg and then Grouty said:

'That'll do for now, Tinker. Come back in half an hour.'

Tinker nodded and withdrew leaving us alone together. It was an honour, of course, but then it was doubtless also an honour to be closeted with Jengiss Cohen. Who needs that kind of honour? Grouty seated himself comfortably.

'What's this about Mackay's movable molars then, Fletch?'

I gulped, hoping it didn't show.

'Don't follow you, Grouty?'

'Oh, don't you? I hoped you'd got them.'

'Just what exactly are we discussing, Grouty, if you don't mind me asking?'

'Haven't you heard, Fletch? Mackay's lost his false teeth. I thought you probably had them.'

I assumed my most innocent look and shook my head sorrowfully.

'Afraid not, Grouty.'

'Pity. You could have made a few bob, selling them back to him.'

What was this? Not what I'd expected. But then I remembered that Grouty's much too fly to do what you'd expect. He was doubtless just trying to trap me. I shook my head mournfully.

' 'Course, if I had heard of their whereabouts, I'd have notified you straight off, Grouty.'

'Not interested, Fletch. Screwing the screws not my line. But those teeth are somewhere in the nick. Keep your ears open. Could do yourself a favour.'

'I certainly will, Grouty,' I said gratefully and then began to withdraw. It's not absolutely necessary to depart from Grouty's presence backwards on hands and knees with your nose scraping along the floor like what the Japs has to do when leaving their emperor but you don't just turn and nip smartly away neither. I had retreated slowly towards the door when Grouty, who'd been helping himself to a succulent mint, turned.

'Hang about, Fletch. One or two things to discuss.'

And then, of course, I realized that I'd been wrong. Grouty's summons had not been connected with Mackay's missing mandibles at all and Lennie and I had gone to a great deal of trouble for nothing. Still, better safe than maimed, as the old saying has it. I felt a definite uplift at the thought that we could now negotiate freely about the teeth but at the same time – what did Grouty want? When it came, it sounded innocent enough.

'The thing is, Fletch, I've had this notion. A football match. Show biz celebrities come up here. Give the lads a boost. Good for morale.'

I nodded, trying to look enthusiastic.

'Yes,' I agreed. 'Lovely.'

Football? Celebrities? How could these things tie in with any of Grouty's rackets? The only boost Grouty had ever been known to give the lads was when Samson and Delilah banged their heads against the ceiling. But Grouty went on placidly.

'Thing is, I know a bloke in The Smoke who'd organize it.

Naturally the first thing we have to do is to get the Governor's blessing.'

I felt a strong impulse to ask Grouty what the hell he was playing at but I suppressed it. Simply not done. Would be just like if James Bond, after having been told that he's got to fly to Discomania, parachute into the president's palace, blow up his entire army, steal his jock-strap and make love to his gorgeous daughter, turned to the Prime Minister and said: what's the point of the daft scheme anyway? I mean, if Grouty had proposed holding a flower show and beautiful ankle competition in the chow-hall, I'd have naturally said it was just what Slade needed. He continued:

'Could be a problem that, Fletch, getting the Governor's OK.'

I shook my head deferentially.

'I'm sure the Governor would do anything for you, Grouty.'

'He usually does. But sometimes these things go wrong and they say, "Whose idea was this in the first place?" The point is I don't want it coming back to me. So *you* suggest it, Fletch.'

'Why me?' I gulped.

'You're a man to be trusted. And I know you'd do it subtle.'

I nodded, without making any special effort to look chuffed.

'And of course if anything did go wrong, it would come back on me, not you, Grouty.'

He smiled agreement – at any rate, his mouth did.

'That's right.'

I sighed.

'You think of everything, Grouty.'

As he waved me imperiously from his parlour, he murmured modestly:

'I try.'

On pattering back to our more humble quarters, I tried not to think about the implications of what Grouty had said. But certain phrases kept echoing in my ears. 'These things go wrong'... What things? Football matches? How could they go so wrong that Grouty wanted to distance himself from the very idea? 'Good for morale' ... Grouty cared about as much for prison morale as Dick Turpin had cared about the solvency of his victims – after he'd robbed them, that is. No, there was more to this – and then I pulled myself up. Fletch! Shtum! Even to yourself! Hear no evil, see no evil – think of yourself as a brass monkey. But as I entered home I could not forbear shivering and not just because the flowery was cold enough to remove from the animal mentioned above an important part of its anatomy. It was because I knew that I was once more caught in one of Grouty's terrible webs.

'Well?' asked Lennie sombrely.

'He didn't want the teeth,' I said thoughtfully.

'What? That's great. Because Barrowclough's been looking for you. I think he wants to negotiate.'

Naturally this cheered me up somewhat and sure enough a couple of minutes later, the screw with the woebegone expression ambled into the dell.

'Hello, Mr Barrowclough,' I greeted him.

He cleared his throat huskily, as if ridding himself of a stubborn cud, and then, glancing behind him to make sure we had reasonable privacy, said:

'Could I have a word, Fletcher?'

'Which one did you have in mind, Mr Barrowclough?'

'Now, please, Fletcher, this is – well, it's a rather delicate matter. In fact, I wonder if you'd mind, Godber, leaving Fletcher and me alone for a moment or two?'

'Certainly, Mr Barrowclough,' agreed the obliging lad and, with a secret wink in my direction, hastened out.

But after he'd gone, Barrowclough did not seem to find it easy to begin his yarn. To encourage him, I said:

'About that word you're looking for, Mr Barrowclough. Could I suggest moolah or spondulix? Or if those don't appeal, how about Steradent or even canine?'

Barrowclough blushed faintly, making him look more like a jersey than usual, but found the courage to begin:

'I'm here at the request of Mr – er – ah – a certain senior colleague of mine. From what you've been saying, Fletcher, I think it's possible you know what I know – that is you know what it is that I know that you know – that is—'

'Come to the point, Mr Barrowclough. Make it sharp like a tooth.'

Barrowclough swallowed.

'The grapevine,' he began, 'says that you can put your hand on what – ah – this senior colleague hasn't got.'

I looked doubtful.

'Well, if he hasn't got it, sir, I don't see how I can put my hand on it. And if he has got it, I don't know if I'd want to.'

Barrowclough shook his head irritably.

'Don't be obtuse, Fletcher. We both know what we're on about. And I'd like you to know that I heartily disapprove of this.'

I assumed a sympathetic expression.

'So do I, sir. But we're just go-betweens, aren't we? Just here to maintain the status quo. And if we don't come to some arrangement, they'll go into the auction on Sunday.'

Barrowclough knew very well what I was referring to: the floating auction held every Sunday in a different place, and which is conducted with such discretion that the screws never manage to track it down, where all the little treasures that have been picked up during the week are auctioned off, mainly for snout, although a good deal of horse-trading goes on too, even though it's a long time since anyone managed to purloin a horse.

Barrowclough swallowed and resumed:

'That's why I'm here, to come to an arrangement. It is my function to ensure that the – ah – the item in question is restored to its rightful place.'

'Would that be a little south of the nose and north of the chin, sir?'

'I think we see eye to eye, Fletcher.'

'Can't chew with an eye though can you, Mr Barrowclough? Isn't there some old saying about an eye for an eye and a tooth for a tooth?'

'How many teeth do you want, Fletcher?'

'Just a way of speaking, sir. What's the offer?'

'I've been authorized to go up to a fiver.'

I tried not to let my delight show. Always bad business practice. I grunted and remarked:

'Then the quicker you go up to it, the better.'

But Barrowclough looked unhappy at this suggestion.

'I feel I should make at least a token gesture towards bargaining, Fletcher.'

84

I nodded briskly.

'Fair enough. Go ahead, sir.'

'Three fifty?' suggested the screw, without much confidence.

'A fiver.'

'Done. Well, I have the – er – fee with me. If you could just hand over the goods, I'll be on my way.'

'Hang about, Mr Barrowclough. You'll surely appreciate that one can't just leave such a valuable commodity lying about. No, it's been transferred to the company's safe deposit vaults. If you'll come back in quarter of an hour, I'll have it for you then.'

'I hope this doesn't mean, Fletcher—'

'No, no, you've come to the right firm. The asset we is discussing is in our possession. It's just not here on the premises.'

Barrowclough sighed. He obviously wanted to close the deal without delay.

'All right, Fletcher, I'll return in fifteen minutes.'

And he turned and plodded from the dell. After a few seconds, Lennie returned and I said eagerly:

'Contract signed. Where's the merchandise?'

'What are we getting for it?'

At that, the demon which haunts all nicks whispered to me: why tell him the truth? But then I recalled the many occasions when Len had seen me right.

'A fiver,' I said jubilantly.

'A fiver,' Lennie echoed, impressed. 'That's more than Tubby Tipton got for old Kershaw's hearing aid.'

'All right, let's not just stand about rejoicing. Where is the goods?'

'In Samson's mouth.'

'What?'

'Can you think of a better stash?'

It was true I couldn't. But nor could I see, in the first moment of reflection, why Samson should agree to carry a set of contraband teeth about in his mouth. It must make talking difficult to begin with, although on second thought, recalling that Samson communicated normally in little more than menacing grunts, this factor would not be too important.

'How did you get them in there? More to the point, how do you propose to get them out?'

Lennie explained. It seemed Samson, as a result of an encounter in The Smoke with an even heavier heavy than himself, normally wore dentures. These had recently stopped giving the trouble-free service to which he had grown accustomed and he had asked Banyard to tune them up or whatever they do to artificial gnashers to make them function more smoothly. Banyard, of course, was a dentist in civil life before his behaviour to certain young ladies under anaesthetic became too uncivil for the civil law and he was committed to Slade Nick to repent of his incivility. Now Banyard suffered many frustrations in the nick, like the food, the confinement, the company – but the worst of all was professional frustration. He was always moaning that by the time he got out he wouldn't know a canine from an incisor. So he was always on the lookout for opportunities to keep his hand in on any criminal ivories that needed servicing. This was strictly unofficial since all cons were supposed to use the prison dentist, probably because the authorities feared smuggling inside hollow teeth or something. But a little work occasionally fell to Banyard.

'But,' I asked, 'what makes you think Banyard will keep shtum?'

'He doesn't know about it.'

Lennie explained further. It seems Samson and Banyard were not on cordial terms. Therefore, Lennie had acted as go-between in the matter of the teeth. Banyard thought he was repairing the teeth of a nice but fictitious old con called Tapley that Lennie had invented for the occasion. He'd explained to Banyard that Tapley was too shy to ask in person, and Banyard was too eager to practise his trade to question the matter. There was still something I didn't understand.

'How come Samson doesn't realize he's not wearing his own teeth? I mean he's thick but not that thick.'

'He thinks they're spares that Banyard had. He thinks he's just got them temporary. So all we have to do is get his teeth back from Banyard and swap them with Samson for Mackay's teeth. Got it?'

'Yeah, I think so. But it's getting a bit complicated, Len.'

'Come on. Let's go get Samson's teeth from Banyard.'

We strolled over to the haughty felon's dell and found him reading *Time* magazine.

'Hello, Banyard,' chirped Lennie. 'We've come about the teeth.'

Banyard put down his paper and pointed his nose at us. Far behind it his eyes looked thoughtful.

'Ah yes – what did you say this Tapley was like?'

'Nice old gentleman,' Lennie explained. 'Fatherly, reassuring.'

'Yes, that's roughly what I thought you'd said. I find it hard to see how anyone could be fatherly or reassuring with a jaw like a gorilla.'

Lennie gulped.

'Ah well – he looks like a fatherly gorilla. Something very reassuring about the great apes, don't you think?'

'Rarely seen such prognathous development,' mused Banyard. 'I think I'll write a paper on it for the *Dental Gazette*.'

I chimed in impatiently.

'You do that. Meanwhile, could we have the fangs, please?'

'They only needed a little adjustment to the left molar process. I've returned them.'

I could see that Lennie, not having the in-bred control of the seasoned veteran which I have, was about to make some exclamation that would give the game away and so I quickly touched his arm and said:

'Oh, really? Tapley was here then?'

'No, but Ives was. I asked him if he knew Tapley and he said he did. So I gave him the teeth to return.'

'Good old Ives,' I said warmly, 'always ready to put himself out for his comrades. Well, in that case, there's no further call for our services, Len. Come on.'

As soon as we were at a safe distance, I said:

'No time to lose.'

'I don't understand it,' Lennie said plaintively. 'Ives knows there's no Tapley in the nick.'

' 'Course he does. So he's put two and two together. His ferret brain's good enough for that. He'll be looking for Barrowclough at this moment.'

So Lennie and I separated and scoured the nick. But there was no sign of Barrowclough or Ives. We met up again in our dell to wait glumly for Barrowclough to come and collect Mackay's teeth. We could hardly tell him to go and prise them out of Samson's head. In due course he arrived and, for Mr Barrowclough, he was in a very disturbed state, almost shaking with anger.

'I wouldn't have believed it of you, Fletcher. I've always been lenient, almost indulgent, towards you and I would have thought I might have expected better treatment in return.'

'What seems to be the trouble, Mr Barrowclough?'

'The tee— that is the merchandise we discussed earlier. They weren't in your possession at all.'

'Are you telling me that you've got them back?'

'I have.'

'And would I be right in supposing that you got them back from someone whose initial is the letter after H?'

'As a matter of fact, yes.'

'Mr Barrowclough, did you pay this someone the fiver we agreed?'

'Naturally.'

'Well, I have some bad news for you. The merchandise you acquired is not genuine.'

'Not genuine? What do you mean, Fletcher?'

'It's paste. It's fake. You'll have to take my word for it, sir. But if you try and pass that off on – the customer we both have in mind, there's going to be trouble – for all of us.'

Mr Barrowclough gulped. I saw his hand move towards his pocket. He patted a lump there.

'You're saying—'

'The item you have did not come from the customer. But I have to have the item in order to swap it for the correct item. Do you understand, Mr Barrowclough?'

'Frankly, I don't. And—'

'Please, sir, take my word for it. Give us another quarter of an hour – half an hour at most – and I guarantee you'll have the right merchandise.'

'I'm not paying another—'

'Not another penny, sir. At this stage, it's in everyone's interest to sort this out.'

Mr Barrowclough sighed deeply. Then he plunged his hand

into his pocket and withdrew an object wrapped in a washcloth. He handed this to me.

'All right, Fletcher. But if you don't get it this time, I won't be able to prevent a fullscale search. I'll be in my office when you're in a position to deliver the goods.'

'Stand on me, Mr Barrowclough.'

The bovine screw sighed again and then turned and departed.

'What do we do now?' asked Lennie. 'Go and thump Ives?'

'Ives can wait,' I said. 'Nip along to Samson and get the dentures swapped. Then we'll take care of Ives.'

Lennie took the unpleasant package and departed. I waited anxiously. In about five minutes he was back. He pulled out what looked like the same washcloth. I seized it gratefully.

'Right. Let's go find Barra.'

'Better not,' said Lennie glumly. 'Those aren't Mackay's teeth.'

'What?' I asked incredulously. 'Whose are they then, the Governor's? Look here, Godber, we can't play musical teeth all afternoon.'

'Samson wouldn't swap,' the lad confessed heavily. 'Said the substitutes was better than his own. He's going to keep them.'

'Oh Gawd!' was all I could find it in my heart to say.

But, of course, we could not sit around just wallowing in despair for long. We had crossed the Ruby Con, which must be a celebrated fraud of some kind involving jewellery, and if we didn't deliver now Barrowclough would have no option but to finger us to Mackay. And then – the mere thought of the retribution that would follow was enough to set up a shuddering spell. Besides, we'd put a lot into this operation and I didn't intend to emerge with empty hands.

'Any ideas, Len?' I asked, after a few minutes' silence.

'Could be,' he said unexpectedly. 'I'll just pop along to the kitchen and you go and have a word with Ives. Tell him—'

And Lennie swiftly outlined his scheme. It was as full of holes as a safe being worked by an incompetent cracksman but I couldn't come up with anything better. Nodding assent, I got up to set the daft thing in motion. As I went in search of the insect, I could not forbear remarking severely to my cellie:

'In future, Godber, try and remember: simple moves are best.'

Ten minutes later, a curious sequence of events began. Ives, who is better known for sliminess than courage, approached Samson who was dutifully attending his feudal lord Grouty as usual, and remarked:

'I think you're a stupid nurk, Samson.'

The big man blinked down at the rodent in surprise. He was not used to being addressed in this way. Indeed, Grouty's heavies were very rarely addressed at all and, when they were, it was usually with considerable deference. So for a moment he assumed that he hadn't heard correctly.

'Say that again,' he said at length with a slight hiss which showed his substitute teeth were not as satisfactory as he seemed to think. Ives made a contemptuous gesture and said:

'Just something I've been meaning to tell you for a long time. You're a stupid nurk. That's my opinion.'

Now Ives is no heavy but he is nimble and he was watching the other closely. As Samson's great hand swung down towards him, he deftly sidestepped and yelled:

'What's more, I'm not afraid of you. And I'll be in my cell if you want me to prove it.'

With which he twirled lightly and slithered away. Samson looked after him for a moment, more in astonishment than anger, but then a frown appeared on his brow and he glanced about anxiously to see if anyone had witnessed his humiliation. The one thing a heavy has to keep intact is his reputation. Don't matter so much about his skull or his ribs but if his reputation gets damaged he's out of a job. He turned and murmured something in Grouty's ear, gesturing after the fleeing Ives. Grouty listened and then nodded graciously, whereupon Samson turned and trundled after his diminutive slanderer.

I wish I'd seen it but in fairness to Ives, who was bearing the brunt of the operation because Len and I had put some very persuasive arguments to him, it was not possible. But we heard about it in detail afterwards and it must have been beautiful.

Samson turned into Ives' cell and was surprised to find the little reptile calmly rolling a snout. Ives glanced up and remarked unpleasantly:

'I've changed my mind, Samson. I don't want you in my cell. Takes a month to clear the pong. So would you kindly piss off?'

Samson shook his great skull in astonishment. If he'd been capable of any degree of self-knowledge he might have realized that this new experience was almost enjoyable, or at least refreshing. No one had ever talked to him like that before. It was a strange new side of life he was seeing and one that opened up mental horizons as he hadn't known were there. Moreover, he liked mauling people and he had never before had such an absolutely clear-cut reason for doing so. Where should he start? As he balled his fist, he debated with himself the varying satisfactions to be obtained from lightly knocking Ives' head off his shoulders, stoving in several of his ribs or just tying granny knots in his arms and legs. He took a ponderous step forwards whereupon Ives leaped agilely to his feet.

'I said, piss off out, you great ape! You get any closer and I'll pull you apart.'

Again, a thrill at the novelty of it ran through Samson's mighty frame. He took another step forwards, bringing him within battering range of Ives. But at this Ives' manner abruptly underwent a transformation. From swaggering bravado he slipped suddenly into quivering terror.

'No, I didn't mean it! I didn't mean it, Samson! Don't do it! Don't!'

But of course it was far too late for that. You might as well set a bulldozer in motion, then jump off it and plead with it not to demolish the house it's heading for. Samson would not have been swayed at that stage by the combined prayers of all the saints. He grinned, a slow happy grin which spread majestically over his titanic countenance – and drew back his fist. Ives was now reduced to cowering against his bed, babbling incoherently. His body was all scrunched up and anyhow it wasn't a very juicy target. First the head, thought Samson, and swung hard. As he did so, Ives took a deep breath and held it. At the same moment, he grabbed a pillow off his bed and held it firmly in front of him. It took the full force of Samson's blow. And the next moment the world – or at least Samson's world – disappeared in a dense yellow fog that had sprung up from nowhere. And the moment after that, Samson's mighty lungs filled with polluted air and then discharged a hair-raising sneeze through the cloud of curry powder which Lennie and I had, a few minutes before, stashed in Ives' pillow. And then followed a scene of sombre grandeur. The great muscleman staggered about the little cell, gasping, choking and sneezing until a kind of clunking sound reached Ives' ears. Whereupon, still holding his breath, the little varmint stooped, scooped up the dentures Samson had spat on to the floor, substituted Samson's own set, and darted out of the cell. The long-shot had come off. We had retrieved Mackay's teeth.

The only fly in the ointment was having to divvy with Ives. What's more, we had to give him a full fifty per cent of the proceeds because he'd taken the big risks. Funny thing is, he never did get much kick-back. When he'd stopped sneezing Samson retrieved what he thought were his new teeth and never seemed to notice that his own old ones had been switched back on him. When Ives did his necessary session of crawling and tearful apologizing, saying he'd just had a temporary bout of insanity when he'd baited him, Samson accepted his apology, and even showed Ives some respect thereafter. As for the curry powder, Ives told him that it was just some contraband that he'd stashed away and since everyone in Slade knows that Ives would nick his mother's eyebrows if he could trade them for anything, Samson accepted that too.

'Not a bad day's work,' said Lennie complacently that evening, as we prepared for lights out.

'Maybe not. But if it hadn't been for your super-clever stash, Godber, we'd have two and a half quid each, not one and a quarter.'

'Be fair, Fletch. You wanted them teeth safe from Grouty too.'

'Oh Gawd!' I said. 'Why'd you have to remind me?'

'What?'

'I don't know what. That's the trouble. Grouty's got some caper on – which is already more than I should have breathed a word of.' I brightened up a little. 'Still, with the money we should be able to buy ourselves a few luxuries for Christmas.'

'Booze?'

'Who knows? I hear there's a firm in B Block has produced some very acceptable carrot wine. They say it's a saucy little vintage with a kick like a mule.'

There was silence as we climbed into our bunks. Far away, we heard a familiar roar approaching.

'That's Mackay,' remarked Lennie, unnecessarily. 'Seems to have got his teeth back. Here, Fletch, I wonder what he'd say if he knew his precious molars had done time in Samson's cakehole?'

'Dunno,' I said thoughtfully. 'He's bound to find out in the end.'

'How come?'

'No secrets in the nick, are there? Haven't you ever heard the old saying, Godber?'

'Which one?'

'Tooth will out.'

6 Planting the seed

Bloke called Runcorn. My very first cellie, he was, at the prison farm near Market Harborough. Never heard of him since so it's possible he kicked the criminal habit and has been going straight. But I very much doubt it. Not because he was evil. He wasn't evil. In fact, he was just the opposite. He had a very tender heart and cried a lot. No, the reason I doubt if he kept straight is two things: one, his appearance which was heavy and two, his intellect which was not. In fact, if brains had been snout he wouldn't have had enough for a roll-up.

We was both seventeen and we made a very odd couple, even odder than those two in the telly series, which I think I managed to see two episodes of the last time I was out. See, I was a normal seventeen-year-old, five foot eight and ten stone. I was a fine figure of an adolescent before years of prison goo and incarceration padded me out like I am now. And Runcorn? He was six foot seven inches tall and weighed fifteen stone. He was the most fearsome seventeen-year-old in appearance that I ever met. When he stumped into the dell the whole place darkened and kind of vibrated with his sheer physical power. I once saw Guy the gorilla, before he escaped from his life-sentence into eternal sleep, in the London zoo, and there was this same feeling about him: sheer physical power. But, like I said, Runcorn was gentle and wouldn't harm a fly. Well, at least, I never saw him assaulting no flies but it has to be admitted that he had laid out four coppers who'd tried to bust into the jewellery shop where Runcorn's mates were harvesting the sparklers. They must have been a low mob because when they heard the bogey-car *hee-hawing* up they all scarpered out the back and left him to face the music. And, because he was a good lad, and it was his first job, instead of belting off himself, he stayed to guard his mates and kept two carsful of police at bay long enough for them to get away. But, of course, they nabbed Runcorn in the end and we wound up together at Market Harborough.

After my rabbit with Grouty, I kept thinking about Runcorn or, at least, about his name. I'll tell you why. One day, I came into the dell after hoeing radishes or whatever and Runcorn was sitting on his bunk sobbing. I have to confess I was not sympathetic. I still thought of myself as Jack the Lad in those days. I'd been unlucky. But I'd learned. Next time, I wouldn't get caught. Oh, I saw a glittering future for Norman Stanley Fletcher in which items like Jaguar cars, busty blonde beauties, swimming pools, pools of booze, pool tables and so on were all within my grasp. But when I tried to share these glowing dreams with Runcorn, he put the mockers on them. Not by what he said, which was hardly anything at all, but just by his mournful, patient, gentle manner. I sometimes wonder if Al Capone would have gone on to rule Chicago if he'd served a spell with Runcorn. Anyhow, on this occasion, I sighed and said roughly:

'What's bugging you, Runcorn?'

He looked up at me, great tears oozing from his big eyes and coursing down his cheeks like mountain streams, and shook his head. I said roughly:

'Look, we didn't choose it but we've got to muck in together. And it's not helped by you flooding the place out every day. Likely to get chronic bronchitis from the damp. Tell me your sorrows. Perhaps I can help.'

'Wish I was like you, Fletch.'

'How do you mean?'

'Not give a monkey's. Wish I was happy like you.'

'You can be, my son. This place isn't so bad. We'll be out in less than a year.'

94

'Not that.'

'What is it then?'

'Only happy till I was seven. Mum and dad broke up then. Never happy after that.'

'Yuh, well – lots of us comes from broken homes. Something you have to live with.'

'Happy family – lovely, Fletch. I've got a pickcher. Want to see?'

I sighed. The family album has never been my favourite form of entertainment, but anything to dam the flow.

'Yeah, let's have a shufti.'

Runcorn rummaged at length. Like I said he wasn't no mastermind and it often took him quarter of an hour to find his shoe. So I waited patiently while he ferreted in his grubby possessions but finally he come up with a little finger-marked snapshot and handed it to me. I looked at it and I couldn't connect at first. It was taken in the garden of a small terraced house. It showed three people lined up in front of the back door. There was a normal looking young couple, smiling as hard as they could for whoever was taking the picture, and between them, holding both of their hands, was a dear little boy, neatly dressed in short pants and jacket. He was very cute, the kid, like something out of a Heinz beans commercial and I distinctly thought to myself: who's the lad? And then I twigged. It was Runcorn before his glands had gone on the rampage. It was incredible, the difference. I looked up from the photo to the spouting giant on the bunk and then back at the picture and the thought just came into my head: great blokes from little Runcorns grow.

So that's what I've been leading up to: planting the seed. That's what my job was now, as per Grouty's orders. I had to plant a Runcorn – that is, an acorn – here in Slade which would grow into the celebrity football match Grouty had set his heart on. But it wasn't that easy. Why not? Because what Grouty had said the danger was for him also applied to me. If there was anything dicey about it – and I was dead sure there was – then I didn't want any chance of it being traced back. So I couldn't just apply for an interview with the Governor and say:

'I've got this smashing idea, sir – a celebrity football match.'

No. Because whenever the bombshell that Grouty was constructing went off, I wanted to be as much in the clear as what he did. At the same time, I couldn't wriggle out of it. It had to be done. But how?

The first idea I came up with was an anonymous letter. At first, it seemed a winner. I could build it up a bit, make out the lads was getting a bit restive and mutinous and, what with the price of roof slates, it might not be a bad idea if a little robust diversion, like a celebrity football match, was set up to damp down the high spirits. I could see the Governor nodding his head and calling his secretary, the delectable Miss Parsons (and 'delectable' to anyone who's done more than a year of his term means any person who wouldn't actually be disqualified from a ladies' athletic team for being the wrong sex) and asking her to bring the bible. The bible is, of course, the Home Office Manual for Prison Governors, or whatever it's called, in which the head of our little state would check to see if celebrity football matches was acceptable to the Home Office or not. And he would, of course, find that they were not banned because if they had been Grouty, who is too fly to make a simple mistake like that, would never have suggested the idea in the first place.

I even drafted two or three versions of this anonymous letter but I never put it in the wooden box for delivery. The snag I kept coming up with was the signature. How should I conclude my friendly message? 'A Well-Wisher'? 'Someone what has the best interests of this nick at heart'? Or, more simply, just 'eager' or 'fan' or 'a prisoner'. They all had the same defect. They were all covers. And the Governor was not Governor for nothing. True, he didn't have his finger on the pulse like the screws who walked the landings and turned the keys. But he'd spent as much time in nicks as almost any long-server in the land. The question would immediately dawn on him: why has this felon not signed his name? If there was no name, there must be a reason for it, and the reason that would immediately occur to the astute Governor would be the correct one: this scheme is bent. No, an anonymous letter was not the way.

Well then, the idea had to be transmitted verbally. It had to be whispered into a real live human ear. Whose? A screw was the obvious choice but was just as obviously disqualified. A screw might remember who'd first suggested it and then, when

Grouty's balloon had gone up, probably with Grouty, Samson and Delilah in the basket hoping to waft over to Holland, that screw would finger me and I'd be in the clartes. No, a screw was out. Who then?

The choice ain't all that big in the nick. If it wasn't a screw it had to be a con and the obvious choice for me was a certain likeable, open-faced lad who I knew had a passion for football and who would doubtless be listened to with respect when he transmitted the idea. No doubt about it, it had to be Len.

That evening, as I lay on me bunk pretending to browse through the *Sun*, I remarked:

'I see they're having one of them celebrity football matches in Carlisle.'

There was no answer and, after a moment, I glanced down round the edge of me paper. Lennie was seated at the table, deep in a book.

'Did you hear me, Len?' I asked, with a slight note of irritation. Without looking up, he asked:

'What?'

'I said, there's a celebrity football match in Carlisle.'

'That's where Gaspard Roo started his first restaurant.'

'What?'

'Gaspard Roo – well, it's spelled R-I-E-U. How's that pronounced in French, Fletch?'

'It's pronounced "THAT" just like in English. What are you reading?'

'*Great French Chefs in England*. Surprising when you consider the state of gastronomic barbarism in this country, how many of them have come here.'

'Less competition, I suppose. Here, you're keen on football, aren't you, Len?'

'More keen on cooking. I'm thinking of going in for hot kewzeen. Trouble is, I'd have to learn French first. All the great recipes are in French.'

'What is this, Godber?'

'Be getting out soon.'

'So?'

'So – don't want to come back. Want to go straight. Need a career.'

'So you think all you got to do is read a book and you'll be whipping up a fine moose for the Prime Minister at Claridges, is it? More likely end up slinging chips at a motorway caff.'

'Everyone has to start somewhere. Jean le Sewer didn't start till he was in his thirties. One of the all-time greats, he is. Invented seventeen classic dishes.'

'When did this daft notion occur to you?'

'Not daft. Work in the kitchen, don't I? That's a start.'

I shook my head incredulously.

'A good start for being a blender in a paint factory. What you get up to in the kitchens has got nothing to do with cooking.'

'Raymond – which I suppose should be pronounced Ray-Morn—'

'That's quite enough, Godber.'

'Always had a good palate, I have. Ever since my Aunty Pauline fed me steak tartare with champagne before she seduced me.'

'Yuh, well – your precocious sex life is no concern of mine. Anyhow, I always thought you was a healthy, normal adolescent, keen on sports and stuff?'

'Only football.'

At last.

'That's what I'm on about, football. What do you think of celebrity matches?'

'That's pantomime, that is. Did you know that The Grey Goose in Bantry has got three stars in the Mitchelling Guide?'

I sighed deeply and heaved myself off my bunk.

'No, I didn't. But I'm sure Egon Ronay would be happy to award your meat loaf three large blots.'

'Where you off to, Fletch?'

I paused at the door to deliver some parting shot.

'Just thought I'd stroll down to the bistro for a spot of lobster soufflay. Failing that, I might be able to persuade Warren to share his Bounty bar with me.'

And I departed haughtily. Drawn a blank there. I ambled down to Black Jock's cell. He's keen on football, less I suspect because of the game's intricate beauty than because it gives him a chance to hack people on the shins. He was playing his guitar which is something he doesn't do well. When he saw me, he waved me a chair and continued twanging. After a while, I remarked loudly:

'Very lovely, Manuel.'

'Do you know any flamenco, Fletch?' he asked eagerly.

'Used to speak it fluently but you don't get a chance to practise inside.'

'It's Spanish guitar music.'

'Oh great, why don't you play some?'

'I was.'

I stuck it out for quarter of an hour or so and was just beginning to wonder if my eardrums could survive any more when Jock gave a final discordant thrum and put the instrument aside.

'Great for pulling the birds,' he remarked complacently.

'You mean you twangs it and they all flees screaming into a pit you've dug?'

But McLaren just grinned happily. Normally, one of the more surly inmates, Jock has periods when he's all sunshine.

'Pity you don't play an instrument, Fletch. We could do duets.'

I immediately saw an opening.

'Well, I has to admit, anything to pass the time. I see in the *Sun* they're having one of them celebrity football matches in Carlisle.'

Jock's eyes lit up immediately.

'Is that so? Hey, wouldn't it be great if we could have one here?'

I shrugged.

'I don't know. Just a lot of well known names and faces – chance to meet famous people – bit of a holiday – probably better grub and all – especially for our team.'

Jock looked enraptured.

'I can see myself out there, stealing the ball from Tommy Cooper and belting it home past Ken Dodd.'

'Knocking the stuffing out of several diddy men as it passes. I suppose it couldn't be too bad.'

Jock shook his head sadly.

'Won't happen. Governor would never allow it.'

'Nothing ventured, nothing gained,' I said with cautious encouragement.

'It would be the biggest event of my stay in this miserable hole.'

'Pity someone doesn't suggest it, then? To one of the screws?'

'I might do it myself?'

My heart beat a little faster but I maintained the casual note.

'Up to you, isn't it?'

'And at the same time I'll propose that we all have a coach-trip to London and a night out in Soho.'

And the obtuse felon picked up his ghastly instrument again and began making the night hideous once more. What else could I do? Without showing my hand? Nothing. But perhaps a seed had been planted.

I had very little confidence though and so, for the next few days, I went through the same routine with all the blokes I was on speaking terms with. But by the end of the week, I felt a dismal conviction that I had failed. The dismal conviction came upon me at the exact moment when, as I was hastening to the loo, a heavy hand fell on my shoulder and I turned to see Samson's massive countenance looming over me. He didn't even bother to say 'Boss wants a word' or something but just jerked his head in the direction of Grouty's cell. With a sinking feeling in my stomach, and a fragile feeling in my bones, I trudged ahead of him to the throne-room.

Grouty was reclining on his bunk with a tumbler of what looked like fruit juice and a temptingly open box of milk and plain chocolates on the table beside him. He was reading the *Radio Times*. Delilah was not in evidence. When he heard us at the door, Grouty glanced up and said:

'Hello, Fletch. Come in and take a load off.'

I did as I was bidden and sat myself on the chair near the bunk. Grouty waved Samson out and then got slowly to his feet. He walked over to his little chest of drawers, opened one of them, extracted what looked like a brown torpedo, snipped the end off, lit it carefully, took a deep breath and then, casually and with style, blew the smoke in my face.

'Football season won't last forever, Fletch,' he said softly. His face through the smoke was like the grin of the Cheshire cat only more threatening. I took the opportunity, in spite of my terror, to suck in a lungful of that second-hand but superb smoke.

'I've been putting the word about, Grouty,' I said earnestly. 'Ain't it took yet?'

'Doesn't seem to have, Fletch. You'll be losing your reputation for reliability – amongst other things.'

'Perhaps my tactics haven't been spot on.'

Grouty nodded thoughtfully.

'We understand each other, Fletch. So I'll put it to you straight. You get this celebrity match set up by this time next week or I'll be displeased with you.'

'Well, that's very straight, Grouty. I appreciate that.'

Grouty turned and strolled about his glamorous dell for a while. I wasn't sure if I'd been dismissed or not. Then he turned and asked with interest:

'Did you ever visit my club in The Smoke, Fletch? The Caribbean?'

I shook my head regretfully.

'No, I never had that pleasure, Grouty.'

'When we're both back home, you must do that, Fletch.'

'Thank you, Grouty. I'd like that.'

'One of the best floors in London. Be a pity if you couldn't dance, Fletch. Oh, you'll have to excuse me now. Six o'clock news. Never miss it.'

As I backed out on trembling but still intact limbs, I realized that the jig was up. I could no longer afford the luxury of trying to keep my name under cover. It would have to be a screw. But if I was going to be dropped in it then I was going to take my least favourite screw, after Mackay that is, with me. Which is why the very next afternoon, I ambled up to Mr Beale who was standing by our gritty football pitch watching Mr Mackay refereeing a practice match.

'Afternoon, Mr Beale,' I said cordially.

The vicious little nurk turned and surveyed me without enthusiasm.

'Afternoon, Fletcher. Football fan, are you?'

I nodded enthusiastically.

'Love the game, sir. And it's so good for the lads. Teaches them things in life. Give and take, fair play, may the best man win—'

And to demonstrate what a keen fan I was I turned towards the embattled pitch and bellowed:

'Put the boot in, E Block!'

Beale shuddered slightly, possibly because my mouth was not too distant from his ear, and stepped to one side of a pace. He remarked:

'I used to play a bit. In goal.'

I looked at him with deep respect.

'Oh, I can see you as a custodian, sir. I mean, nothing would get past you, I'm sure, Mr Beale.'

He shrugged modestly.

'I suppose I was fairly useful. Essex Methodist League. Runners up in 'sixty-nine.'

'Really, sir?' I looked at the turmoil on the field and shook my head sadly. 'In my opinion what our lads need is more motivation.'

'What kind of motivation?'

'Oh, I don't know, sir. Well, for example, if one of those showbiz teams came up here. Now that would work wonders for morale, that would.'

For a while, we watched in silence a con artist from E Block stumbling incompetently about the field. I was desperately wondering how I could make it plainer when at last I got a nibble.

'Show business?' asked Mr Beale absently.

'Yeah, you know – one of these teams with a sprinkling of celebrities in it. I was reading in the *Sun* they had one of them matches in Carlisle the other day.'

Beale nodded thoughtfully.

'Could be an idea, Fletch. Bit hard to arrange from up here.'

I said sorrowfully,

'Would be, wouldn't it?' but then I clapped my hand to my brow as if dazed by a great thought. 'Hang about, I used to know a bloke in The Smoke who did that sort of thing. 'Course he might have gone into some other line by now but you never know—'

Beale drew himself up into a more official posture.

'Shouldn't you be at work, Fletcher?'

'Was on my way, sir. But I can never resist the smack of the leather.'

'Off you go, Fletcher.'

'Certainly, sir.'

Crafty sod. I knew what it was. He'd suddenly twigged that the idea was a winner. And he didn't want to share the glory with a con. 'You're welcome to it all, mate,' I muttered to myself, as I headed off towards the farm.

For the next three or four days nothing happened, except that Samson eyed me closely whenever we passed as if measuring me for a coffin. Get on with it, Beale, I thought. I wasn't to know at that stage that my acorn was already on the move. The next stage of its journey occurred in the Prison Officers' Club.

There, the usual scene of hectic gaiety was in progress. That is, Mackay and Beale were drinking glumly at the bar and Chalky, whose boils had abated, was serving them. There was no one else in the place.

'Another lager and lime, Mr Beale?' asked Mackay, gazing vengefully about the empty premises.

'My round, sir,' insisted Beale, with his usual toadying generosity. 'What will you have – another half in here?'

'I'd prefer a large Scotch,' admitted Mackay. 'Didn't Miller say he was going to drop in for a drop?'

'I believe he did, sir. But then he remembered that he had to write a letter to his cousin in Worcester. He told me to apologize to you.'

'A great deal of letter-writing seems to be occurring amongst the prison officers these days, Mr Beale. Have you noticed?'

'Now that you mention it, I have, sir.'

'I wonder—' Mackay gazed about at the cold, cheerless room with its whitewashed walls and its ludicrous bull-fighting poster on the walls. 'I wonder, Mr Beale, if it would be a good idea to extend the facilities?'

Beale looked dutifully questioning.

'How do you mean, sir?'

'We could put in a few writing tables. Perhaps we should try and make the atmosphere of this place more like that of some fashionable London West End club like – er – the Reform Club or – one of them. What do you think?'

'Do you think the premises is adequate for that, sir?'

'Don't see why not. Could have writing tables anyway. Damn it, Mr Beale, I want this club to be used!'

'Naturally, sir.' At this point, Beale decided that it would be prudent to change the subject. He didn't want to see Mackay chewing the carpet as Hitler was supposed to have done when he got upset. 'How's the team shaping, sir?'

'The team? They're never here, are they? That's just what's cheesing me off, Mr Beale.'

'No, no, sir. I was referring to the football team.'

'Oh them! They've got about as much spirit in them as the booze you get in a clip-joint.'

'Ha, ha, that's very well put, Mr Mackay. Still, in my opinion, there's a certain amount of talent in those villains. But they lack motivation.'

Mackay snorted.

'Well, we can't hardly join a league, Mr Beale, and play away matches, can we now?'

Mackay thereupon gurgled happily for some time at this new witticism. Finally, Beale, having maintained a fawning grin while Mackay gurgled, felt it was safe to pursue the subject.

'The thing is, I had a thought the other day, sir. I happen to know of a fellow in London who organizes charity matches. You know the kind of thing, sir, team with a sprinkling of celebrities in it – people like – um – Michael Parkinson and Basil Brush and so on—'

'Basil Brush is a stuffed fox, Mr Beale,' objected Mackay.

'Is he? I've never actually seen him. Well, show-business celebrities. Now this chap might be willing to bring a team up here.'

Mackay took a big swig of Scotch. A gleam of interest showed somewhere far back in his dull but savage eye.

'Show business?' he said thoughtfully.

Beale smiled with inner triumph.

'Work wonders for morale, sir.'

But like I said, I did not know until much later that this conversation had taken place. All I knew at the time was that every day that passed, Samson seemed to take a keener interest in my person and that each time I lay down in my bunk of a night I prayed that the next day would bring good news. But no such news was forthcoming. However, all unbeknownst to me, my acorn had taken another leap forwards.

*

Mr Treadaway, the Governor of Slade Nick, was a different class of person altogether from the screws. I think he went to one of them posh public schools like Harrow or Eton which, by all accounts, is a bit like prison, with the boys cheating and beating each other rotten, eating filthy slops and having to learn Greek and Latin into the bargain. I know he was a senior officer in a guards regiment and then, when he'd finished serving his country, he entered the prison service in order to punish it. Ha, ha. But I have to say this for him – he was no sadist. You might think that the Home Office would not appoint sadists for governors but one nick I was in the Governor delighted in thinking up fiendish punishments for the inmates and sometimes personally administering them as well. No names, no pack-drill but you can stand on me that it happens. I was in another nick where the Governor was a jolly bloke that was always smiling and dreaming up improvements for his cons and they responded with affection. Once two of them went over the wall, and when they'd got far enough from the nick, started hitch-hiking. Who picked them up? The Governor himself who happened to be out driving alone. That's the key word, alone. Because as soon as he clapped eyes on his passengers, he said:

'Hello, Stubbins. Hello, Aitchison. Out late, aren't we? Well, I should be able to get you back to your bunks for lock-up.'

And he turned his car round and drove them back to the nick. The point is, there was two of these villains and they could easily have taken the Governor if they'd wanted. But they liked and respected him and so they went docilely back to their cells. Now, I'm not saying Treadaway would have got the same results in that situation. But he was not disliked. He was a little man, somewhat fussy and not very forceful. He was more concerned about his nick and its good name than about the welfare of the men but he was generally reckoned to be fair.

So the next stage in the progress of my acorn occurred two days after the conversation in the Prison Officers' Club when Mackay was giving the Governor his weekly report on the running of the nick.

'Well, Mr Mackay?' asked Treadaway, who was seated at his big desk in his office, which has barred windows like the cells so that no con could get out if he managed to break in, if you get me. 'Well, Mr Mackay, what kind of week have you had?'

'Pretty much as usual, sir,' returned Mackay, with the twisted leer he always reserved for the Governor. He was under the impression that it was a charming smile but the Governor tended to keep his eyes down on his desk-top and, if he had to glance up, could be seen to shudder slightly.

'No special incidents or anything to report?'

Mackay shook his head vaguely.

'Just routine, sir. Caught a felon called Rodgers making a knife in metalwork. He'll be up in front of you tomorrow. I recommend you make an example of him, sir.'

The Governor tut-tutted faintly.

'You do have a tendency to be a trifle vindictive, Mr Mackay. We're here to help regenerate these fellows.'

'If you say so, sir. But in my opinion you cannot make the leopard change his spots.'

'But these chaps are not leopards, Mr Mackay. Anything else to report?'

'Only a firm in A Block making illicit drink.'

The Governor shuddered fastidiously. He was a teetotaller as a result of having seen the ruin brought about on an old friend in the Grenadier Guards who became a dipsomaniac and was cashiered out of the regiment. Mr Treadaway can never recall without horror the scene when the whole regiment was lined up in a hollow square and the Colonel whipped the pips off his friend's shoulders. After that, he took the pledge and so he is particularly hard on cons caught with, or making, hooch.

'They never learn, do they, Mr Mackay? Well, I'll certainly give that bunch something to think about. Be a long time before they use my prison for moonshining again. Well, that will be all unless you have any suggestions, Mr Mackay?'

'As a matter of fact, I do, sir. It concerns the prison football team.'

'Oh good. I'm always concerned about the men's physical well-being, as you know, Mr Mackay.'

'In my opinion, the team lacks motivation, sir.'

'Yes, I've noticed they seem a trifle lack-lustre. What can we do about it?'

'I suggest we set up one of these celebrity fixtures.'

'I don't think I know your expression, Mr Mackay.'

'It's quite common practice, sir. We get one of these teams up from London with a sprinkling of show-biz personalities in it. People like Michael Parkinson and Basil – uh – Bob Monkhouse or someone. That would give the men a challenge and stimulate them at the same time.'

The Governor tapped thoughtfully on his desk-top. He was not green and it was his job to inspect any ointment the screws put before him with care to see if there was any flies in it.

'Look here, Mr Mackay,' he said at length. 'Did this suggestion issue from the prisoners?'

'Oh no, sir. All my own idea.'

'Very well, I'll give it some thought, Mr Mackay.'

Now this conversation took place on the morning of the seventh day since I had last seen Grouty. In other words, my time was up. And, as I have explained, I was in complete ignorance that my acorn had made any progress at all. So I spent the afternoon of that day in deep gloom. I knew that promptly at half-past five, when the week was up, Samson would arrive in the dell, looking for me. And I knew that after that – well, I didn't know exactly what would happen after that – but I was pretty sure that my mobility henceforth would be restricted.

I'd been roughed up once or twice in my life but I'd never been worked over by someone like Samson who was said to hold the East End record for both shin-breaking and razor slashing. I have to admit it: I was getting into a right old panic. I even thought of flight but where can you fly to in the nick? Wild schemes for a last-minute bust-out flashed through my head but I knew there was no chance. Of course, I could go to Barrowclough and demand protection. I might even get it. But not for the rest of my life. And the one thing any heavy has to do is make sure his wishes are respected. For this reason, he will take care to track down anyone who does not respect them and give him what's coming to him sooner or later. If I went to Barrowclough, I would never have an easy night's sleep until Samson, or some new thug, eventually found me and did the job. After that, I might get a very great deal of sleep, hospital if I was lucky, or in the churchyard if I wasn't. No, it was no good looking for help. I spent the afternoon visiting friends and putting out feelers.

'What's this about the celebrity match, Jock?'

'What celebrity match?'

'Thought I heard a rumour that we was going to have one. Didn't it reach you?'

'No.'

And so on. But there was no comfort to be found anywhere. So I went back to my dell, as the dread hour approached, and occupied myself in writing my will, just in case the worst happened.

At about a quarter past five I heard heavy steps along the landing and I thought dully:

'He's quarter of an hour early. Not fair, that isn't.'

I even wondered if I could persuade Grouty to allow me the last fifteen minutes' use of my legs. Then a wave of calm resignation took over. I felt like some hero who goes to the firing squad with proud defiance, conscious that he has done his duty and secure in the justice of his cause. I saw myself waving away the last cigarette and standing with a faint proud smile as they tied the bandage round my eyes. The footsteps got closer and closer. I rose to my feet and faced the door, a faint proud smile on my lips. Round the corner into the cell came – Mr Beale.

'Evening, Fletcher,' he grunted.

I sighed and returned the greeting. Even Beale looked mellow and human compared to the fury that was approaching.

'Evening, Mr Beale.'

'You're keen on football, aren't you, Fletcher?'

I remembered that, in another life, I had taken something of an interest in the sport even if Orient never did seem worthy of my loyalty.

'Yeah, I am – right, sir.'

'Thought you'd be interested to know. My suggestion for a celebrity match has been approved by the Governor. There'll be a notice going up on the board soon.'

Did I really hear a faint unearthly sound like angels singing in the background? No, probably I just imagined it. I gulped. For a moment, I was unable to speak. Then words came. Even in that hour, I kept my cool.

'Is that right, Mr Beale? I'm very glad for you, sir.'

Beale cleared his throat and glanced about. He looked a trifle abashed and, now that I was beginning to feel I belonged to the world again, I knew just why.

'Er – Fletcher, do I recall you saying you knew someone in The Smoke who organizes these things? Of course, I could set it up myself but if you do have a contact—'

'Oh yes, I'm sure I can help you there, sir. I'll get the name for you, Mr Beale.'

'You don't have it?'

'Not on me, Mr Beale. Be just a case of writing a letter. Take a few days. Will that be all right, sir?'

'Oh, I don't know. I'll probably do it myself. Still, you might as well send your letter, Fletcher. Just as well to have a back-up.'

'Will do, Mr Beale.'

'Well – you can tell the lads if you want. I'm sure they'll be pleased.'

'Oh, they will, sir. No doubt about it. I may say it means more than you can possibly realize to me too, Mr Beale.'

'Keen fan, eh? All right, Fletcher.'

And the bearer of sweet tidings turned smartly and strode away.

So, just one more hurdle to be crossed. I had to persuade Grouty that it was really fixed and to leave me intact until the notice went up. I was pretty sure I could manage it but it was still with a sense of foreboding that I glanced up and saw Samson filling the doorway.

'Come on,' he grunted.

And a couple of minutes later, I was back in Grouty's opulent dell. The master was seated at his comfortable little desk occupied in writing a letter. Samson gave me a slight shove, which was not reassuring, and then closed the door and stationed himself in front of it, which was definitely terrifying. Eager to straighten the situation out, I began at once.

'Listen, Grouty, you'll be—'

But the suave heavy held up a hand for silence.

'Please, Fletch, I'm writing a letter. Don't want to lose my thread.'

'But, Grouty, I just thought—'

'Shut up, Fletch!' He did not raise his voice but there was something in it which commanded instant silence. He went on. 'No sweat. We'll have our little chat.'

So I stood and waited. It seemed like a long time and must have been five minutes or so. Then Grouty folded his letter carefully, placed it in a nice blue envelope, stuck it down and wrote the address. Finally, he turned and looked at me. He smiled and I tried to judge whether his eyes were taking part in it or not.

'Like to know who I was writing to, Fletch?'

'Wouldn't dream of prying, Grouty.'

'This bloke I know in London – the one who sets up celebrity matches.'

'You mean – you know?'

Then an amazing thing happened. The emperor of Slade Nick held out his hand to me, a simple subject. And now I could tell – there was no doubt about it – his whole face was smiling.

'Well done, Fletch,' he said.

Of course. I needn't have worried. If there's any news going, who does it go to first? Grouty. He'd probably known it was on before Beale did.

'Yuh, well—' I stammered, trying to look modest but successful, as I took his hand lightly and shook it.

'I knew you wouldn't let me down, Fletch,' continued the mighty one. 'Have a walnut whip.'

And he reached into his locker and produced a box of the succulent sweet-meats. I took one reverently.

'Thank you, Grouty. One of my favourites, them is.'

'Too sweet and bland for me. I'd give you the box but they come in useful for tips. Now then, Fletch, what we need is someone reliable as trainer for the home team.'

'Yeah, that's the next step, Grouty. Well, if you want my—'

And then I stopped abruptly. No! It couldn't be. Not after what I'd done for him. He wouldn't pile more on. He couldn't. And then I saw it. His eyes had abandoned the smile and were boring into me in the old thermal-lance glare. But I wasn't going to give in without a struggle.

'Not me, Grouty. I wouldn't be no good at it. Besides, I've done my bit. You wouldn't ask any more of me?'

'No, Fletch, I wouldn't ask. I insist.'

I sighed deeply and took a bite of my walnut whip. The delicious taste cheered me slightly.

'In that case, Grouty, it's my privilege.'

7 Up the home team

It could be worse, I thought as I padded out on to the field for the first day's training for the big match. I could be playing!

Then again there were certain privileges which went with my new dignity: lighter duties, extra grub, a tin whistle. But no matter how I tried to bolster my spirits, a sinking feeling remained. I was in the thick of it now, committed, and whatever stroke Grouty was planning was almost certain to land on my neck.

I had another cause for disquiet. The fact is, I was not really qualified for training a football team. Of course, the lads under me were also not really qualified to make up a football team but that was small comfort. My previous experience of coaching had not extended much further than standing on the touchline when Orient was engaged in one of its hopeless struggles and bellowing: 'Get the lead out of your boots!' and similar encouragements. There had been no problem about my selection as trainer. Grouty had seen to that. One or two lads had grumbled a bit but a quiet glance from the Leader and a gentle movement in their direction from Samson had been enough to ensure my 'election'. The night before I had combed the prison library and come up with a tattered volume called: *The Art and Practice of Football for Youth Leaders* and, as I led my motley youth out on the field, I tried to recall its precepts. The first few days, of course, would be devoted to trials and it was only when I'd selected the team that the hard grind would begin.

There is a meteorological peculiarity about the district around Slade Nick which I have never seen mentioned on the telly or in the papers. The sun never comes out and this small area has five times the national average of rain and ten times as much fog. But on that particular day, we all felt a lift at the weather. Naturally, there was no sun but the cloud-base was quite high and you could spot a screw at a hundred yards. This made it almost Costa Brava conditions for us and Black Jock let out a cry of delight.

'This is the life, eh, Fletch?'

There were twenty-two felons in my first try-out batch and they included, in addition to McLaren, Oakes, Warren, Samson

– whom I thought I'd try in goal since his ape-length arms could probably stop anything without him having to move – McMillan and, inevitably, my cellie Lennie Godber.

'Right, lads,' I said, after I'd lined them up. 'You all know why you're here. Now this pitch, as you can see, is not the green baize you get at Wembley and other great stadiums. Some of you might claim it looks more like an old gravel pit than a football pitch. But it's the best we've got and the main thing to remember is that if anyone gets too badly slashed from rough tackling he stands a fair chance of ending up in the infirmary. In other words, you can't lose. But can you win? We do not yet know the exact composition of the star-studded team that is coming up from The Smoke to meet us but some of them will be professionals. For this reason—'

'Get on with it!' bellowed a con called Hampton who was jumping up and down.

'Plenty of time for that, Hampton,' I reproved him. 'See if you're still as perky at the end of the day. Right, we'll start with a few warming-up exercises. Touch your right toes with your left finger-tips and then the other way round. Ready, go. Down, two. Down, two. Down, two. Come on, Oakes, you look like a busted windmill!'

I kept them at it for a while, push-ups, deep-knee bends and the like while I noted their form. Jock was fit. So was Lennie. Samson was strong but musclebound. Some of the others was OK. But several were hopeless, none more so than Oaksey who, for some reason I couldn't fathom, seemed to have his heart set on making the team.

'All right. On your feet. Now the next exercise—'

'Come on, Fletch,' called McLaren irritably. 'We need some ball practice.'

'All in good time, sonny Jock. Got to get you in shape first. Right, round the pitch twice.'

There was a groan of discontent from the candidates but they obediently set off at a jog. I noted that before they'd completed a lap Oaksey was trailing badly. I heard a familiar step from immediately behind me and, without turning, said:

'Afternoon, Mr Mackay.'

Then I turned and confronted the screw, who was working his neck like a cam-shaft.

'Afternoon, Fletcher. Hard at it, are we?'

'We are indeed, sir. I'm quite out of breath.'

Mackay contorted his mouth into what he imagined to be a jovial smile but really made him resemble a hedgehog with toothache.

'You're a strange choice for trainer, Fletcher.'

'It was the prisoners what decreed it, sir. Took a vote, see.'

Mackay nodded.

'I heard, yes. Yet you're a man who's always despised physical activity.'

I permitted myself a brief smile.

'Not in others, sir.'

Mackay tapped his nose meaningfully.

'You're up to something, Fletcher. Don't think I haven't noticed.'

'Really, Mr Mackay? Well, when you find out what it is perhaps you'd let me know. I thought I was just communicating some of my football expertise to the lads.'

'Football expertise? All right Fletcher. Here's a simple problem. If a dog ran on to the pitch, and the ball was deflected off it into the net, would it count as a goal?'

'Wouldn't care to be dogmatic about that one, sir.'

Mackay shook his head sorrowfully.

'All I can say, Fletcher, is that with you moulding it, our team will be fortunate if it even sees the ball.'

'Won't matter, Mr Mackay. They'll be trained to such a pitch they could win blindfolded.'

The screw snorted and strode off.

I kept up the exercise for a while longer and then I divided the lads into two teams and let them have a practice match. I watched critically as the shambles on the field moved towards utter chaos. McLaren, although showing definite skill in dribbling, used a technique for warding off tackles which involved jabbing two fingers into the tackler's eyes. Even as I watched, a brutish con called Musk, who had just experienced one of these unpleasant evasive actions, jumped on McLaren's back. I blew my whistle, hurried over and separated them.

'Jock,' I rebuked him. 'You don't handle the ball and that goes for eyeballs too.'

'I never touched him,' grumbled the dusky dribbler.

I started them off again. Lennie obtained possession. He passed to Oaksey but put the ball several feet behind. Oaksey turned and then, forgetting his direction, kicked the ball towards his own goal. His mistake was catching and a moment later, all twenty field players were charging down on Samson in the goal. Samson took one look at the approaching panzer corps and lurched off behind the goal line. I blew my whistle.

'Look,' I said, when I had at last assembled them all around me. 'I don't want to have to issue compasses.' I divided them up again into two teams. 'Now you lot go this way and you others go the other way. Is that clear?'

Slowly, as the afternoon wore on, a little form began to emerge.

'Er – Fletch,' said a diffident voice behind me.

I recognized it as that of my farm-assistant, Rudge. Without turning, since I was busy making notes on my clipboard, I said:

'What?'

Rudge came round to my front.

'Well, I wouldn't mind – you know – trying out for the team. I can play a bit.'

I looked up at him and shook my head cynically.

'Oh, that's what they're all telling me. Since this game was announced, Slade Prison suddenly has a hundred schoolboy internationals.'

'No, straight up—'

Just then a loose ball came bounding towards us. To my amazement, Rudge trapped it neatly, flicked it up on to his toe, from there up on to his knee, from one knee to another and then down to the other toe. It was a display of ball control worthy of a league player. I gulped but it doesn't do to sling compliments around so I just nodded and said:

'Oh yes. Very fancy. Different though isn't it, when you're in the park. And someone tried to take it off you!'

And then, intending to surprise him, I lunged for the ball. But with no sweat at all, Rudge cleverly flicked the ball between my legs while swivelling out of reach of my tackle. My knee, deprived of the opposition it was expecting crashed down on to the sharp stones and I emitted a yell of pain.

*

What with my slashed knee, and aching muscles from jogging about the field after the lads, I was ready for kip that night.

'Thank Gawd, I'm not playing,' I remarked to Lennie who was just then cleaning his teeth at the bowl.

He turned and bubbled through his toothpaste:

'How would you shay the team ish shaping, Fletch?'

I took up my clipboard.

'Well—' I began, but I was rudely interrupted by a sound not unlike that of a sinking oil tanker and which I recognized as Lennie gargling and spitting. I waited patiently for the sounds of the deep to subside and then resumed, 'We have a lot of strength at the back. One thing we're not short of is stoppers.' But then I shook my head and sighed. 'What we need is a bit of creative mid-field flair.'

Lennie replaced his toothbrush neatly in its plastic case and turned.

'From the little I saw of him, Rudge could provide that. Revelation he was.'

I nodded.

'Says he had a trial for Brentford, before he went to Borstal.'

'I can believe it.'

Bunny Warren scampered into the dell.

'I don't want to be in the team, Fletch,' he announced.

'Well, that's very convenient, Bunny, because I don't want you in it.'

'Rugby's my game.'

'Really? What do you play, the ball?'

'Straight up. They play Rugby in my local. That's the game where you roll a ball at some pins, isn't it? Or am I thinking of hockey?'

And he scampered out again. I sighed deeply.

'At least he doesn't want in. Half the nick does.'

'I bet you've had some offers, haven't you, Fletch.'

'What are you suggesting, Godber? That I'd accept bribes?'

'Wouldn't you?'

'Not when it's a matter of honour. Besides Grouty wants the best eleven I can find.'

Lennie cleared his throat.

'And – er – have you chose the final team yet?'

I shook my head.

'No. Too early.'

Lennie rummaged in his possessions and withdrew a familiar object.

'Like a bit of KitKat?' he asked hopefully.

'Oh ta,' I said, taking the proffered stick of juicy succulence and munching it.

'About the team, though, Fletch. You must have a fair idea by now. I mean in your mind – a nucleus, like.'

I picked up my clipboard again and frowned at it.

'Well, yeah, it's taking shape.'

Lennie rummaged in his kit and brought out his housewife.

'Just about to mend some socks, Fletch. Any of yours need darning?'

For answer, I raised my unbooted foot and revealed the big white mushroom of my toe sticking out. Lennie immediately pulled off the well-ventilated garment and set about stopping the rot. After a while, he remarked mildly:

'I thought I played quite well today.'

'Oh yes?' I returned absently.

Lennie sounded aggrieved.

'Well, I thought so. I was good in the air. Scored one, didn't I?'

I shook my head positively.

'That was Urquhart's goal. Just hit your ear on the way in.'

'Did not,' returned Lennie indignantly, laying aside the sock. 'That was a cunning deflection, that was.'

And he demonstrated exactly how he had directed the ball into the goal. So the evening passed. Lennie finished darning the sock and we made ready for bed. Right on time the lights went out and I mounted to my upper berth while Lennie crawled into his lower. He still hasn't come right out and said it. I wondered how long it would take him. From the cages outside, we heard the usual din of men bawling and choking, getting fainter as the nick once more shook itself down for the night. Then finally it came, a small voice from beneath me.

'So – er – how do you rate my chances then, Fletch?'

'Hm? Nearly asleep I was. What did you say, Len?'

'I asked how you rate my chances.'

'Chances of what?'

'Of making the naffing team.'

'Oh, those chances? Slim.'

There was a long pause. I could hardly keep from laughing out loud.

'In future, darn your own socks!' snapped Lennie.

For the next few days, training proceeded to the point where I went to Beale and asked him if he'd kindly referee a trial match for us. Naturally, he was flattered and agreed. I had reasons for wanting to keep this interfering screw involved with the game. Well, he turned out to be a competent referee, I'll say that for him. And the lads generally speaking were beginning to look as if a football was not an utterly mysterious object to them. Now and then they even came up with something quite smart. I was watching from the touch-line and noted with approval how Lennie dribbled the ball competently downfield, beating a tackle, and clipping it smartly across to Rudge. With those two, I was beginning to see makings of a forward-line. Rudge trapped the ball cleanly, avoided a bruising tackle with a twist of his lithe body and then booted an exactly placed pass through to the wing, where Oakes was positioned. He made a lunge at it, missed completely and allowed it to trickle into touch. It was always the same. Oakes might have all that it took to grab a payroll but he couldn't steal a ball from a lame geriatric. As I spat in disgust, I saw Mr Treadaway, the Governor, attended by Chief Toady Mackay, approaching. I quickly wiped my mouth and tried to look like a responsible coach.

'You seem to be getting in the spirit of things, Fletcher,' remarked the Governor pleasantly, heaving abreast.

I smiled politely.

'Oh, good afternoon, sir.'

'How do you rate our chances?'

'Well, sir, don't know what we're up against yet, do we? Have you heard any more about who's coming?'

Naturally, there was a lot of speculation in the nick and a certain amount of snout had been wagered. I had myself staked a quarter of an ounce against Bunny Warren risking a hundred to one odds that whoever else was in the team James Callaghan would not be. Bunny seemed to think he was a winger for Liverpool. I was hoping the Governor might supply me with a little advance information which might come in handy for making bets. But he turned to Mackay and said:

'They seem a little vague at the moment, don't they, Mr Mackay?'

Mackay nodded deferentially.

'There's some talk of David "Diddy" Hamilton, sir. And possibly one of the Goodies.'

I could not resist. I smiled brightly at the Governor and said:

'That will be a rarity up here, won't it, sir, a goodie?'

The Governor smiled uncertainly and then turned back to Mackay.

'Is that all, Mr Mackay?'

The screw shook his head positively.

'Oh no, sir. But these people have commitments, you know, and it's hard to pin them down till the last minute.'

Suddenly I saw Lennie misbehaving, sportswise that is, and I cupped my hand to my mouth and bawled:

'Your head's going down, Godber!'

The Governor shuddered. Perhaps my mouth had been a little close to his ear. Mackay frowned and for a moment I thought he was going to reprimand me. But he had other things on his mind. He turned to his chief again and announced proudly:

'We've had a letter from Michael Parksonson.'

'Oh?' said the Governor, clearly impressed. 'Is he coming?'

'No, sir, not actually coming. But he wrote to say that he would have come, but he isn't. Still, we have his letter. On file.'

The Governor shook his head sadly.

'Didn't you mention the comedian chap? What's his name, Jimmy Tarbrush?'

'Buck, sir,' Mackay politely corrected him. 'Tarbuck. Unhappily, he's indisposed.'

The Governor sighed.

'Well, let's hope we get some celebrities. Come along, Mr Mackay, I suppose I'd better inspect the facilities for our guests.'

Of course, I did not accompany them but I have ascertained how their tour continued. It was not exactly rich in drama or interest. Mackay escorted the Governor to the ordinary prison changing-rooms where the only sign of special preparations was two lilac screws, Whittaker and Whalley, painting the walls.

'This will be the visitors' changing-room, sir,' explained Mackay to his chief. 'And our lot will change next door.'

The Governor, a frugal man, asked anxiously:

'We're not painting that as well are we?'

Mackay shook his head firmly.

'Certainly not, sir.'

The Governor then raised a matter which seems always to be cropping up in a prison governor's life.

'What about valuables, Mr Mackay?'

'They'll leave them in the coach, sir.'

The Governor nodded approvingly.

'Very wise.'

The Governor then paused and looked hard at the two felons occupied with paintbrushes. Surely one of them – no both of them – had exceedingly black and finely curved eyebrows?

'Who are these fellows, Mr Mackay?' he asked curiously.

Mackay smiled complacently.

'Whittaker, sir. And the other's Whalley. I picked them for the job because they have an artistic bent.'

'Bent, anyway,' muttered Whittaker under his breath.

The Governor nodded, still troubled by something odd in the two criminals' appearance but he couldn't decide what it was.

'Carry on,' he said, and turned to go.

Mackay hung back a few paces and, when the Governor was out of earshot, snarled:

'Take that eye shadow off, Whittaker.'

The official pair then emerged from the changing-rooms and moved along the wall. As they neared the grim door leading to his beloved Prison Officers' Club, Mackay said hopefully:

'After the game, sir, I thought we'd have a little reception for the visitors here at the Prison Officers' Club.'

The Governor shook his head positively.

'Oh, I don't think so. It's such an inhospitable place.'

Mackay suppressed a start of anger. He could not, after all, rebuke his chief. He paused to recover his calm and then tried again.

'You haven't been there, sir, since we brightened it up. I acquired some more horsebrasses and the M.O.'s wife has recently donated a stag's head.'

'No, no, Mr Mackay, they'd be far more comfortable in the Plough and Sail.'

As they passed on, Mackay's lips could be seen moving slightly: 'one, two, three, four, five . . .'

One night, about a week after training had started, and shortly before lock-up, the convict Banyard suddenly felt a call of nature. Laying aside the *Dental Practitioners' Gazette* with a sigh, he lowered himself from his bunk, put on his carpet slippers and trudged out of his cell and along to the latrines. But what was his indignation upon finding, when he arrived, that admission was being illegally denied him! A huge bulk, immediately recognizable to Banyard as his fellow convict Samson, barred his way.

'Stand aside, please,' droned Banyard in his best public-school accent. 'I wish to enter the toilet.'

'It's engaged,' growled Samson.

'Rubbish. Let me through. I will ascertain that for myself.'

'You can't go in.'

'I most certainly can. And you have no right to stop me. I've never heard of such impudence. Have you been appointed official doorman to the latrines by the Governor? Well? Have you?'

While this unequal argument was going on outside, Grouty and I were having a little discussion inside. When summoned to it, I'd expected it to be just the two of us and I'd been a little surprised to find that Oakes was there too, apparently with Grouty's full permission.

'Right then, Fletch,' said the Warden of Slade Prison, 'let's hear the team.'

'Wasn't easy, Grouty, to make a decision but I think you'll be pleased with what I've come up with.'

'I'm sure I will, Fletch. Hello?'

This last remark was in response to a sudden hubbub from just outside the door. It consisted of a voice raised high in shrill protest, which I thought I recognized as Banyard's, followed by a sharp thud and a cry of pain. Then all was silent again. Grouty nodded in satisfaction.

'I told Samson I didn't want to be interrupted. Well then, Fletch, the team?'

'What? Oh yes. Well, I've got Ronnie Simkin in goal. He's the lesser of two evils seeing that he can't jump while Bill Allison can't stoop but Ronnie's tall at least. Then the team itself is Tommy Armstrong, Steve Callaghan, McLaren, Nifty Small, Mini Cooper, Young Rudge – who's going to carry a lot of our chances I can tell you – Wellings, McMillan, Urquhart and Lennie Godber. Substitutes will be Wilfred James, Adams and Samson out there in case it gets ugly.'

I looked hopefully at the Overlord, seeking some sign of satisfaction with my selection. But Grouty just nodded as he took a long drag on his cigar.

'Seems a fairly well balanced side.'

I brightened up.

'Well, I think so, Grouty. We've gone for a blend of youth, experience, flair and brutality.'

Grouty nodded and tapped a head of pure white ash from his enormous Havana. I noticed that it dissolved into pure dust before it reached the floor. He smiled but it was too dark in the latrines for me to be certain whether his eyes were participating.

'Only thing was, Fletch, I didn't hear Oaksey's name in there.'

Oaksey? Was that what he was doing here? But he'd make a worse footballer than George Washington a con artist. Obviously, he must have bunged Grouty one. What the hell did Oaksey want to play for anyhow? He'd only make a fool of hisself. I'd put in a lot of work on the team by this stage and I was quite proud of my efforts. We might have a chance against the dudes from The Smoke. But not with Oaksey in it. On the other hand, if Grouty was really determined—

Playing for time, I said cautiously:

'Ah, well, yes, see – I think Oaksey would be the first to admit that he's just not a footballer.'

And now the second heavy of Slade Nick spoke for the first time, briefly and to the point.

'Yes, I am,' said Oaksey.

I swallowed.

'Oh, a footballer, certainly. What I meant to say was, Oaksey, that you're not as fit as some of those young lads.'

Oaksey smiled faintly.

'Yes, I am,' he said.

I gulped.

'Let me put it another way. You see, Grouty, I was just going on the basis that Oaksey can't tackle, pass, trap or dribble. I have to admit he throws-in well.'

Grouty nodded.

'We need a good thrower-in. He plays.'

'Well, if you're absolutely sure, Grouty—'

'I am, Fletch. Candidly, I'm surprised that you didn't spot Oaksey's talent yourself.'

Well, of course, that did it. Norman Stanley Fletcher doesn't have to have his house blown down to see which way the wind's blowing. I raised my trusty clipboard and peered at it in the poor light.

'Oh, silly me,' I exclaimed. 'Your name was here all the time, Oaksey. It's just that I'd spelt it M-c-M-i-l-l-a-n.'

Grouty nodded and then peered about with distaste.

'Could do with a proper conference room in this nick. Must have a word with the Governor about it. Looking forwards to the match, Fletch.'

'Me too, Grouty,' I enthused. Then I turned to the new midfield ace. 'Had my eye on you from the start, Oaksey.'

He smiled and the conference broke up.

I entered our dell deep in thought. Lennie was waiting for me and made no attempt to conceal his excitement.

'Well?' he asked.

'Well, what?'

'Well, who's in the team?'

'One very distinguished person, Sydney Oakes, top villain from Manchester.'

'Oakes? He's got no more footwork than a stuffed trout – 'bout as fast too.'

'Grouty wants him in the team.'

'Why?'

'That is just what we should *not* be asking ourselves, Len.'

'What, you mean—'

'Don't mean nothing. Except that when Grouty whispers low "thou must" it's up to us to get on with it, isn't it? You should have learned that by now.'

'But it'll ruin the team!'

'I been thinking about that. The forward-line I've picked is quite strong now. I'll move Mini Cooper up a few yards to cover for Oaksey's blunders and pass the word about not to pass him any direct balls. Best we can hope for is he don't get possession too often. Because taking the ball off Oaksey makes taking candy from a baby look like a desperate caper.'

Lennie sighed and shook his head.

'I was beginning to think we was contenders. Anyway, Fletch, who else is in the team?'

'Well—'

But at this point, there was a dramatic interruption. There was a strange sound from the direction of the door, a sort of cross between the snort of a buffalo that's just spotted Buffalo Bill galloping up on his tail and the whimper of a frightened kitten. Naturally we both glanced up and beheld a terrible sight: Banyard's nose. Now this object is fearsome enough in its normal state. But at present it was very far from that. Since Banyard was nursing it with both hands, you might be surprised, if you've never been confronted by the appendage yourself, that we could see it at all. But we could and gruesome was the spectacle. It was swollen to at least fifty per cent more than its normal robust proportions and had turned a very ugly shade of blue. The blue was picked out dramatically, but far from attractively, with red which was soon recognizable as blood. More blood was oozing through Banyard's cradling fingers and dripping to the floor of our hitherto immaculate dell. Accustomed though I am to the fearsome sights of the nick, this one brought a gasp to my lips and Lennie, less seasoned, let out a small cry.

'What's happened to you?' I asked, and then I remembered. 'Did you try and bust in the loo just now?'

Banyard nodded and exclaimed in a kind of strangled drone:

'We buss forb a dakshun group.'

'What?'

Banyard sniffed revoltingly, removed one paw from his proboscis, dipped it quickly into his pocket, removed a handkerchief and applied it to the wounded member. After that he spoke a little more clearly.

'We prisoners must form an action group and put an end to this tyranny. It's an outrage. I was gratuitously assaulted by that monster, Samson. I'm quite certain that the man Grout is behind it. We must teach him a lesson.'

I heard Lennie draw in his breath sharply even as I rose like a rocket, pulled Banyard into the cell and pushed the door shut after him, having first glanced quickly up and down the landing to make sure no one could have heard.

'Sit down,' I urged Banyard, offering him a chair, 'and pipe down.'

'But look what they've done to my nose.'

'Do we have to? Listen, Banyard, it's about time you learned a few home truths. Grouty runs this nick. You've still got arms and legs, haven't you? After crossing him that's a high score. Look on the bright side. When the M.O. sees that, he might put you down for a nose transplant.'

'I intend to complain to the Governor.'

Lennie, meanwhile, had been ferreting in his possessions. He came up with a small brown bottle.

'Want some iodine, Banyard?' he asked the afflicted dentist.

Banyard ungraciously shook his head.

'Rhino-pharyngeal tissue is too delicate for iodine. Godber, you'll support me, won't you?'

I answered for Lennie.

'You go on this way, and six of us'll support you – all the way to the cemetery.'

'Well, I don't intend to be intimidated.'

'Better than being amputated.'

Banyard rose to his feet haughtily. I had to admit there was a certain gory grandeur about him. He looked like a bull elephant that's just tangled with a flock of ivory-hunters.

'Well, I'm sure there are some men in this prison who—' and then he paused, listening. Just that moment, I heard the foot-steps too. I reached for him but it was too late. Banyard had stepped over to the cell door and pulled it open, revealing Mr Barrowclough who was passing on his rounds.

'Could I have a word with you, Mr Barrowclough?' he asked formally.

The screw with the bovine features recoiled.

'Good heavens, Banyard, what's the matter with you?'

'Fell on the landing, Mr Barrowclough,' I said hastily. 'Know how slippery it gets, down by the sinks.'

'I did not fall,' announced Banyard.

'Oh?' I exclaimed innocently. 'I thought that's what you said. But you weren't too clear. What happened then? Catch your nose in a lamp bracket?' I turned again to Barrowclough. 'Anyhow, no need to bother you, sir. We'll bandage it for him. I've got an old shirt that should be big enough.'

Mr Barrowclough, his eyes swivelling nervously from me to Banyard, like a cow being propositioned by a brace of bulls, began to retreat towards the cell door. But Banyard, the idiot, lurched after him.

'Don't go, Mr Barrowclough. I want your support. The man Grout is behind this.'

At that point Lennie and I naturally jumped Banyard and wrestled him back to the chair while I exclaimed loudly:

'Shock, that's what it is. He's been raving like this ever since he arrived. You needn't worry, Mr Barrowclough. We'll look after him. Carry on with your rounds, sir.'

Barrowclough had by now definitely paled. He stammered:

'Perhaps I'd better. He's in good hands with you, Fletcher, I'm sure. Yes – delirium – undoubtedly—'

And Barrowclough was gone. Banyard opened his mouth to bellow after him and Lennie promptly clapped his hand over it, while I hissed:

'You ignorant great nurk! Don't you know even the screws is cowed by Grouty? If you don't come to your senses, Banyard, there'll be no more frolics under the laughing gas for you.'

It seemed at last I had made an impression on him. He waved us off feebly and, when we'd released him, made no further move to elude us. He just sat dabbing at his nose morosely. Finally, he sighed deeply and said:

'Very well then. I suppose you'd better enlighten me as to the corruption that apparently is prevalent in this prison.'

I nodded emphatically.

'I think we better had, Banyard.'

And I started to enlighten him. Meanwhile, Barrowclough, still palpitating from the fright Banyard had given him, decided this was one night when he could use a snifter. Consequently, after he'd finished his rounds and after lights out, he made his way to the dingy hole in the wall known laughably to Mr Mackay as the Prison Officers' Club. When he got there, he found the usual cheerful bedlam in progress. Mr Mackay was on the telephone and Beale was standing at the bar. Barrowclough joined the junior screw who glanced at him and grunted:

'Not many of the chaps in tonight.'

Barrowclough shook his head mournfully.

'There never are. It's a desperate place, this. The only reason I come here is, it's either this or going home.'

Beale nodded. Just then Chalky came out of the store room.

'Drinks, gents?' he chirped.

'What'll you have, Mr Beale?' asked Barrowclough heavily.

'Do you run to another lager, Frank?'

'Certainly.'

Mr Barrowclough issued the orders and then resumed.

'No, it's not the most exhilarating place in the world but it beats home.'

'I'm single myself,' Beale admitted. 'Was married but now I'm divorced.'

Barrowclough smiled faintly.

'Really? Well, look at it this way. 'Tis better to have loved and lost, than to spend your whole ruddy life with her.'

Mr Beale considered this sage advice in silence. Mr Barrowclough glanced over to where Mr Mackay was rasping down the telephone.

'Who's Mr Mackay talking to?' he asked.

'Bloke in London. I think it's something to do with the celebrity match. Between you and me, he's had one over the top.'

'They certainly do drink, don't they?' asked Mr Barrowclough with just a touch of envy.

'Who?'

'Er – Scotsmen – I was thinking of. I suppose it's because there's so much whisky up there.'

At this point, Mr Mackay hung up his phone and reeled over to them. He looked none too chuffed and his speech was decidedly slurred.

'That was Bainbridge, I was talking to.'

'Really?' asked Mr Beale politely.

'Yes, Bainbridge, their team captain. More blasted bad news. We've lost David Diddy Hamilton – or is it David Hammy Diddleton? Anyway, he was the last important celebrity on the team. We'd have done better getting our stars from amateur nights in the pubs of Carlisle.' He glared about resentfully. 'Where's everyone gone?'

'There was no one else here,' said Mr Beale with a faint cough.

'Well, why not? Why don't they make this place their home the way we do? We love it here, don't we?' His bleary eye focused on Mr Barrowclough. And he continued,

'Oh, well done, Frank. You've decided to honour us with your presence. Least I can do is buy you a drink. Large Scotch, is it?'

'Er – just a bitter, thanks,' demurred Mr Barrowclough. 'Sorry to hear the news about the team. But we still have the Goody, don't we?'

Mackay grunted vengefully.

'Anyway, he didn't say we hadn't.'

'In my opinion,' said Mr Barrowclough tactfully. 'This celebrity match is undoubtedly a good thing for the prison by and large. The men have talked about little else. And there's been a noticeable dropping off of violence of late. I mean, apart from Banyard's nose—'

'Whose nose?' asked Mackay quickly.

Mr Barrowclough, aware that he'd been indiscreet, immediately back-pedalled.

'Whose what?' he gulped.

'Nose? Didn't you say, nose?'

'Knows what?' asked Barrowclough with pretended innocence. 'You're asking me who knows what?'

'No, I'm not,' returned Mackay irritably. 'I'm asking you what nose? You heard him, didn't you, Mr Beale?'

'I thought he said nose,' admitted Beale.

But Barrowclough shook his head earnestly.

'No nose that I know of,' with which he hastily changed the subject. 'I was watching the team train today. Fletcher's certainly done an impressive job. I think we stand a very good chance.'

For some time after that the three screws discussed football. But Mr Barrowclough could not clear from his mind the image of poor Banyard's battered nose. After a lull in the talk, he said hesitantly:

'I wonder, Mr Mackay, did you ever hear of Parkington?'

'It's Parkinson, Frank, and he's not coming either.'

'No, I was thinking of Chester Parkington, a prison officer at Parkhurst Prison. Do you remember the case?'

Mackay screwed up his face, a thing he does well.

'Rings a bell,' he admitted.

'As I recall it, Mr Parkington ran afoul a powerful snout baron in Parkhurst – decided to cut him down to size, you know – and shortly after the particular criminal's release, Mr Parkington had a very nasty motoring accident in suspicious circumstances. Of course, nothing was ever proved but poor Parkington was crippled for life.'

Mackay snorted.

'All nonsense, Mr Barrowclough. These outcasts are all cowards at heart. Firmness is the only thing they understand.'

Mr Barrowclough nodded uneasily.

'Then you're saying that you wouldn't stand for bullying by one of these barons?'

'I'd personally conduct the perpetrator to solitary confinement, Frank.'

'I see. It's just that I have an idea that Grout—'

But Mr Barrowclough never had a chance to conclude his remarks because at exactly that point, Mr Mackay bawled:

'Chalkey! Fill them up again.'

And after that talked non-stop for half an hour about his youth in the Lanarkshire coalfield.

While these jollifications were unfolding in the whitewashed paradise of the Prison Officers' Club, Lennie and I were having a little goodnight chat between bunks.

'I just want you to know,' my young cellie remarked bitterly, 'I've had it with you.'

'What?' I asked innocently.

'Been waiting all evening – ever since we shifted Banyard – for you to tell me – and you haven't.'

'Tell you what, my old son?'

'Whether I've made the team or not. You knew I wanted to know. The last two weeks, you've really pissed me off, Fletch. Never miss an edge, you don't. You've been like a tin pot Napoleon, drunk with bleeding power. I've degraded myself, giving you KitKat and darning your socks. Just to make your naffing team. We've been cellies for God knows how long. You'd think that would count for something.'

'But what you is forgetting, Len, is that if you make the team automatic, tongues would wag. There would be dispersions of favouritism. And that is why you had to prove yourself more than the next man.'

I heard Lennie scrambling out of his bunk and, sure enough, the next moment saw his face loom up beside me in the moonlight.

'Well, didn't I? And I didn't mind doing more laps than anyone else, doing more press-ups than anyone else, working my goolies off – but I still don't see why I had to stay behind and lace everyone else's boots!'

'You're in the team,' I said quietly.

But Lennie was wound up now.

'This whole prison's wetting its knickers, just because some so-called celebrities are coming here.'

'Don't you want to play then?'

There was a pause. I chuckled. I could just see the expression on his face. He looked dazed.

'What?'

'I said you're in the team.'

A broad grin appeared.

'Straight up?'

'Striker.'

'Oh great – ta, Fletch.'

'Yuh, well—'

There was a silence while he savoured the news. Then he cleared his throat and said tentatively:

'I was just wondering, Fletch. Who's the captain?'

'Why d'you want to know?'

'Well, I just wondered if I was a contender, like.'

I sat up in bed and said earnestly:

'A captain, Len, has to possess certain attributes that set him apart from the rest of the team. That's why I chose Black Jock.'

A fleeting look of disappointment crossed his face and was followed by one of puzzlement.

'Black Jock – what attributes has he got?'

I settled myself back on my comfy pillow again.

'He had half an ounce of snout and he's given it to me.'

8 The big match

'Bunny,' I asked, with as much patience as was left to me by the afternoon of the great day, 'what the hell are you doing?'

The dyslexic felon was standing on a step-ladder trying to tie a flag to the top of a goal post. He looked down at me with a puzzled expression.

'Just putting this flag here, Fletch.'

'With your personal colours on it?'

'Mr Mackay told me to set up the corner flags.'

'The corner of the field, you nurk, not the corner of the goal. Haven't you ever been to a football match?'

' 'Course I have,' he retorted indignantly. 'I used to attend the cup final every year regular.'

'Well, you don't seem to have observed much.'

'Yes, I did. But I was working, see? So what I observed was mainly the bulges in hip pockets.'

I sighed.

'Take it down, Bunny. And set it up over there.'

Grumbling, he complied. I gazed about the field. I had to admit it was quite a satisfying sight. I mean, nothing could make our gritty pitch in the grounds of the prison look like even a second-division stadium on the day of the home match.

There were no stands filled with colourful and cheering supporters, no expanse of well tended lawn, no ranks of coppers ready to quell riots – and then I smiled. Funny one, that. You had to come to a nick to get a football match without uniformed fuzz. Of course, there were a number of screws on duty but no one anticipated that kind of trouble. No, to the lads it was too much of a treat. The spectators was straggling out now, nearly an hour before the scheduled time for kick-off, so as to miss nothing and get a first butchers at the celebrities when they arrived. Groups of cons were marking the sidelines and the penalty areas. Others were attaching nets to the goal posts. The weather was excellent. There were several distinct breaks in the cloud cover through which a pale radiance suggestive of sunlight filtered down. Lennie approached me.

'Fletch, I been thinking. You know that move we planned where I take a corner and Rudge—'

But I held up my hand and silenced him.

'The time for tactics is over, Godber. Now it's up to the will and the skill.'

He nodded.

'Well, I've got plenty of both. You won't regret having selected me, Fletch.'

'I have every confidence in you, Len, boy. It was your Kit-Kats pulled me through this trying period. So – hey up, here they are!'

Lennie turned eagerly and looked towards the massive swinging gate, which I was already facing, and where a big coach had pulled up. Just the sight of it gave me a thrill which I knew Lennie was sharing. It was big and green and had large windows all along the sides, quite different from prison transport. It brought with it a breath of freedom, of the big, comfortable world outside.

The two screws on gate duty approached it, just for routine, because they knew as well as we did that it was the celebrity team inside. After a brief exchange with the driver, the screws returned to their checkpoint and operated the mechanism for opening the outer perimeter gate. As soon as it had swung open, the coach started up and swung round the field, stopping outside the changing-rooms. By this time, Lennie and I, with a crowd of the other lads, had hurried over to it and were clustered round the door when it opened and the visitors began to emerge. There was an excited hubbub from our lads.

'Hey, that's Oliver Reed, isn't it?'

'Don't be a nurk. Oliver Reed always travels with at least five birds with him.'

'Is that Morecambe and Wise?'

'More like Bournemouth and Dim.'

Gradually, a note of discontent and even anger crept into the exclamations.

'Well, where's the bleeding celebrities?'

'This must be the netball team. Where's the flaming football team?'

And such like. I sighed. I was not surprised by the visitors but I had hoped there might at least be one familiar face. Suddenly, I saw Bunny dart forwards and grab the hand of one of the last of those emerging from the coach. To my astonishment, a look of pleasure, which Bunny's approach has never been known to occasion inside, came into the face of the team member. The two shook hands and a moment later Bunny was towing the bloke over to me and Lennie.

'Fletch,' he announced, with ill concealed delight, 'may I have the honour of presenting my very good friend, James Callaghan. You owe me twenty-five pounds of snout.'

It was a tricky situation.

'Pleased to meet you,' I said coolly, shaking hands with the young blond bloke, who had nothing much in common with the Prime Minister in his appearance. 'That your name, James Callaghan?'

'Uh-huh,' grunted the other and then, making me suspect that he and Bunny had somehow planned the whole thing, he pulled out a driving licence and showed me. But I was not wrong footed.

'You a celebrity, are you?' I asked.

He shook his head.

'Scene shifter. We ain't all celebrities.'

'Twenty-five pounds of snout, Fletch,' crowed Bunny, almost dancing about with delight.

'Hang on, Bunny,' I said. 'Let's see the terms of the agreement.'

Bunny produced them and I took the bit of paper from him and handed it to Len.

'Would you mind just reading that, Lennie?' I asked with dignity.

'*Norman Stanley Fletcher wagers Bunny Warren,*' Lennie read, '*that James Callaghan will not be one of the celebrities in the celebrity team what is coming to play the Slade Prison team. The bet is a quarter ounce of snout to twenty-five pounds giving odds of a hundred to one.'*

'Thank you, Len,' I said. 'Sorry, Bunny.'

'What do you mean, sorry?' exclaimed the little rabbit crossly. 'He's here. He's James Callaghan.'

'But,' I pointed out, 'by his own admission he is not one of the celebrities. Nor is any of the others that I can see. Better luck next time.'

'But – but—' stammered the outsmarted one. James Callaghan said:

'See you later, Arthur. I've got to change.'

And he trotted after his team towards the changing-rooms.

'I suppose you think you're very clever, Fletch,' said the smarting Bunny. 'It's just taking unfair advantage because you happen to be able to read and write.'

'Unfair, I know, *Arthur*,' I consoled him, 'but when was life ever fair? You'd better get over to the pitch if you want a good position to see the match. I think Mr Mackay wants to see me.'

I hurried over to the beckoning chief screw. Mackay was with one of the new arrivals, a bloke in his thirties who had something in his manner which, if he'd been a con, I might have considered was just a shade lilac.

'Fletcher,' Mackay rasped, as I pulled up, 'this is Mr Bainbridge who has organized the – er – Show-biz Eleven.'

Bainbridge flashed me a brilliant smile and raised a floppy hand from the elbow.

'Pleased to meet you, dar— er, Mr Fletcher.'

I took the manicured extremity and flapped it weakly.

'How d'you do?'

Bainbridge winked roguishly and then leaned forwards and confessed:

'Actually, there are only ten of us. We were supposed to pick up Tony Macaulay at the Mill Hill Roundabout. He's a songwriter. I expect you've heard of him?'

I shook my head regretfully.

'Can't say I have.'

'Anyway, he never turned up, which is why we're a little late.' He looked about him. 'It's not a fun palace, is it, ducks? Still, I expect there are lots of lovely chaps here.'

Mackay cleared his throat huskily which produced a fastidious shudder from Bainbridge. The screw rasped:

'Yes, well we'd better get on. As you can see, Mr Bainbridge, we don't have floodlights.' He called to his junior who was hovering nearby. 'Mr Barrowclough, can you show the visitors through to the changing-rooms?'

As Barrowclough bustled towards us, Bainbridge asked me:

'Any chance of borrowing one of your chaps?'

'Yes, how about one of your subs, Fletcher?' added Mackay.

I nodded.

'If you like, sir.' And then, as always happens with me, the big idea bounded out of nowhere like a case of Scotch tumbling from a passing lorry. Smoothly, I added: 'But what about Mr Beale, sir? He's been telling us he can play a bit. Keen as mustard, he is.'

Mackay swallowed the hook. As Barrowclough ushered Bainbridge and the other visitors off towards the changing-rooms, he said:

'I'll have a word with him.'

Mackay turned to go but I stopped him.

'Forgive me asking, Mr Mackay, but who the hell are they? I mean, me and the lads, we was led to understand that this team would contain a sprinkling of celebrities.'

Mackay squared his shoulders and tried to look confident but I could see he was making the best of a bad job.

'So there is, Fletcher. Now the chap with the red hair – he reads the weather on Anglia Television.'

'Really?' I asked, as if deeply impressed.

'Absolutely. And two of the others are scriptwriters.'

'Scriptwriters, is it, sir? That is something. Hardly ever see them out and about, do you?'

'However, for someone who really is . . . known to the public. I have his permission to tell you that Mr Bainbridge himself has just finished a pantomime season at the Alhambra, Swansea.'

'I can't wait to tell the lads, Mr Mackay. They'll be right chuffed.'

'We've done well, I think, Fletcher.'

'A glittering line-up.'

'Right, you'd better get the team changed.'

I turned and went over to where my blokes were standing in a gloomy group. One of them asked:

'Who are they then?'

'One's a weatherman. The other's Widow Twanky. Now go and get changed.'

While they were changing, I had a little job to do. I made my way into the main nick and up to Grouty's palatial cell. He was reclining on his couch, reading a book called *Crime and Punishment*, which struck me as a bit masochistic. But Grouty has strange tastes in reading matter.

'The team is here, Grouty,' I announced, after I'd been admitted by Delilah.

'Oh, good, Fletch.'

'Be coming down to see the match, will you?'

'No, I've already seen one, Fletch. When I was at school.'

'But – I thought—'

'You needn't worry, Fletch. I've asked Ives to keep me informed of its progress.' Then, as he waved me out with a lazy movement of his right hand and returned his eyes to the page, he murmured, 'May the best team win.'

'Course I'd known there was more to this match for Grouty than mere entertainment but I had expected him to grace it with his presence. I hurried on to the changing-rooms trying to stop myself from thinking what I could not help thinking: that whatever it was Grouty had been planning all these months was going to happen soon. Anyway, nothing I could do about it, and the less I knew the better.

Immediately inside the door of the changing-room sat Oakes. He was gazing straight ahead and seemed to have forgotten all about the football boot he was holding in his hand. Of course, with his form, he had every reason to be tense. I said encouragingly:

'Never mind, Oakes. Just do your damndest.'

He started and then swallowed. Then he began putting on his boot, muttering:

'I'm all right.'

I wasn't too sure. Still. I went on to where the main team was getting their gear on and called for attention. When I had secured it, I gave them a pep talk.

'Now, lads, I know you're all disappointed because they're all nobodies but the fact remains that these blokes have come a long way to give us a game. So let's give 'em a game. Let's show 'em. Don't need the hard stuff, do we?'

There was a kind of mutter from the men which was hard to make sense of but sounds none too encouraging. Then McLaren asked darkly, which is something he does well:

'What about Mr Beale?'

'Naturally,' I advised him, 'you can kick holes in him. In fact, I've got a little plan which might come in useful. Tell you about it in a minute. Now then, you blokes, remember all I've taught you and whatever happens, don't let them panic you into playing football.'

There was an appreciative laugh and the lads resumed putting on their kit. I went off to assemble my bucket, sponge and liniment and, as I passed McLaren, I beckoned slightly with my head. He rose and followed me towards the cupboard where my trainer's equipment was stored.

A few minutes later, we took the field. A ragged cheer, not devoid of irony, went up from the cons ranged along the touch-lines. Then, out of the changing-rooms, trotted the visitors. There was a moment of silence before the lads caught sight of Beale amongst them. Faintly at first, and then more loudly, the words of the old song swelled out:

'*There's no business like show business, like no business I know—*'

'Quiet, you men!' bawled Mackay and his powerful larynx was enough to make the command heard above the song. The singing trailed off. I went and took my position on the bench between my substitutes. McMillan grumbled:

'What am I doing benched with that wanker Oakes on the park?'

It was a question that I'd been trying not to ask myself. I said soothingly:

'You'll get on, son. Don't fret. Here, have a snort of liniment.'

Like I've said elsewhere, anything with a kick in it is eagerly consumed by prisoners. McMillan raised his head and I bunged some liniment into his nostrils.

Mackay, who was naturally refereeing, blew his whistle for captains and the kick-about on the field came to an end. The two captains joined Mackay on the centre line and the screw said importantly:

'Well, gentlemen, let's have a good clean contest, shall we?'

McLaren shook his head at the formula.

'This isn't a boxing match, Mr Mackay.'

'That,' affirmed the screw, 'is what I'm anxious to avoid.'

Bainbridge, the visitors' captain, patted his hair nervously and Mackay gave a little chuckle to show that he'd just been joking. A moment later, he pulled a coin from his pocket and, tossing it in the air, shouted:

'Call!'

Bainbridge called heads and the coin came up heads. Bainbridge turned to signal his decision to his team and McLaren stooped swiftly, scooped up the coin and began to trot away towards his men. Mackay immediately called him back and demanded the coin. With ill grace, McLaren handed it over. Mackay blew his whistle and the great match began.

A moment later, I picked up a familiar vibration from behind me. Without turning, I said:

'Afternoon, Mr Treadaway.'

Then I turned and had to suppress a chuckle at the surprised look on the Governor's face. How had I known it was him? Fact is, I couldn't tell you myself, just some amazing extra-sensual perception we old lags acquire. Treadaway recovered and said:

'Afternoon, Fletcher. How's it going?'

'Well, it's a little early to tell yet, sir. We're only ten seconds into the game.'

'Which one of them is the Goodie?' asked the Governor with interest.

'Well they is all very well behaved, sir. But if you is referring to the telly Goodie, he didn't make it. However, we do have a weatherman from Anglia. In his opinion it's going to rain.'

Just then the Governor caught some move on the field which, because I'd turned politely to converse with him I'd missed myself, and called:

'Oh, well played, Slade!' Then to me: 'Who was that?'

I looked back at the field.

'Urquhart, that was, sir. Class player.'

The Governor nodded sadly.

'Oh yes. He's going out next month. Pity that. He'd be valuable if we have another fixture.'

'Well, he's a keen lad, sir. If I put it to him, perhaps he'll agree to stay on.' But I didn't want the Governor to think I was being insolent, so I quickly continued: 'More games on the agenda, are they, Mr Treadaway?'

'I don't see why not. If this one goes without a hitch. Good for morale. What's that noise?'

I heard it too, like rain drumming on a tin roof. I glanced down.

'It's your dog, sir. Peeing against my bucket.'

'Oh, bad dog,' exclaimed Mr Treadaway, bending to chastise the mangy old animal. The opportunity was too good to miss. Quickly filling my lungs, I bawled:

'Come on, Oakes! Get stuck in!'

The Governor, whose ear was about level with my mouth, jerked very satisfyingly.

At the far end of the field a little dispute had broken out. The ball had gone into touch and Barrowclough, our linesman, had put up his flag to indicate that it was the visitors' ball. But Black Jock snarled:

'Are you blind, Mr Barrowclough? That came off him!'

'Oh, I'm sorry,' apologized the docile screw. He changed the flag to his other hand causing the visiting player to exclaim indignantly,

'Here, I never touched it!'

'Oh, didn't you?' asked Barrowclough, perplexed, and shifted the flag back again.

Beside me the Governor, peering at this, exclaimed:

'What's going on down there?'

'I think,' I explained, 'it's a message in semaphore. Oh yes, it reads: *Sink the Bismarck.*

So the lads charged about the field in pursuit of the elusive football. Now and then someone got it on the tip of his boot and sent it spinning wildly away, usually in the direction of an opposing player. But, just before half time, my long weeks of training and deep-laid tactics paid off. McLaren took a corner for us and managed to place it, as planned, where Rudge could volley it at a sharp angle up to Lennie's head. With just a twitch of his sensitive cheek, Godber put it away. The whistle blew and we were one up.

During the five-minute break, I could not keep my eyes from wandering uneasily about the field. I did not want to see what I was afraid I might see, something dodgy, and the fact is I did not see anything dodgy. The coach driver, a small chap with a pencil-thin moustache, wandered over to the screws guarding the exit gates and exchanged a few words with them. But he would be hardly likely to pull a machine gun and spring the whole nick. Besides, I knew Grouty. If a stroke was coming up it was going to be subtle. No, there was nothing visible. Still, I was relieved when the whistle blew again for the second half.

It was very satisfying. Only a couple of minutes into second half and another of my tactics paid off. This one was not connected with scoring goals but with settling scores. Lennie booted the ball upfield and, to my delight, Beale intercepted. Immediately McLaren and Armstrong closed in on him and tackled simultaneously. I could practically hear the crunch as they sandwiched the screw. As Beale went down, Mackay blew a blast on his whistle. McLaren and Armstrong, with that acting skill which is another talent fostered by incarceration, immediately stooped with expressions of great concern and hoisted the breathless Beale to his feet.

'I saw that!' bawled Mackay, panting up to them.

'Saw what?' asked the two tacklers, voices tinkling with innocence. To further demonstrate their grief at being unjustly suspected, they made gestures towards the heavens, which had the effect of releasing Beale who thudded heavily to the ground once more.

Mackay whipped out his notebook and pen. He snarled at McLaren,

'I'm going to have to put you in the book for that. What's your name McLaren?'

'McLaren,' admitted McLaren.

And now the third member of the complicated play arrived on the scene. It was me, Norman Stanley Fletcher, with my bucket and sponge.

'I'll take care of this, Mr Mackay,' I promised.

While the savage screw was engaged in booking McLaren, I

bent down over the afflicted Beale, thus concealing him from view, and tried to revive him. I did this by bashing him several times about the head with my ice-cold sponge. Finally, to my great relief, he responded.

'Wha— wha— wha—'

'Where does it hurt, Mr Beale?' I asked anxiously.

'The ribs,' he gasped hoarsely.

The moment had come.

'The ribs, eh?' I asked. I poised a horny finger. 'What, you mean, just – here !'

'Aaaaaaarrrrghhhh !' was all Beale replied.

'Fletcher !' snarled Mackay, 'What the hell are you doing to Mr Beale?'

I stood up.

'Think he's busted a rib, sir. Won't be able to play no more. They can have McMillan or Samson if they want.'

There was a kind of scrabbling at my feet and then a faint voice spoke :

'Okay – I'm okay – play the game – must play the game—'

Mackay kneeled beside the heroic Beale.

'Quite allright, Mr Beale. You've been injured. No one'll think the worse.'

Beale got laboriously to his feet.

'Your permission, sir – like to keep playing—'

Mackay nodded his head in admiration.

'I admire your spirit, Mr Beale. That's the difference between them and us. Carry on.'

And so battle was once more joined. For the next quarter of an hour or so it was indecisive. The excellence of my forward-line was matched by the unexpectedly tenacious defence of the visitors. We couldn't seem quite to get the second goal we needed as insurance. The only good thing was that their attack was so feeble I had small fear of them breaking free. But then the show-biz side managed, for the first time in the second half, to actually penetrate our territory. I wasn't worried when their left winger chipped the ball neatly into the centre, because Urquhart was marking their striker and had the situation in control. Besides the striker was a good thirty yards from the goal. I could see what he should do, back-heel to his midfield player who'd come up to press the attack on the right. To my amazement, he simply booted it straight at Urquhart. To my even greater amazement, Urquhart obligingly opened his legs or so it seemed and let the ball through. To my horror, Ronnie Simkin in goal, confronted with a ball which, by the time it got near him, was hurtling along with all the power and ferocity of a clockwork duck, threw himself dramatically in the wrong direction and the ball trickled in. One all.

'Naffing hell!' I exclaimed. Then I rose irately to my feet and bawled, 'You been bribed, Simkin?'

'No, I've not!' he bellowed back, picking tiny rocks out of his knees.

'Well, don't sound so uppity. That's what you're in for!'

'Fletcher!' roared Mackay. 'Show some sportsmanship.'

'Why?' I said under my breath. 'No one else is.'

But then someone began to and to my surprise it was none other than Oakes who, up to this point, had seemed more like an Oakes tree – ha, ha – than a human being. See what I mean? Rooted to the spot. I don't suppose he'd moved more than about five yards from his midfield position and, to my recollection, he'd never once had possession of the ball. But something about the show-biz equalizer seemed to galvanize him. He started raging up and down his wing like a tiger, tackling every chance he could, and even gaining possession now and then. It was a heartening sight.

I rose again to my feet and shouted:

'That's it, Oaksey. Stuff 'em!'

As if in response to my encouragement Oaksey flung himself into a long sliding tackle against the ginger-haired weatherman from Anglia who was dribbling past with the ball. It was brave but ill conceived. Oaksey missed the ball but found the toe of the weatherman's boot and crashed down like a – well, why not? – like a felled oak. I groaned. I could see it must have hurt. It seemed I was right because Oaksey did not rise again. Mackay's whistle blasted out and once more I seized my bucket, sponge and liniment and trotted forth to minister. When I got there the weatherman was crouched anxiously beside Oaksey.

'You all right?' he asked, obviously concerned.

Oaksey, I was relieved to discover, was not unconscious,

although his face was contorted with pain. He shook his head.

'Don't know yet.'

'You come into the game with a bang, you did, Oaksey,' I said admiringly. 'Can you stand?'

We helped him to his feet but as soon as he got any weight on the injured leg, he collapsed again.

'Think it's the cartilage,' he groaned. 'Old trouble. Had it before.'

Mackay said irritably:

'You'll have to get him off.'

Samson joined us.

'It's all right, Fletch,' he grunted. 'I'll give you a hand.'

Oaksey put one arm around my neck and one around the massive Samson and together we hobbled off the field and across the intervening distance to the changing-rooms. As we slowly advanced, I glanced about the field with apprehension. I now had a very definite prickling feeling all down my back. I was very conscious of the fact that it had been Grouty's man, Samson, who had come forward to help me with Oakes. I tried to push back the dangerous thoughts and concentrate on the sounds of battle that were wafting back from the field. We finally got Oaksey into the changing-room where, wincing from the pain, he sat down gingerly on a bench.

I said:

'I'd best fetch the M.O. for you, Oaksey.'

He shook his head firmly.

'No.'

'But you're in pain.'

'I'll be all right,' he maintained. 'That doctor knows naff all about orthopaedics. I'll just have the early bath.'

'Yeah, but—'

'You heard him,' growled Samson.

'Oh, sure,' I said quickly. 'Well, I'd best be getting back to the field then. Mustn't deprive the lads of my encouragement. You coming, Samson?'

'What? Oh – uh – yeah.'

Together we left the changing-rooms. But I saw that, as I returned to my bench, Samson showed a tendency to hang back. When I was seated again, I noticed two things. One, that Samson was still near the door to the dressing-rooms. He was running on the spot, as if keeping himself limber, but I wasn't very convinced. The other thing I noticed was that the driver of the coach was nowhere to be seen. Probably gone for a slash, I said to myself hopefully. Then I fixed my eyes on the field, determined that, whatever happened, that's where I would keep them. Only safe way.

Happily, during the next quarter of an hour, nothing untoward happened. But, the game picked up considerably. I'd put McMillan in to replace Oaksey and he was showing surprising form. We now definitely had the edge and most of the action was taking place in the visitors' penalty area. It was obviously only a matter of time until we scored again. Then the moment came. Rudge, in possession, expertly beat two defenders and headed for the goal. Lennie, according to our pre-arranged tactic, raced for the far post. When he was near it, he shouted:

'Rudgie! Rudgie!'

With perfect timing and placing, Rudge crossed the ball to him. As Lennie rose in the air to head it, so exciting was the moment that most of the spectators rose too. But I covered my eyes with my hands. I'd seen what none of the others had. Lennie was closer to the post than he'd intended. As he jerked his head to one side ready to hammer the ball in, his bonce hit the post. I could hear the clunk from where I sat. There was a disappointed roar from the crowd as Lennie folded and the ball went into touch.

'Fletcher!' came the urgent bellow of Mackay.

I looked up. Sure enough, Len was stretched out on the field. I grabbed my implements again and started towards him, muttering: 'I'm getting more exercise than wot they are.' But by the time I reached the goal Lennie was on his feet again. He looked all right at first glance, but when I got near I saw that his eyes were glazed. I'd seen that look before, concussion.

I took out my sponge and started sponging his face but he brushed it away impatiently.

'Our ball!' he shouted. 'Corner kick. Come on, where are they?'

Since he was facing the wrong way, it's not surprising that he couldn't see the action which, in any case, had come to a halt.

I put my arm over Lennie's shoulders to steady him.

'Where's the ball?' he asked. 'Where's the team? Come on, Slade. Let's stuff them!'

'Easy, Len, boy,' I said.

Mackay nodded wisely and stationed himself in front of Lennie. He held up one finger directly in front of Lennie's face.

'Godber? How many fingers am I holding up?' he asked.

'Dunno, sir,' gasped Lennie. 'Where are you?'

Mackay sighed and lowered his hand.

'The lad's concussed,' he pronounced. 'Take him off, Fletcher. Somebody go down to the Plough and Sail and fetch the M.O. Do you know what to do, Fletcher?'

'I'll look after him, sir, don't worry,' I assured him. 'Come on, Len. Easy does it, boy.'

'Just a moment, Fletcher,' rasped Mackay. 'Where's your substitute?'

I looked at the bench where Adams should have been sitting. He wasn't.

'Anyone seen Adams?' I asked. 'How about you, Tippett?'

Tippett was his cellie. He nodded.

'His toothache come on. Went back to his cell for some pills the doctor gave him.'

Mackay had been listening to this.

'He'll be no use with toothache. There's Samson over by the changing-rooms. Tell him he's on, Fletcher.'

'Will do, Mr Mackay.'

And I set off, piloting Lennie, who showed a tendency to keep going in a straight line, towards the changing-rooms. When we got near Samson, who looked to me very much as if he was minding, I said:

'Go on, Samson, you're on.'

The heavy's eyes widened and he scowled.

'What?'

'You're a sub, ain't you?'

'Let Adams go on.'

'He's got toothache. Got to be you.'

'I can't.'

'Well, if you don't, Mackay will be over to find out why not.'

Samson licked his lips. The one thing heavies try to avoid is having to make decisions. They don't have the equipment for it. That's why they attach themselves to governors like Grouty. But, of course, Grouty was tucked up in his cell and Samson was on his own. Which was it to be? Stick to his post, as by now I'd twigged he was doing, or bust orders and go on the field? I could practically see the cogs turning in his eyes. Finally, he nodded.

'Right.'

He started trotting towards the field but he'd only gone a few yards when he stopped, turned and made a gesture towards me.

'What?' I called.

For a moment he just stared. Then he shook his head hopelessly, turned again and continued on to the pitch.

'Len,' I said sadly. 'I'm afraid we is entering a right nest of hornets, but I can't think of any way to avoid it.'

'Where's the ball?' he asked, gazing straight ahead.

'Come on.'

Pushing him gently ahead of me, I followed him into the changing-rooms.

I didn't really need to see it. I'd just about guessed the caper by then even though I'd been trying not to. I had to admit, it was quite neat. There was the coach driver, in his underwear and tied to one of the loos. And there was Oaksey just pencilling in the last traces of a moustache like the driver's with a piece of burnt cork. Oaksey was now wearing the driver's civvies while his own prison uniform was scattered carelessly on the floor to make it look like a rush, spur-of-the-moment job instead of the meticulously planned one it really was.

Naturally, as soon as he heard us, Oaksey looked up in alarm and, when he saw who it was, his face contorted in anger and he swore. I held up a helpless hand:

'Not our fault, Oaksey. We never saw nothing, did we, Len?'

'Saw what?' asked Lennie. 'The ball?'

'Why didn't that goon Samson stop you?' snarled Oakes.

'Because he had to go on as a substitute. Not his fault, any more than it's mine. OK, you better tie us up too.'

'Can't.'

This surprised and alarmed me.

'What? Why not?'

'Haven't got any more flaming rope.'

'Well, use our uniforms, braces, anything. You got to, Oaksey.'

'Hang on,' said Oakes. He turned to the tied up driver. 'What do you think?'

'You'll have to take them with you,' the small man replied.

'What?' exclaimed Oakes, appalled at the thought.

'Got no choice, have you? Otherwise, I'm in it as well.'

Not liking the drift of this conversation, I began backing towards the door, pulling Lennie with me.

'Listen, Oaksey,' I said, 'I don't mind doing anyone a favour and being tied up. But I'm not going nowhere.'

Inevitably, I suppose, Oaksey shipped out a gun and a real one too, not one of your hobby-shop specials which usually do more damage to the shooter than the shot. The driver must have brought that in for him and all.

'You'll do what I say, son,' insisted Oakes.

I sat down wearily on a bench. I hadn't the heart to say more than:

'Oh, bleeding hell.'

'Sorry, Fletch,' said Oakes, not unpleasantly, 'but you better understand this gun is not for show. I've got naff all to lose now. Burned my boats.'

Lennie exclaimed:

'It's our ball – came off their man. Corner!'

'What's up with him?' asked Oakes, glancing suspiciously at Lennie.

'He's concussed. Hit his head on a goal post. So he won't say nothing. He can't even see anything. All you got to do is tie me up. He'll just sit there quiet.'

'No,' called the driver.

'Sounds all right to me,' admitted Oaksey. 'I don't want to be lumbered with these two.'

'Well, you got no choice. Remember, I got friends outside too. Only way to protect my alibi proper is for you to take them with you.'

I walked over to the driver, aware that Oaksey's gun was following me every step.

'Listen,' I said, 'I don't grass. Anyway, how's Oaksey going to get that ruddy great coach through the gate? Crash it?'

Oaksey came over to us.

' 'Course not. I'm not daft. It's been fixed. Dines here has got permission to go down to the village and fill up with petrol before he takes the team back to The Smoke.'

I nodded. It was a good scheme. Might work.

'But,' I pointed out, 'they may just take a look in the coach. And they won't be too chuffed if they see Len and me there going along for the ride.'

Dines grinned.

'You travel in the luggage compartment.'

'What?' I turned indignantly to Oaksey. 'You wouldn't do it, Oaksey.'

He shook his head grimly.

'I wouldn't if I could help it – for my own sake. Fact is, you shouldn't have come in here, Fletch.'

'Hadn't no choice, with Mackay's eagle eye on me. No, why insult eagles? Naffing hell, Oaksey, I'm due for release in less than a year. Len here, even less. They'll never believe we didn't go along voluntary. You're about to ruin our lives.'

He grinned.

'Well, when we're in the clear, I'll give you a note for the Governor.'

I sat down again.

'Ha, ha,' I said.

Oakes went to the door and very cautiously peered out. I tried to remember the set-up. From the pitch, it was possible to see the door to the changing-rooms. I reckoned it would have looked suspicious if the coach had been parked in such a way as to block them completely. But that meant there was a space of five or six yards between the door to the dressing-rooms and the conceal-ment of the coach when anyone on or around the pitch would be able to spot us. Wasn't going to help Oaksey's plan having me and a concussed Lennie along. I mean, alone, he could pick his moment and then just stroll over in his disguise. But with us, he'd have to make a dash for it. And Lennie wasn't in very good dashing shape.

Of course, I knew what I *could* do. I could take Oakes. When he had his hands full, opening the luggage compartment, or when he was distracted, like now. I glanced up at him at the door, his back to me. I'm very deceptive in my physical appearance, as many a villain has lived to discover and regret. When the need arises, I can move like a cat and strike like a bear. Yes, I could take Oakes. But I knew I wasn't going to. It was still them and us. It wasn't Oaksey's fault that we'd got mixed up in his caper. I had no right to hinder his bid for freedom. Besides, Grouty would be very dischuffed if I cocked-up his doubtless profitable plans. I wondered how much Oakes was paying him.

'Come on!' snapped Oakes.

I rose and propelled the docile Lennie to the door, keeping us out of sight naturally.

'Right,' said Oakes. 'McLaren's about to score. When the ball hits the net, we move. Ready—'

'Hang about, Oaksey—'

The gun swung round dangerously.

'Fletch, if you—'

'The hat,' I said quickly. 'The driver's still got his hat on. Need that, won't you?'

Oaksey glanced over at the driver and nodded. He went and got the hat and then gagged the driver quickly. Then he returned. By that time, McLaren had muffed his shot and the game had moved into a skirmishing phase again.

'Thanks, Fletch,' said Oaksey.

'Rudgie!' Lennie suddenly shouted. 'Over here! Rudgie!'

'Keep him quiet!' snarled Oakes.

I put my arm over Lennie's shoulder.

'S'alright, Len. It's a penalty.'

'It is an' all,' said Oakes with surprise.

'What?'

'Tommy Armstrong just handled. Mackay's giving a penalty. Right, this is it. When I say, go—'

The distant uproar from the pitch had abated as everyone waited to see if the visitors would go ahead.

'Go!' said Oakes, and he darted out from the changing-rooms and headed for the coach.

I took Lennie's arm firmly in mine and followed him. We was about halfway to the cover when there was a roar from the field, doubtless meaning they'd scored. As soon as he heard it, Lennie stopped dead. His arm tore loose and I continued on to join Oaksey behind the coach.

'Naffing hell!' he exclaimed. 'You've left him behind.'

'He just stopped. Shall I go back and get him?'

I made a move but Oaksey grabbed on.

'Hang on! They could see you – call him!'

Lennie was just standing there, in full view, gazing with a puzzled expression at the pitch.

'Len!' I called. 'Len, over here. You got to change, remember?'

He turned and looked in my direction. But I doubted if he was seeing me. It was a very dicey situation. Oakes was worked up and he had a gun. I certainly didn't want to get caught in the crossfire when the Governor opened the prison armoury and issued firearms. Len looked back at the field.

I had a brainwave.

'Here, Len, I've got it, the ball. It's here. Come and get the ball, Len!'

He turned at once and trotted over to me. Oakes had been busy. He'd pulled up the hatch of the luggage compartment, revealing the low dark space.

'In there,' he ordered. 'Quick.'

'The ball's in here, Len,' I urged, and he allowed me to pull him after me into the miserable hole. Immediately, the hatch slammed shut and we were in total darkness. Then I felt a slight movement as Oakes climbed into the big vehicle. The motor whirred and died. Then it whirred again and our grimy quarters began to throb gently. A moment more and with a jerk that no professional coach driver would have made the machine started to move.

'Can't see the ball, Fletch,' complained Lennie. 'It's too dark in here.'

9 Alarm

So there I was, shut up with a loonie, because that's what Lennie was in his concussed state, in a kind of mobile black hole of Calcutta. The first thing I thought about was oxygen and very vivid recollections came into my mind of about a hundred films I've seen where the depth-charged sub sinks to the bottom of the ocean. Then the crew have to sit around awaiting rescue. The captain says: 'Stay quiet and don't move about so as to conserve oxygen.' And everyone sits around for hours and then days conserving oxygen. And it gets hotter and hotter and they all begins to sweat and pant and turn blue. Then one of them snuffs it, murmuring: 'There'll be more oxygen for you lot now. Bye.'

And they turn blue some more and two more snuff it and so on and just when you think you can't stand it no more and have to leap out of your seat and buy a choc-ice to keep going, there's a clunk on the side of the sub and one of the survivors opens a weary eye and gasps: 'That's the rescue sub. We is saved.' And a very faint croaking cheer goes up from the handful still alive. Just as I reached this point in my mental replay, there was a clunk on the side of the coach and I gasped:

'That's the rescue coach, Lennie. We is saved.'

But what I would like you to understand is what an amazing contraption the human brain is. Because that clunk on the side of the coach came only about half-a-minute after we'd set off and by that time I'd had a mind's-eye re-run of every sunk-submarine film that was ever made, usually with John Wayne as captain. But, you are probably wondering, what was clunking on the side of the coach?

I will tell you. In fact, seeing that not much action and drama is possible in the luggage compartment of a coach, I think it would be best if I forgot about Len and me for the time being and concentrated on events outside our miserable moving prison.

The clunk on the side of the coach was caused by the impact of a football. The ball had been kicked against it by McLaren as a gesture to show his disgust because the visitors had followed up their penalty goal by scoring another one almost immediately. McLaren was booked for causing the clunk by Mackay but, other than informing you that the visitors ultimately won by five goals to one, I don't propose to devote any more of this narrative to the great celebrity football match.

So now Oaksey was very cautiously piloting the big coach round the narrow road towards the manned gates. He was naturally exceedingly nervous. On the field, Samson had stopped playing football (which helped the visitors get their fourth goal) and was staring fixedly at the coach. Fortunately, the screws present, knowing that Samson's brain is of the kind that normally only ticks over and often seizes up completely, were not surprised by his conduct and twigged nothing. Now Oaksey could see, through his windscreen, the screw Cox leave his box, walk out ahead of the coach and put up his hand. This was not on the books. Dines was supposed to have fixed it so that the gates was opened without any hassle. For a second Oakes panicked and his foot went down on the accelerator. The temptation was strong. If he was nabbed with a gun on him, he might get another five years added to his sentence. He knew that the vehicle was massive enough to crash through the gates and then he would be free! Free! No law-abiding citizen can get even an inkling of the power of that word to a con doing a long stretch. The prisoner sometimes feels that he is being squeezed to death by the walls closing in on him. He craves for freedom like your dope addict for a fix. He must have it – and Oaksey could see the open moors beckoning beyond the gates. But he wasn't the crime king of Manchester for nothing. He'd kept his head in tough spots before and the voice of reason was still whispering to him: you bust through and you'll be lucky to get five miles. They'll have helicopters landing on the roof and tanks blocking the roads. So even as he started to press down on the throttle, he stopped again. He crawled smoothly up to Cox and braked to stop. And then, because he had the villain's instinct to make things look even more natural than they really needs to, he wound down his driver's window, stuck his head out and said:

'Yeah?'

Cox said:

'It's a Texaco station. You go straight down the road, through the village and it's on the left-hand side.'

'Ta,' said Oaksey genially.

Cox went back to his controls, works them and the big gates swung open. Oaksey started his coach again, put it in gear, engaged the clutch, started to roll and a moment later he was through the horrible gates at last and – FREE! Soon he was bowling along an undulating road over the moors. A little later, when he had turned several corners and was well clear of the nick, he was belting along with his foot down as far as it would go.

In the luggage compartment, Lennie and I was being shook about like silver spoons in a fleeing burglar's bag.

Meanwhile, back at the old plantation, the darkies were singing – well, anyhow, Jock McLaren was cursing. The match was over and recriminations were naturally bursting out. Simkin was backing away from Black Jock who was advancing on him with a set expression.

'Don't look at me, McLaren,' pleaded Simkin. 'There's eleven men on a team.'

'But only one of us let five goals through, didn't he?'

'That'll be quite enough, McLaren,' said Barrowclough, who, providentially for Simkin, was passing at that moment. 'Good heavens, surely you play the game for the sake of the game?'

'Where I come from,' snarled McLaren, 'we play the game to cripple the other team.'

'Yes, well you did your best. You're the only player that was booked seven times. You'd have been banned if it had been league football. Has anyone seen Fletcher? He should be supervising things.'

'He took Godber to the changing-rooms, sir,' volunteered Urquhart, 'but that was some time ago.'

'I'll see if he's still there.'

And Barrowclough hurried off to the changing-rooms. About two minutes later he emerged from them again and, moving with unusual speed, hastened to where the Governor, Mackay and Bainbridge were holding a post-mortem on the match.

'Good close game,' Bainbridge was saying. 'Five to one isn't bad against professionals. Your chaps did well.'

'Not my chaps,' insisted Mackay. 'I'm strictly impartial.'

'One or two of them are rather sweet,' maintained Bainbridge. He turned to the Governor. 'I suppose one can't reach them on the telephone?'

'Not yet,' retorted the Governor grimly, 'but if the penal reformers have their way, it could be the next stage.'

At this point Barrowclough arrived breathlessly on the scene and tapped Mackay on the shoulder.

'Mr Mackay—'

'Just a moment, Frank,' urged Mackay irritably over his shoulder.

'Yes, but you see—'

'I'm talking to the Governor, Mr Barrowclough.'

'I see that, but something rather important—'

'Whatever it is can wait.'

'There's been an escape.'

'All right, I'll attend to— WHAT!'

Two minutes later, pandemonium! Anyone who's done a reasonable amount of bird knows what it's like but it's hard to describe for someone who hasn't experienced it. In the first place, bells start ringing like a hundred ambulances converging on a disaster. Then doors starts slamming and keys grating in locks. Screws dash all over the place trying to look as if they was hot on the trail of the fugitives. Other screws start rounding up all the cons still on the premises and herding them into their cells. The sounds of the bells is picked out by the angry bellowing of the officers, angry because a stroke has been pulled and each and every one of them is afraid that somehow he will get the blame for it. But the strongest feeling about the whole circus is the excitement of the lads. In some funny way, the escape of one is the escape of all and each con as he is locked up securely in his own cell, feels that part of him is with the fugitives, out there in freedom. This feeling is intoxicating, and is given more strength, of course, by the fact that it represents a victory for us against them. So there is no question, on these occasions, of writing letters or reading the *Sun*. No, what you find is each and every con standing at the door of his cell, banging his iron mug against it and singing:

'*Tie a yellow ribbon round the old oak tree – It's been three long years, but the lads are free!*'

The only exception was Harry Grout who, as his cell door was slammed and locked, never stirred from his bed. Through his earphones he was listening to a commentary on a first division match between Liverpool and Leeds United.

A little later, Prison Officer Miller knocked urgently but respectfully on the door of the Governor's office. There was no answer but since he knew his tidings were important, he opened the door discreetly and entered. Inside were two standing men and one seated one. The seated one was Dines, now attired in an ill fitting guard's uniform, and the two standing ones were Mackay and the Governor. The Governor was the first to see the new arrival.

'Yes, Miller?' he asked.

'Three missing, sir,' the screw said crisply.

'What?' asked Mackay, swivelling incredulously. Then he turned back accusingly to Dines. 'You said that Oakes was alone.'

Dines shook his head wearily.

'I didn't say Oakes. Dunno who it was.'

'Your description fits. It must have been Oakes. But you didn't say anything about any other two.'

'I didn't *see* any other two. Maybe they got on outside – I dunno.'

'Look here, you—'

'Just a moment, Mr Mackay,' the Governor said sternly. He turned to Miller.

'Who are the other two, Miller?'

'Fletcher and Godber, sir.'

The Governor looked flabbergasted.

'Fletcher? But he was in charge of our team!'

'Good cover, sir,' growled Mackay.

'Yes, but hang on, Mr Mackay. Both of those two are due out in a year. Is it likely that they'd abscond now?'

Miller cleared his throat respectfully.

'Well, I can assure you, sir. They're not in the prison. We've searched thoroughly.'

'Oh, all right,' the Governor looked irritable, as well he might. He turned to Dines and shook his head. 'You can wait in my secretary's room for the present, Mr Dines. But we'll probably want to talk to you again.'

'Bleeding hell,' grumbled Dines as he got to his feet, 'next time I gets offered a job driving to a prison I'll take the day off.'

He slouched out of the office.

'Well, Mr Mackay?' asked the Governor. 'What do you think?'

'Hard to say, sir. Naturally, we've asked Criminal Records if they know him but it's not likely. Could be just inspired opportunism by Oakes.'

'The Home Office won't like this. I was hoping after last summer's riot that we might have a smooth patch.'

'They'll not get far, sir. Police in four counties have been informed. There are road blocks on all major roads south and east. The local police are out looking for the coach and I've detailed some of our men to help them.'

'I had a premonition—'

'I beg your pardon, sir?'

'If you remember, Mr Mackay, I was opposed to this absurd celebrity match from the start. Moreover, I shan't forget that it was your suggestion.'

Mackay swallowed at this manifest injustice.

'Mine, sir? Oh, no, sir. The idea came from Mr Beale, sir.'

The Governor smiled a mirthless smile.

'Indeed?'

Meanwhile, the visitors' team were sitting glumly in the screws' canteen sipping foul tea. The red-haired weatherman was complaining:

'If I don't get back to the studios this evening the whole of East Anglia may have a drought.'

Another pseudo-celebrity moaned:

'I told my agent I'd be home this evening. She gets very annoyed if I don't keep my word.'

A colleague said reassuringly:

'So what? You could use a new agent. You haven't had a decent part this year.'

'A bit difficult, though. We're married.'

Barrowclough entered.

'I hope you're all . . . reasonably comfortable, gentlemen.'

Bainbridge hastened over to him.

'Can you tell me what's going on? No one else seems to know. We've lost our coach and we're going to miss the train too if we don't leave soon.'

Barrowclough shook his head unhappily.

'I'm sorry, sir, but the police want statements from all of you. You see this job could have all been worked out in advance.'

Bainbridge tossed his head angrily.

'I bet if we'd brought Michael Parkinson or the Goodies you wouldn't have held them for questions.'

'Probably not,' agreed Barrowclough, with a faint and uncharacteristic touch of irony. 'But of course you didn't, did you?'

By now, the hue and cry extended far beyond the grim walls of Slade Prison. All over the surrounding countryside police cars raced over the moors searching for the missing cons. But the cops in them were not very hopeful of success. They knew they were dealing with a pro, and a pro would have found some way to switch vehicles. How right they were.

Oakes knew exactly where he was going. It had all been planned in careful detail for weeks in advance. Just fifteen minutes, and about as many miles, from the gates of the prison, he turned into a side road. As he came to a certain corner, marked by two fine oak trees (nice touch that, he'd though when it was first suggested), he slowed down. Immediately around the bend he saw what he'd hoped that he would see: a car and a caravan parked on the verge. As his cumbersome coach, moving slowly now, came into view, a woman stepped out into the road, waved and then pointed. Oakes saw a muddy path, just big enough for the massive vehicle, leading off towards one of the rare stands of trees in the neighbourhood. Signalling acknowledgement to the woman, he turned the vehicle with difficulty on to the track and continued on down it. After a couple of hundred yards he saw a five-barred gate ahead. He was just coming to a halt when a man stepped out from the bushes beside the road and heaved the gate open, beckoning Oakes through. The coach rolled on into a field where it was completely hidden from the road.

'First stage accomplished, right on schedule,' Oakes said to himself as he switched off the engine and got out of the coach. But by the time the man had come up to him, his expression was stern.

'Who's the bird, Alf?' he asked.

'My sister-in-law, Sheila,' explained Alf.

'Well, what the hell's she doing here? Was supposed to be a solo job.'

'I thought it would be more natural,' said Alf apologetically. 'You know – married couple, like – touring the Lake District.'

'Very good, Alf.' But then the lightning which kept a large group of bent men in Manchester subdued flashed from his eyes. 'You thick nurk! Who tours in February?'

Alf gulped.

'Anyhow, we'd best get weaving. The car—'

'Hang about!' said Oakes sharply, whereupon he went round to the side of the coach and started to open the luggage compartment. Alf watched in amazement.

'You didn't bring a bleeding suitcase?' he asked.

'Shut up and help me.'

Together they raised the door and guess what came out? Well, of course, you don't need to guess because you already know: me and Len. Stiff, battered and blinded by the daylight after the total darkness, we emerged.

I once read a story about a man that got accidentally locked in some dark dungeon. Now, for some reason I can't remember, he had food and candles with him. So he burned the candles and ate the food. And he tried to dig his way out but he wasn't making much progress. Meanwhile his food stocks got lower and lower and he conserved the candles and often sat about in the dark. And finally his food supplies was used up. And he began to get very hungry. So finally he ate what was left of the candles. And then he gave up digging because he knew he wasn't going to make it. And then he began to feel weak and knew he was starving to death. And he started screaming in anger and fear and just then the door opened and his wife or whoever it was had come home and let him out. He looked like the Prisoner of Zenda as he staggered from his dungeon, fell on his knees in front of her and exclaimed: 'Thank Gawd. I'd just about had it.' And she replied: 'Codswallop. You've only been in there since this morning when I went out to see mum.' Or something along those lines. Maybe I haven't got it quite right, but the point of the yarn, which I can confirm from personal experience in that coach, is that time is very elastic stuff and can stretch incredibly if the circumstances is right or rather wrong. I really thought I'd been bouncing along in the luggage compartment for hours and hours, maybe days. I gazed about greedily and said:

'Where are we, Africa? Don't look much like the Sahara.'

'Shut up, Fletch,' said Oakes.

'Here, who's this?' asked Alf. 'I wasn't told about this.'

'You shut up too.'

'No, I mean, Oaksey,' I said humbly. 'I won't give no trouble but where are we? Is it Cornwall?'

'Don't be a nurk. You've only been in there twenty minutes.'

I laughed at this cruel joke.

'Hear that, Len? Twenty minutes, he says.'

'Where's the ball?' asked Lennie, gazing straight ahead.

'Oh no,' I groaned.

'Bring him along,' ordered Oakes roughly. 'No time to waste.'

I took Lennie's arm and we followed Oakes and Alf, as I later discovered his name was, down the muddy lane. At the end of it we came to the caravan. Sheila was waiting there. I suppose she was an average looking woman in her thirties but if you'd told me she rated top billing at the Palladium just for standing on stage and smiling I'd have accepted it. After three years, she was like Rita Hayworth, Betty Grable and Lauren Bacall rolled into a big beautiful ball. Even Lennie was affected. He stopped dead and remarked:

'Look, Fletch, a woman.'

'I know, my son. Shock snapped you out of it, has it?'

'What's a woman doing on the pitch?'

'Naffing hell!'

'Is he all right?' asked Oakes doubtfully.

'I dunno. Not a brain surgeon, am I? He should see a doctor.'

'Then the sooner we get rolling the better. Fletch, you and your punchy friend in the car with us. Move it.'

But Alf interrupted anxiously.

'Only room for three up front, Oaksey. Got the back seat full of camping gear – make it look more natural, like.'

Oakes shook his head irritably.

'Then it's got to be you, Fletch. Not having you signalling out the caravan. He can ride in the back with Sheila.'

'Here,' protested the lady indignantly, 'don't want to be locked up with a loony.'

'Len's not a loony,' I told her. 'And he wouldn't hurt a fly, particularly one wearing nylon tights.'

'That's all very well but—'

'Shut up!' snapped Oakes ungallantly. 'You shouldn't be here at all. Since you are you'll do what you're told. In the back.'

'Charming!' said Sheila feelingly, but she entered the caravan. I helped Lennie in and seated him. Then Alf shut the caravan door and locked it from the outside.

'Get the lead out!' urged Oakes, scanning the road winding away over the hills anxiously.

A few minutes later and the outfit was on the road, three of us squashed uncomfortably and, I couldn't help reflecting, somewhat conspicuously on the front seat. Wouldn't take no Lord Peter Wimpey to ask himself why three blokes with a caravan behind their car should want to be crushed up like we was. But I never mentioned it to Oaksey.

'Look at it, Fletch,' enthused Oaksey. 'Freedom.'

'Oh, is that what it is? Thought it was just a lot of barren moor.'

'Cheer up. Done you a favour, son. We're free and clear.'

'Like the bleeding fox with the pack yapping on its heels.'

'Not very appreciative, are you?'

'Wasn't done no favours, was I? I didn't ask for this fiasco.'

'What do you mean, fiasco?' asked Oakes indignantly. 'Sweet as a nut this is.'

'So far, maybe. But don't you think they'll have the roads blocked?'

I heard a quiet chuckle from Oakes.

'The thing is, we're going north. To Scotland. Never figure that, will they? Never figure on Dumfries.'

I sighed.

'Oaksey, you've obviously got good reason to do something this drastic. Me, I've got under a year to do and the kid even less. You've not helped us, son. I ain't got the readies for plastic surgery and a first-class ticket to Acapulco. And I do not relish wintering in Dumfries.'

'I'm a bit upset you feel that way, Fletch,' said Oakes reproachfully. 'I had to bring you, though. You can see that.'

I contented myself with a grunt. Meanwhile, about ten feet behind us, Lennie was sitting gazing straight ahead. After a while, he asked:

'Where are we going?'

Sheila, who'd been watching him closely from the other end of the caravan, shrugged. Then, realizing he hadn't seen the gesture, said:

'No one tells me anything. But I heard something about Dumfries.'

'Dumfries?' said Lennie eagerly. 'Queen of the South, their team is. Scottish League Division B, as was. Dumfries two – Hamilton Academicals nil.'

'How d'you get like that?' asked Sheila curiously.

'Like what?'

'Sort of crazy.'

'Dunno,' said Lennie vaguely.

'Shouldn't you be in Broadmoor? That's where they put the loonies, isn't it?'

Lennie considered this question for a while in silence, then countered with another one.

'You from Dumfries?'

'Don't be daft. I'm from Manchester.'

'Manchester three, Tottenham Hotspur one,' remarked Lennie.

'What?'

'Score, last time I saw Manchester play. That was one of the best seasons they ever had. Is that the whistle?'

Sheila glanced nervously out of the window but all she saw was moorland.

'What whistle?'

'For half-time. My head hurts.'

'Not right,' muttered Sheila to herself. 'Locking me up with a loonie.'

But Lennie, whose hearing was apparently unaffected, said reproachfully:

'I'm not a loonie. Striker, I am.'

Sheila, not being clued-up about football, didn't like the sound of this. She made a tisking noise with her lips and lit a cigarette. They rolled along in silence for a while. Then Lennie asked:

'Is it injury time yet?'

'What?'

'Injury time—' a faint light of reminiscence appeared in his eyes. He raised his hand to his head. 'That's it, I was injured. Got a bump on my head.'

About fifteen minutes later, a police car full of uniformed policemen overtook them very slowly so that its occupants could look carefully in through the caravan's windows.

Alf, had noticed the bogeys when their car was still little more than a dot on the horizon.

'What do I do, Oaksey?' he asked anxiously.

'You slow down to begin with.'

'Slow down?' asked Alf, surprised.

'Unless you think you can outrun them in a chase. You silly nurk, if you can't beat them, fool them. Slow down to about twenty-eight and when they overtake, flash them a smile and a wave.'

'Yeah, but when they see you and Fletch—'

'Which they won't do, will they? Because we are going to be under the camping gear at the back. Come on, Fletch, over the seats.'

'Here, Oaksey, I'm not built for—'

'Move!' said Oaksey and I noticed that he had his gun in his hand again.

So we both climbed into the back and dug ourselves in under the heaps of canvas and stuff back there. I reckoned we was pretty well concealed but what if the law—

'What if they stop us in any case, Oaksey?' asked Alf just at that moment.

'What else?' said Oakes. 'We shoot our way out.'

Be ironic that, I thought, as we crouched under the gear, to end up dead in a shoot-out with the law. Ironic because all my working life I have been very strict about violence. I've never worked with any firm that's gone in armed. I've never carried any weapon of any kind. Most I've ever permitted myself is a shove to clear someone out of the way if I was on the run. And now I was likely to wind up like Bonnie and Clyde riddled with bullets. Would they make a film about us if that happened, I wondered. *The Legend of Norman and Len.* Would there be a stone on the moors marking the spot where the great gunfight had happened? Then I thought of my wife and kids. Not much of a memorial to leave them. And how would they ever know that I hadn't turned brutal? Rotten that.

In a while, I heard the sound of the law car creeping up on us and I could tell from how slow it was going that the fuzz inside were having a good shufty. Would they see Len in the back, I wondered? Another few moments and I heard the police car's powerful engines rev up and soon it was getting fainter and fainter ahead of us.

'What's the scene, Alf?' asked Oaksey, without moving.

'Just like you said, Oaksey. I waved at them and they waved back. You can come out.'

So we did.

'Smart thinking, Oaksey,' I complimented him. 'You didn't get where you is for nothing.'

He didn't respond. I could see he was shaken and thoughtful.

'How long till we're on the motorway, Alf?' he asked.

'Another half hour or so.'

Oaksey sighed with relief.

'Got a good chance of making it then.'

Maybe, I thought, and maybe not. In any case, I don't want to be around when you find out. I'd been pretty badly shaken by our brief encounter with the law car. It occurred to me that Alf was almost certainly tooled-up like Oaksey and, for all I know, the woman was too. Up to now, it had seemed to me my most serious problem was how to avoid doing a stretch for gaol-breaking. Now I realized that my life was in danger. It had gone far enough.

'Oaksey,' I said firmly, 'stop the car and let me and Len out.'

Oaksey smiled at what he took to be my little pleasantry.

'Certainly Fletch. Or how about you take the car and we'll walk?'

'I ain't kidding, Oaksey. I want out.'

He sighed.

'I appreciate how you feel, old son. But you gotta understand my position.'

'Your position, Oaksey, is that you got quite enough to do to get clear without worrying about us.'

'Something in what you say, Fletch. Might even have considered dropping you. But I told you our destination, which, I admit, was stupid. So there's nothing I can do.'

'Didn't hear your destination, Oaksey.'

'Didn't you hear me say Dumfries? Naffing hell, I've done it again.'

'Don't matter what you said, Oaksey, because as far as I'm concerned it's still them and us. So I ain't heard nothing. I been tied up in the back the whole time if we gets picked up. But since I'm not too anxious for that either, chances are you'll be on your way to Rio before we talks to any bogeys. So let us out, Oaksey.'

'Can't be done, Fletch.'

'Yes, it can. You know why? Because it's your best bet. Now you drop us off right now, Oaksey, and we stay shtum. I give you my word. But you keep us with you, I also give you my word, I'll give you nothing but trouble. Make every attempt I can to contact the law. So you're going to have to watch us like a hawk or you're going to have to shoot us. You don't really want a murder rap, do you?'

'Don't want that, Fletch.'

'So what do you say?'

He didn't say anything for a while. Then:

'Alf? What's your opinion?'

'Don't like it.'

'Why not, you dumb nurk?' I exploded. 'Oaksey knows I'm no grass. But I'll tell you what I am, a heavyweight. I should think you'd get another five miles an hour out of this contraption on the motorway without Len and me.'

'Could be right there,' admitted Alf.

'You win, Fletch,' said Oaksey to my inestimable relief. 'Next suitable place we find.'

'Course, it's always the same, never find a suitable place when you want one. I mean, you're driving through an empty forest and you decide you need a Jimmy Riddle. Suddenly there's houses on both sides of the road and a stream of traffic and you're practically busting your bladder before you come to even a driveway which provides some cover although almost certainly an old lady out walking her dog comes upon you and screams abuse even then.

That's how it was. Oaksey, naturally enough, wouldn't halt the outfit on the open moor where it could easily be spotted across miles. But for miles and miles we never came to a stand of trees or an embankment or any cover at all. Then finally, just as I was beginning to think it was going to be Dumfries after all, the road dipped into a little gully and for about ten yards we were out of sight from anything but traffic and there was hardly any of that.

'This is it,' snapped Oaksey. 'Pull up, Alf.'

We ploughed to a halt. I reached for the door handle and, as I grasped it, felt a very hard hand grasp mine.

'One more second, Fletch,' said Oakes softly. I turned impatiently to remonstrate but my words were halted by one of the most grim expressions I've ever seen on a human face. 'If you shop us, you don't live, Fletch. Understood?'

I nodded.

'Understood, Oaksey.'

'Right. Let's move it.'

And we all tumbled out of the car and hurried round to the door of the caravan which was at its rear. Alf got out his key, climbed on the step, unlocked the door and flung it open.

'All right, Len, out,' I said firmly.

10 On the run

'Hurry up, Len!' I called. 'I'm freezing.'

'Naffing hell,' came a reproachful voice from the clump of bushes, 'what do you think *I* am?'

'Well it was your choice, wasn't it? And I don't know why you're so modest all of a sudden. We've been cellies for over a year.'

'Different, out in the open.'

'Well, hurry up!'

I gazed disconsolately about at the vast moor stretching in every direction. We was about a hundred yards from the road. Now and then a car whizzed past, full of comfortable citizens on their way home to a blazing fireside and tea and crumpets. Where was we going to go? I sighed and reached into my pocket for the fag-end I thought I'd stashed there. Couldn't find it. I tried the other pockets. Then I remembered. It was in the lining of my trousers, in a special pocket near the ankle. I ferreted about and found it – wet and soggy! With an ironic grunt, I chucked it away. Then, realizing the bogeys might soon be combing the moors I crawled after it, found it and buried it carefully.

Len emerged from his cover but I noticed his lips was blue and he was shivering convulsively.

'What are we going to do, Fletch?' he chattered.

'First thing is to get you warm. Only thing is, we don't have no matches, no blankets, no hotwater bottle, no nothing.'

Lennie grinned which, in his present half-frozen state, did not produce a pretty sight.

'Got some of those – matches, fags and this.'

And he pulled triumphantly out from under his coat a large thermos bottle.

'Where'd you get those?'

He shrugged.

'Old habits—'

'Right, we'll have a quick swig to warm us up and then we'll go somewhere where we can light a fire.'

We both had a slug of coffee and very welcome it was. Then we set off, away from the road. Before long I noticed that Len was shuddering as he walked. The lad was in poor shape. But we must have walked a couple of miles before we came to a possible place. It was a ruined shepherd's hut, just four walls, two of them crumbled almost to the ground, and no roof. But in one corner of it there was a big pile of brushwood and under that was some bigger branches which seemed dry.

'We'll have a bit of a blaze, Len,' I said encouragingly.

He looked around anxiously.

'What if they notice the smoke?'

'Have to take that chance. Can't have you freezing to death. You may still be in a state of shock from the concussion – never mind the other shocking experiences you've had recently.'

'Leave off, Fletch.'

'Here, help me with these sticks.'

It wasn't long before we had a good fire going. Then we sat round it, smoking, sipping coffee and trying to get warm, which wasn't all that easy, in spite of the fire, because of the way the wind swept through the ruin.

'Feeling better, Len?' I asked hopefully.

'I think so.'

'Thank Gawd for that. We both need clear heads if we're going to get out of this mess.'

Lennie shook his head glumly.

'But it wasn't our fault! *We* didn't go over the wall.'

'The screws don't know that, do they? They'll have had a

little conflab by now. "Who's idea was this football match, Mr Beale?" "Fletcher's, sir." Then they'll put two and two together and make three.'

'Three?' asked Lennie.

'Three years. So we can't let them catch us. Can you see Mackay's face when we say: "As a matter of fact, sir, we was on our way back." '

We brooded in silence for a while. Then Lennie suggested:

'How about finding a village and giving ourselves up to the law?'

I shook my head.

'Same thing applies. Your ambitious village bobby isn't going to pass up the chance of collaring us, is he? Commendation for him. Probably a new bicycle and all.'

'So what do you propose, Fletch?'

'Only hope that I can see is Oxo Cummings.'

'Who?'

'Pickpocket I know who works the Oxo up in The Smoke.'

'What's the Oxo?'

'Oxo cube—'

'Oh, right – the underground. But how do we get to The Smoke, Fletch? We've got no money and every cop in England will be looking for us.'

'Cummings *works* in The Smoke but he lives in Carlisle. Not a greedy man. Works one week in four, so it's three to one he'll be at home.'

'Carlisle? I suppose we might get that far. Then what?'

'Oxo owes me a favour. We hole up with him and write letters.'

'To pass the time, like? Seems to me we'd be as well off in the nick as holed up with Oxo Cummings for the rest of our lives.'

'We stay with Oxo for a month or so until we can be sure Oaksey has reached his tropical paradise. Wouldn't want him to think we'd grassed—' and at that thought I could not suppress a slight shudder. 'Then, we writes to the Governor, tells him the whole story and offers to give ourselves up on the assurance that we won't be victimized. Oxo can post the letter from The Smoke so it don't give no leads.'

'Why should the Governor believe us?'

'I think he would, Len. You only has a few months of your

regular term to serve. It's been done before. I read about it in the paper.'

Lennie shook his head doubtfully.

'Sounds like a very hazardous scheme to me.'

'Can you think of a better one?'

Lennie had to admit that he couldn't. We had a last gulp of coffee and then put out the fire and concealed its remains with heaps of brushwood. We left our rude shelter. Lennie looked around. In every direction the undulating moor stretched to the horizon.

'Which way is Carlisle?' he asked.

'Well, taking into account the prevailing winds in these parts, the migration of birds, the moss growing on the trees and the way the sun seems to be setting if only we could see it, I haven't a clue.'

'We could go round in circles till we froze to death.'

I pointed towards a conspicuous clump of trees in the distance.

'What we has to do is pick a landmark and keep going till we reaches it. Then another one – and so on.'

'But what if it's the wrong direction?'

'Can't be helped. Sooner or later, we'll hit a road. Then we follow it until we reach a signpost and then we're in business.'

We set off towards our first landmark. After a little while, Lennie asked:

'Here, Fletch, how did I get this bump on my head?'

'You hit a goal post when you was rising for a header.'

'Was that it? Did I score?'

'*Score?*'

'Yeah, score. A goal?'

'Save your breath. You're going to need it.'

We plodded on for the best part of an hour. Lennie was in better shape than me from all his football practice, but neither of us was on top form. By the end of that hour, our legs was aching and we was breathing hard. Only good thing, we were no longer cold. Funny, the way it is? I mean, everything's relative, ain't it? Inside, it seems like the worst thing that can happen to a man is to be locked up. But as we stumped on across those forbidding moors, I kept thinking wistfully of our cosy cell in the nick. What could have been finer than to have been climbing on to my bunk with a steaming mug of tea and a week-old copy of the *Sun*. No matter how bad things are, I realized, they can always be worse.

'There's a road!' exclaimed Lennie excitedly.

I'd been paying more attention to my boots sinking into the soggy earth than to the way ahead. Now I glanced up and, sure enough, about a quarter of a mile ahead of us was a narrow country road.

'Come on, Fletch!' called Lennie, frisky as a kid out on a picnic. 'Race you to it!'

And he galloped off ahead. I stumped after him at a measured pace. He reached the road and sat down on a mossy boulder near it to wait for me. I was just catching up when I heard a sudden roaring sound.

'Len!' I bellowed, throwing myself to the ground. As I did so, I saw him throw himself backwards off his big stone. And then a police car, going like the clappers, shot past ahead of us.

'Don't think they saw me, Fletch,' he said, when I'd come up. He looked rattled.

'Either that, or they're radioing for a helicopter. Take more care, Godber. Remember, we is on the run.'

Our eyes met for a long look. Then he gulped and said:

'Never thought I'd be that, Fletch. It's like Humphrey Bogart in *The Putrified Forest* – ever see that?'

'Oh yeah – that's where he climbs the mountain and half the American army shoots him off it, ain't it?'

'No, that was—'

'Godber, is this the right moment for movie nostalgia? Unless you is keen to spend the night on the moors, we'd best get cracking.'

'We can't just walk down the road with the cars out.'

' 'Course not. We keep it in sight but we stays under cover.'

It was easier said than done. The road was just a smooth ribbon winding across the empty landscape. We had to keep sprinting from hummock to hummock or taking shelter in what few trees there were. Also there were a lot of bogs about and once I went up to my knees in thick, black mud. But finally, ahead, I saw what we'd been aiming for – a crossroads. We approached it cautiously. Fortunately, the four approach roads were all visible for a good distance and, when we were satisfied that there was nothing coming, we went quickly up to the little signpost. It listed four directions: Warblebank, Brocklebank, Howrigg and Rosley.

'There you are, Len,' I said proudly. 'Told you it would work. Which way is Carlisle?'

'How the hell should I know?'

I was dismayed by his question.

' 'Course you should know. Didn't you tell me you used to hike around here, when you was a boy scout?'

'That was years ago. Think I remember Rosley but just the name.'

I sighed.

'We got to be scientific about this. When they brings you from the station to the nick, you're going away from Carlisle. You passes a signpost to Warblebank on the right, isn't it?'

'On the left. Brocklebank's on the right.'

'You absolutely sure?'

'No, I'm not. And anyhow the road curves all over the place. Truth is, we're no better off than we were.'

I sighed deeply.

'Any of that coffee left?'

We went into a clump of bushes and had a smoke and the last of the coffee. Then I buried the thermos. Lennie said irritably,

'They're not going to comb the whole of Cumberland.'

'Don't leave a trail and you won't need no bail,' I reminded him. 'Now, what's the first thing you see? Quick!'

'Bleeding moor!' snapped Lennie.

'Right: *B* – we heads for Brocklebank.'

Lennie nodded grimly.

'Very scientific. It's a privilege to watch your methods.'

'Main thing is to make a decision and stick to it. We'll come to another signpost sooner or later.'

But by the end of another hour, I was beginning to wonder. We'd been walking parallel to the road, at a distance of about quarter of a mile, and the way had been rough. We'd clambered over piles of boulders, waded through marshes, ploughed through acres of brambles. I was getting near the end of my strength.

'No good, Len,' I panted, leaning against a tree. 'Got to have a rest.'

'There's a farm down there,' he said.

'What?'

He was peeping over a large boulder, looking down into a little gully. I joined him. He was right too. A trim little house, a farm-yard, two or three barns and, best of all, an orchard.

'Right, my son,' I said, setting off towards a footpath leading to the farm, 'down we goes.'

'You crazy?'

'Just realistic. There's no car in the yard. No sign of life and we is going to need some nourishment. Looks like we'll have to spend the night on the moors and who knows about tomorrow? Without food, I'd freeze to death.'

'What about me?' complained Lennie bitterly. 'I haven't got your lining of fat and I'm still in my football shorts.'

'So, we have to take a chance. We'll just slip into that orchard and fill our pockets with apples.'

There was quite a lot of cover and we made it to the orchard without trouble. But when we got there a disappointment awaited us. The branches were bare. The crop had been har-vested.

'Come on,' said Len, 'let's get back on the road.'

'Hang on, Len,' I protested. 'I'll flake out without something in my belly. That barn's open. The apples is probably stored in there.'

'And if someone slammed the door on us, so would we be. Tighten your belt.'

'Fallacy, that is. Just makes it hard to breathe.'

And I dashed – well, limped – out of the orchard into the farmyard and then on into the barn. Len followed me. Sure enough, we found the whole crop laid out neatly on wooden shelves. We were in the process of filling our pockets when we was disagreeably surprised by a voice from behind us saying:

'I've got a shotgun here – two barrels. I'd be grateful if you'd turn round slowly.'

I heard Lennie's gasp of dismay but I was careful not to make a sound myself. I've always had a healthy respect for firearms.

'Please do as I say,' said the voice. 'Turn around.'

There didn't seem a lot of alternative. We both swung round very gently.

'Don't you want us to put our hands up?' I asked grimly.

'Good idea. Put your hands up.'

'Quick thinking,' whispered Lennie in disgust as we obeyed.

There wasn't a lot of light in the barn but I could see that the bloke holding the very businesslike shotgun was a lean man getting on in years. He was dressed in baggy grey trousers with braces over an open shirt. Looked like a typical farmer.

'Are you the ones that have been stealing my seed potatoes?' he asked interestedly.

I shook my head.

'Never touched your seed potatoes. Have we, Len?'

'No, we haven't,' agreed the lad.

'The thing is,' I said, with what I hoped would sound like tolerant amusement at the ridiculous situation, 'we ain't thieves. No, we was out – out training, and we got a bit peckish.'

'Training?' asked the man.

'That's right. This is the Carlisle Kid – heard of him, ain't you?'

'No.'

'What? Your local champ? He's fighting Duke Bilkes next week in Dumfries for the Northern Counties Championship. I'm his trainer, Dick Barton.'

'Dick Barton? That's a familiar name.'

Too bleedin' familiar, I reproached myself silently. But it's not all that easy to come up with an alias when your back's to the wall.

'Yeah, it's common in my part of the country. Anyway, now you—'

'Keep your hands up.'

'Certainly.'

'You're saying he's a boxer?'

'Future world flyweight champ. No doubt about it.'

'What are you doing in my barn?'

'Well – like I said – we've been doing road-work all afternoon and – the lad was hungry – so—'

'Don't believe a word of it,' said the old geezer disappointingly. 'Walk ahead of me, out of the barn and into the house.'

I couldn't refrain from heaving a deep sigh as we obeyed. Once in the house, and keeping his gun very convincingly pointed at us, the man ushered us into a cosy parlour which had a beautiful coal fire glowing in the grate, and told us to sit on a sofa there. We obeyed. Then he went to the other end of the room where there was a telephone on a small table.

'Now,' he announced. 'I'm going to phone the police. I'll have to dial, of course, but I'm pretty handy with a shotgun, so I wouldn't advise you making any false moves.'

Holding the gun with one hand, he took the receiver off the phone with the other and began to dial. Lennie and I looked at each other in despair.

'Hang about!' I said loudly. 'I'll tell you the truth.'

The man stopped dialling.

'Then you did steal my seed potatoes?'

I shook my head wearily.

'Wouldn't know where to fence them. But Lennie and I are, or should be, in Slade Prison.'

The man frowned and looked from one to the other of us. He replaced the receiver.

'You mean you're not thieves? You're escaped convicts?'

'Yes. I mean, no. We're both.'

'But you're not the thieves that have been stealing my farm produce?'

'Certainly not. Never been near your bleeding farm until about ten minutes ago.'

The man looked thoughtful.

'I see.'

Then, to my surprise, he put down his gun. I felt Lennie tense beside me and whispered:

'No rough stuff, Len.'

Then to our captor, I said earnestly:

'Before you picks up that phone again and calls the law—'

'What? Oh, I'm not going to phone the law. Escaped convicts, eh? You must be starving. How would you like some bacon and eggs?'

I thought to myself: it's all the hardship we've been through has affected my hearing.

'I beg your pardon?' I said.

The man was grinning now. He had a long, thin face which made him look a bit like a joker in a pack of cards. Perhaps that's what he was, a joker.

'Food? Aren't you hungry?'

'I could do with a bite,' I admitted. 'What about you, Len?'

'Wouldn't say no,' the lad admitted.

'Splendid. I'll open a tin of beans too. And make some but-ered toast. I think there's some peach flan in the fridge. It will ake me about ten minutes to prepare it.'

And he began to stride out of the room.

'Excuse me, sir——' I called before he reached the door.

He turned.

'Yes?'

'Can we put our hands down now?'

'What? Oh, of course. Pull that sofa up to the fire. Warm yourselves up. Oh, and could you put my gun back in the rack up here? Dangerous things to leave lying about.'

And he was gone. Lennie and I looked at each other.

'Is he a loonie?' asked Lennie.

I shook my head.

'The more important question at the moment is: can he cook? Come on, let's get this sofa over to the fire.'

We pulled it over and then sat and toasted ourselves. Soon, from the kitchen, came the incomparable sound of sizzling bacon. Lennie reached over and grasped something.

'He told us to put this away,' he said wistfully.

I looked round. He was cradling the shotgun in his arms.

'Better do so, hadn't you?'

'You don't think——'

'Len! No shooters – ever. Besides, it would not show suitable gratitude to our host if we was to blow his head off. Put the gun where he said.'

Lennie did so and then rejoined me. Above the delightful sounds from the kitchen came the man's voice:

'There's some booze in the sideboard. Help yourselves.'

'It's a dream,' said Lennie.

'Perhaps we froze to death on the moors,' I added. 'And this s our heavenly reward.'

'Whisky or sherry?' asked Len, inspecting the contents of the sideboard.

'Large one,' I suggested.

'Which?'

'Both.'

*

Twenty minutes later we sat back after a feast such as neither of us could remember for ages. To wash down the lavish and delectable edibles we had drunk a full bottle of very good French wine. And all the time the thin-faced man had beamed on us like a telly mother watching her infants stuffing themselves with beans.

'Feel better now?' he asked.

'Much,' I said, burping politely.

'I've packed you some things to take with you – cold chicken, loaf, chocolate. I would put in a bottle of champagne but it might slow you down. There's plenty of drinking water in the streams.'

Lennie said faintly:

'Very decent of you.'

'You don't know how lucky you are,' he said, shaking his head meaningfully.

'It's beginning to dawn,' I returned.

'No, I mean, my wife—'

Surely, I thought, he's not going to offer us her and all.

'How do you mean?' asked Lennie.

'If she'd been here, I'd have had to turn you in. But happily she's spending the day with her sister in Wigton.'

'I understand, sir,' I said soberly. 'Your old woman does not share your humanitarian impulses.'

'No, no, we neither of us have any humanitarian impulses. It's just that she doesn't know.'

Again Lennie and I was forced to exchange a bewildered glance.

'Know?' I asked weakly.

'I'll show you,' said the man.

He strode to a corner of the room, knelt down, fiddled with the skirting board and a section came away. He reached into the hole and withdrew what looked like a typical family album. In spite of his remarkable generosity, I felt slight dismay. Poring over blurred mugshots of ugly aunts is not my favourite pastime. He brought the album over to us, holding it to his chest protectively.

'I should be glad,' he said, 'that you haven't recognized me. But, such is vanity, I'm a little disappointed. You don't recognize me, do you?'

Lennie and I peered at him dutifully. He certainly had a distinctive jem mace but not one I could recall having seen before.

' 'Fraid not, sir.'

'Houdini Hopson? Name mean anything to you?'

He'd been good to us. He deserved some kind of reward.

'I think that rings a bell,' I said, putting on a thoughtful frown. 'Used to get top billing at the Palladium, didn't you? Escape artist?'

He shook his head sadly.

'*What is fame? An empty bubble?* Can't remember who wrote that, but it's certainly true. I was an escape artist alright, but not on the stage.'

And he thrust his album into my hands. Lennie came and peered over my shoulder and I began to turn the pages. They contained clippings from newspapers, mainly provincial ones. The cuttings were very old, brittle and brown at the edges. Some of them were dated and the latest were from the mid-fifties. They were a record of the criminal career of one 'Houdini' Hopson who seemed to have been a solo house-breaker and a bit of a climber. But a lot of the accounts were about his amazing gaol-breaks.

'There's one in there from the *News of the World*,' boasted 'Houdini', 'and two from the *Yorkshire Post*. Seven escapes in all. I'm not sure it's not still a record.'

'Very impressive, Mr Hopson,' I said admiringly.

'Symes-Jesperson,' he said quickly. 'Walter Symes-Jesperson. That's what I'm known as now. Been straight for quarter of a century. Had a little stashed away. Bought this place. Married a local girl.'

I nodded.

'So you is one of the very few that really kicked the habit. Never been tempted to have another go?'

He smiled wistfully.

'Often. Funny thing is, it's not the loot – it's the challenge. Always wanted to try absconding from one of the new high-security wings. But suppose I didn't make it? Anyway, I've got a pretty decent life here. Farm does quite well, except that there's been a lot of pilfering lately. And Betty – that's my wife – is a brilliant architect. Actually, she brings in most of the money.'

'And she doesn't know a thing about your . . . magnificent past?'

'Good Lord, no. Had a close shave once. She designed a small local prison and I couldn't resist pointing out how simple it would be to escape. But I managed to pass it off as part of my keen interest in games and puzzles.' He sighed deeply and contentedly. 'It's been a tonic talking to you chaps. Great strain keeping a whole dimension of your life secret year after year.'

'Must be. Well, it certainly wasn't no tragedy for us that it was your barn we tumbled into. But now, I suppose we'd better hit the road again.'

'Yes, but hang on. I want to hear your story. How did you do it – tunnel?'

Lennie gave a little snigger.

' 'Fraid you'll be disappointed to hear—'

But I cut in quickly.

'No, he won't! What you talking about, Len?'

It had occurred to me that the great 'Houdini', having wined us and dined us in the belief that we were fellow escape wizards, might get the hump on learning that we were just victims of someone else's caper. He might even be so affronted that he'd think better of his assistance and get on the blower once we'd left. Best spin him a yarn.

'I was only going to say—' Len tried again.

And again I interrupted.

'What my young colleague was going to confess to you, Mr Houdini, was that we're not in your class. We couldn't have pulled it off on our own. We was part of a team. Four of us, there was.'

'Houdini' nodded sympathetically.

'Need at least that many for a tunnel. Only time I ever teamed up, one of the lads grassed just as we were about to move. After that, I always went solo. Found it was more efficient too. Where did you tunnel from? The latrines?'

'Yes,' said Lennie.

'No,' said I at exactly the same moment.

'Houdini' looked at us doubtfully.

'No,' I explained desperately. 'It wasn't a tunnel but, like Len said, it did start in the latrines.'

'How do you mean?'

'Well, it was in the latrines that we noticed— You tell him, Len.'

Lennie gave me a quick reproachful look but he'd twigged how I was thinking by then.

'Me? It was you what had the big idea. Don't you remember, Fletch? We was having a snout by the windows in the latrines one day and you suddenly saw, out the window— But the credit's down to you. You tell him.'

'If you insist, Len. Well, like the lad says, Mr Houdini, I was just idly gazing out the window and I happened to see—' But, by this stage, nothing at all convincing had occurred to me. Still, I had to keep talking, so I said the first thing that came into my head: '—pig swill.'

'Pig swill?' asked 'Houdini' with an uncomprehending frown. I chuckled.

'Ah, don't sound like the path to freedom, does it? But wait till you hear. Tell him, Len.'

Len smiled and nodded as if recalling the whole amazing caper but I knew he was trying desperately to think of a continuation.

'What does pig swill make you think of, Mr Houdini?' asked Lennie idiotically. 'Makes you think of pigs, don't it? Well, that's what it made Fletch think of because we had a prison farm at Slade. I take it you've never done time there?'

'Houdini' shook his head. Lennie continued.

'So the next step was to get Fletch a job on the farm, working with the pigs.'

'Wait a minute,' said 'Houdini', 'you haven't told me the plan yet.'

'We're coming to it,' insisted Len. 'And now Fletch will tell you what it was.'

'Houdini' transferred his interested gaze to me. I could have strangled Len. But I had no choice.

'The plan, Mr Houdini,' I said dramatically, 'was to get hold of some pig-skins.'

'Houdini' looked mystified.

'Pig-skins? Why?'

'I'll tell him, Fletch, shall I,' volunteered Len.

So he'd thought of something. But so had I by this stage and I wanted to get it over quick.

'It's all right, Len. Like you said, it was my caper. What we did, Mr Houdini, was to kill pigs, just one now and then. Not very nice, I know, but it was them or us and the bacon was welcome to all the lads. We made it seem like the pigs died of natural causes or accidents. Took us six months to get four pig-skins with the help of two of our mates – the other two in the team – what worked in the butchers' shop. Then we just waited until market day when the truck came to pick up our spare pigs for auction and, in amongst the grunters, there was four of us riding out through the gates.'

'Amazing!' said 'Houdini' with fervour. 'Never heard anything like it. And I suppose the first time the lorry slowed down, the four of you just jumped off?'

'Right. Buried the skins and then split up. Incidentally, I hope we is not stinking out your nice house? Those skins ponged something dreadful.'

'Houdini' sniffed earnestly.

'Can't smell a thing.'

'Wind on the moor must have freshened us up. So now we'd best be on our way. Oh, just one thing, we somehow lost our maps. You couldn't let us have a shufty of an atlas, could you?'

'Of course, of course,' said 'Houdini', not moving. 'Pig-skins – that must be a classic. Of course, I remember on one of the escapes I constructed a rubber mask—'

'Please, sir, they is combing the moors for us at this moment.'

'Sorry. I can't resist ingenuity. Please send me a full account of it poste restante, Carlisle. Would you do that?'

'Word of honour, Mr Houdini. And now, the atlas.'

He stood up.

'Have a last nip before you go. Of course, I'd ask you to stay the night but Betty will be home in an hour or so. She hates night driving. So it's impossible.' He frowned suddenly. 'Are you planning to spend the night on the moors?'

'Can't check in at the nearest Trust House, can we?' said Lennie reasonably.

'But you'll freeze to death. Look, I've got an old tarpaulin upstairs. I'll get it for you. Oh, and naturally if you should happen to be caught, you found it somewhere else.'

'Naturally, sir. Very good of you,' I said gratefully.

He started to hurry out of the room. Lennie called after him:

'Mr Houdini? That atlas.'

He turned.

'Ah yes. You'll find it in the bookcase over there.'

And then he left the room and we heard him pattering up the stairs.

'Talk about lucky break,' said Len feelingly.

'We'll have plenty of time for that,' I said, 'and we is not in the clear yet. Where's that atlas?'

We went over to the bookcase and started searching. It was very full of reading matter. Took us about two minutes to find the atlas and then we carried it to the table under the light and began searching through it. We had just found the right page when there was the sound of a car crackling up the pebbled drive.

'What's that?' asked Len.

'It's either Mrs Houdini or the law and neither of them is what we needs. Come on.'

We rushed to the door but heard the car pulling up immediately outside it. There was a frantic voice from the top of the stairs.

'It's my wife! She's early. Out the back door – quick!'

'The kitchen!' I said.

We ran back through the house and into the kitchen. There was the back door. I unlocked it and pulled it open. Then we started belting down the back path. Suddenly Lennie stopped, turned and ran back towards the house.

'Len!' I called, softly but urgently. 'Have you gone bonkers?'

He disappeared into the kitchen again. A moment later and he emerged and came flying towards me. As we both charged off, he gasped:

'Couldn't leave that chicken behind, could we?'

And he waved a plastic carrier bag for me to see.

We ran and we ran and we ran and then we ran some more. And then my heart started pounding me in the ribs like Samson working over a grass and I fell to the ground. It was about five minutes later, Lennie subsequently informed me, that I heard his voice calling soft but anxious:

'Fletch, Fletch, don't snuff it. I'll never get to Carlisle without you.'

I sat up indignantly.

'That's nice,' I said. 'All you care about is your own skin.'

He grinned.

'Knew you was all right. I'd listened to your heart. I think it's safe to rest for five minutes.'

We had a snout and talked things over. Where were we? We'd never had a chance to look at the atlas and we were no longer anywhere near a road. We had to face it, we had no more idea of our location than we had done when Oaksey had dropped us. Also, the light was definitely fading.

' 'Fraid, it's going to be a night out for us, Len,' I said soberly.

'At least, we've got some food in our bellies and some more in here,' and he indicated the shopping bag. 'We'll just have to find the best shelter we can.'

Then, after a pause, he said:

'How's Mr Houdini going to explain all the cooking that's gone on? And there's his scrapbook out. She'll see that. It could be the end of their marriage, Fletch.'

'He'll have had time to stash the book. And the food—? Have to hope he's a smooth talker because if he isn't—'

Lennie gulped. It wouldn't be long before this section of the moors was buzzing with fuzz. I got to my feet.

'All we can do is keep fleeing.'

After that we walked and we walked and we walked and then we walked some more. We got beyond tiredness. Feet? I had a dim sense that somewhere beneath me two objects was thumping regularly into the ground but they no longer seemed attached to me.

'I heard, Len,' I managed to gasp, 'that soldiers can sleep on the march. Shall we take turns?'

'Can't march any more, Fletch. Let's stop here for the night.'

'If we do, we'll never see the morning. Get's very chill in these parts and we never did get that tarpaulin.'

'Can't go much further.'

'First cover of any sort we find, we'll stop there. Think of it as training, my son. Left, right, left, right, left—'

And we plodded on. It must have been about half an hour later, when there was hardly any light left, that we came to the wood. It wasn't much of a wood but it provided a little shelter from the wind. We staggered into it and, after about a hundred yards, came to a pile of brushwood and some scattered logs. I stopped.

'This is it, Len,' I said. 'We can build a nest like what gorillas do in the jungle.'

'You're thinking of birds,' said Len wearily. 'There's no flying gorillas, is there?'

'Never mind,' I urged. 'Just help me.'

We dragged two logs close together and piled brushwood over and around them. The result wasn't exactly like the Hilton but it might keep us alive till dawn. Utterly bushed, we sat down on one of the logs to eat our supper.

'Anyhow,' I said encouragingly, 'we've got a feast fit for a Home Secretary, thanks to Mr Houdini.'

I took the plastic bag and ferreted inside. Then I slung the bag away.

'Naffing hell!' exclaimed Lennie feebly. 'What you about, Fletch?'

'Not your fault, Len, what with the haste and all but you must have grabbed up the wrong bag.'

'Well, what's in it?'

'I'm no farmer, my son, but at an educated guess, I'd say it was seed potatoes.'

'Naffing hell!'

'Let's get some kip.'

We began to arrange ourselves for the night. When we'd stretched out, I put my arms around Len.

'Here,' he said indignantly. 'We was never more than cellies, remember?'

'Don't be a nurk. Way to keep warm, isn't it? Only way we've got.'

So we lay in each other's arms for a while. I was nowhere near sleep when the first snore from Len showed that he'd made it. Suddenly, I disengaged myself and sat up.

'Whatcha do that for?' asked Len reproachfully. 'Just drifted off, I had.'

'Shut up, Len!' I hissed urgently. 'Listen!'

He sat up then and we both listened hard. No doubt about it, there was a sound which was very like a car engine.

'It's not far away,' whispered Len. 'What do you think it is?'

'Better find out, hadn't we?'

We emerged from our pathetic nest and, keeping low, moved as quietly as we could towards the source of the sound. It was now almost pitch dark and we kept stepping on twigs and branches that crackled. This didn't matter too much because, as we approached, the roar of engines was loud enough to drown out any noise we was making. Also, as we got nearer, it got lighter from what seemed to be the headlights of one, or more, vehicles. It got so bright that we finally sank down on to our bellies and just wriggled forwards. Now we could hear sharp voices. Finally, very gently, I parted the last remaining shrubs and we peered out at an amazing sight.

'Naffing hell,' exclaimed Lennie. 'It's the bleeding coach!'

Sure enough, there beneath us was the very vehicle in which we'd effected our unwilling escape from Slade Prison. So all this time, all this long weary afternoon of blundering about on the moors, we'd just been making our way back to our starting point. It was enough to make a gorilla weep.

But the coach was not the only vehicle in the clearing. There was also two police cars and the place was swarming with uniforms. The two cars had their engines running and their headlights beamed on the coach. It looked like they'd only just found the stolen vehicle.

'Let's get out of here, Fletch,' urged Lennie, tugging at my sleeve.

'Wrong, my son,' I whispered back. 'Best place we could be. The one thing they'll be sure of is that we is miles away by now. Unique opportunity to study police methods.'

So we just lay and watched. Then, to my horror, Mr Mackay appeared from the other side of the coach. I must say at that my instincts was to leap up and scarper. But I controlled myself. The screw, whose anxious expression could be clearly seen in the light of the headlights, approached one of the uniformed men.

'Mackay, Slade Prison,' he introduced himself. 'Any developments, sergeant?'

The cop shook his head.

'Nothing. They'll be long gone by now. I am Sergeant Townsend.'

'Well, did you check the ground for tyre tracks?' asked Mackay officiously. 'For the getaway vehicle.'

The sergeant gave him a bleak look.

'D'you know, we never thought of that.'

Mackay gulped visibly.

'I didn't mean to imply—'

The sergeant held up a hand.

'If you lot did your job as well as us, the buggers wouldn't be out, would they?'

Mackay jerked his head from side to side a few times. Then, with renewed courage, said sternly:

'This is not an everyday occurrence.'

Townsend shook his head wearily.

'You expect one con to tunnel out. Or go over the wall on a rope ladder. But three of them, driving out in a bus!' The sergeant turned to one of his constables. 'C'mon lad. We're through here.'

'What about the coach?' asked Mackay.

Townsend shrugged.

'It's all yours. We're finished with it.'

The policemen all returned to their cars and climbed in. Then the engines started and the headlights swung round, giving Len and me a bad moment, and then the uniformed men roared away up the muddy lane. I saw that the Slade Prison van was left and that, in addition to Mackay, the screws Collinson and Miller were also present. Miller approached Mackay.

'What next, sir?'

Mackay shook his head wearily.

'Have to get this coach back, I suppose. You take the prison van. Collinson and I will bring the coach.'

'And then,' I whispered to Len, 'we can get back to our nest for some kip. Proves one thing. Houdini soft-talked his old woman or they'd know about us from the radio by now.'

'Glad for his sake,' said Len.

Miller removed himself to the prison van, got in, started the engine and followed the police cars out of the clearing. Collinson said to Mackay:

'Can you handle this thing, sir?'

'Oh yes,' said Mackay confidently, 'did tank training in the Argylls. Get in, Mr Collinson.'

And the two screws climbed into the coach. Its headlights came on and, at the same moment, headlights came on in my mind.

'Len!' I whispered urgently. 'What is our plans?'

'Get to Carlisle,' he returned.

'And then?'

'Get back into nick.'

The engines of the big coach started.

'Exactly. No time to explain. Just follow me.'

And I grabbed his arm. The coach had started moving now, backing towards us so that it could make a three-point turn. I jumped up, pulling Lennie with me, and dashed out of the under-growth towards the vehicle. Lennie had long ago learned to trust me and gave no trouble. We ran to the side of the moving vehicle and I bent down, trotting along beside it, and pulled open the luggage compartment.

'Inside!' I snapped.

Lennie never hesitated. He clambered into the moving cavern and I followed him. I lowered the side as Mackay completed his turning manoeuvre and the vehicle began to bump forwards down the rutted path.

'Fletch!' said Lennie. 'What is this?'

'Forgot to tell you, my son, when we went on this outing. I only booked us day returns.'

11 The gaol-break

'Here, Fletch,' said Lennie nervously. 'We could suffocate in here.'

'We didn't last time.'

'What, was we in here before?'

'Don't you remember?'

'No. Remember the coach – when it arrived like – and then the game – and then the next thing I remember clearly is. . .'

There was a long silence while I tried to think up a plan. No, that's wrong. My trouble was that I had too many plans and none of them was any good. I didn't want to admit to the lad that I'd acted more or less on impulse when I'd dragged him into the dark hole where we now was. If you want to get somewhere, take a bus. We'd wanted to get back in the nick and the bus was going that way. But how was we to get back in our cells? I tried to think what 'Houdini' Hopton would have done. 'Course, he'd always been travelling in the opposite direction but the general principle was the same. Let's see, assuming we got into the inner yard, which I was counting on, then all we had to do was get past about ten screws, some of them guarding gates, without being spotted, bust through five or six massive doors, make our way through four or five barred walls and hope they'd left our cell door open and a hot water bottle in the bed. I shook my head irritably. The kid was right. Jokes couldn't solve everything and one of the things they couldn't solve was how to penetrate several tons of steel. So what *would* 'Houdini' have done? Well, he might have started with disguise. Perhaps we could nick some screws' uniforms and then—

At this point my careful planning was shattered by a torrent of anguished words from Len.

'I just want you to know, Fletch, before you ruins my life, that it's the thought of Ingrid that's kept me going for the past few months. Why do you think I've been studying cookery the way I have? Because I'm determined to go straight and make a decent life that I can invite her to share with me. And I was thinking of you too, Fletch, because you're going to find it harder than me on the outside, being older and all. So my plans naturally included giving you a helping hand once I'd got my French restaurant established. I thought maybe you could work there as a head waiter until I'd made enough to set you up in a little business of your own. I just want you to know that I think more of you than what you seem to do of me.'

At this point, I clapped my hand over his mouth and hissed in his ear.

'Pipe down, Len! You is getting hysterical and making such a flaming row Mackay might hear us.

'Gawd, Godber! Here we is rolling towards a desperate gamble and all you can think about is matrimony. Tell you what, if we make it back to our cells, we'll have a heart to heart before kipping down. How's that?'

'Fair enough.'

There was another period of silence. Far as I could judge, we was bowling along at a fair clip now. Shouldn't be long before we reached the outer gate.

'How we going to do it, Fletch?' asked Godber.

'What?'

'You must have some plan, like.'

I swallowed. The simple trust in his youthful voice was touching. It was also daft.

'Naturally, I've got a plan,' I said, trying to sound brimming over with confidence.

'What is it then?'

'Well – the so-called celebrity team is probably in the screws' canteen, getting such miserable hospitality as it provides, while they waits for their transport to be returned. That's why Mackay will probably drive this thing right into the inner yard which means that the worst of our obstacles – the outer wall – will be no problem. Our chauffeur will drop us at the door.'

'Then what?'

'Hm?'

'Inside the walls isn't inside the cells, Fletch.'

' 'Course it isn't. Don't think I'd forget that, do you?'

'So?'

'So the next stage has to be worked out very ingenious. That's what I've been doing. It involves nicking uniforms and keys, building a thermal lance out of scrap and making ourselves invisible.'

'You mean, you haven't got a clue?'

'Right.'

'Well, I have.'

'Did I hear you correct, Godber?'

'It's easy. Once we're in the inner yard, we wait till the coast is clear. Then we nips out and hides ourselves behind the dustbins and just waits till morning exercise. Then we join the lads when they come out.'

'And what do we do when the screws pounces on us and asks where we spent the night?'

'Tell them, in our cells, of course. They can't prove any different. Can't have us for gaol-breaking if we is inside doing what we is supposed to be doing.'

Much as it went against the grain, I had to admit that Len

was right. 'Course, there'd be a good deal of hounding and snooping. We'd have endless sessions of interrogation and probably finish up copping minor punishment of some kind. But in the end they'd just have to forget the whole thing. Never heard of any cons done for gaol-breaking when they was caught in their correct places inside the nick. And the best part of it was, Mackay would never know that he'd brought us safe home again. Or was that the best part? Wouldn't it be more satisfying if the complacent nurk *did* know? Truth is, it was at exactly at this point in time that I first conceived the idea for the present exciting book you is reading on the train to Glasgow or wherever.

But my literary plans were not given the chance to develop much that night. The idea had just lit up in my head, and I was grinning in the dark at the thought of Mackay's eyes popping out as he turned the pages of the special advance copy I would send him, when the coach made a sharp turn to the left and slowed to a crawl.

'We're approaching the outer gates,' I whispered to Len.

'Do you happen to have any Bisodol on you?' asked Len. 'I feel sick.'

'Control yourself. Think of something delightful.'

'Holding Ingrid in my arms?'

'Not that delightful.'

The brakes were applied, not too expertly, and I slid against Len. I just had time to hiss: 'From now on shtum – until I give the word!' when the coach stopped. The engine, however, was left running and I figured the screw on gate duty was coming out to check. A moment later, I heard his voice.

'Oh – it's you, Mr Mackay.'

'It is, Mr Cox.'

'Who's that with you, sir?'

'Prison Officer Collinson.'

'Anyone else?'

'Who were you expecting, Mr Cox? The Dagenham Girl Pipers?'

'I wasn't – no, sir. Shall I look in the luggage bay?'

I felt Lennie's hand squeeze my arm – hard.

'Good idea, Mr Cox.'

'Thank you, sir.'

'Except that, as you could have guessed, this vehicle has been combed by half the county's CID. If you found a flea in there you could be sure it would have had its prints taken.'

'I . . . understand, sir. You mean, it's not necessary?'

'It is not, Mr Cox. But if you'd shown half as much vigilance earlier, this whole ghastly cock-up would never have arisen.'

'But I had no reason to suspect—'

'There's *always* reason to suspect, Mr Cox, which is the first rule of being a prison officer. Anyway, save your excuses for the Governor tomorrow.'

'Yes, sir.'

'And now, if it wouldn't be too much trouble, perhaps you'd let us in?'

'Of course, sir.'

There was a fairly long pause and then we heard the grinding noise of the heavy gates being mechanically operated. A moment later and the coach started easing forwards again. I noticed that Mackay's driving seemed to be better. We bounced a bit along the rough prison road but before long came to a halt again. I knew exactly where we was. The coach was pointed straight at the massive main gates of Slade Prison. This was it.

Before long the voice of one of the gatekeepers reached us.

'Mr Mackay?'

'Who's that, Spiller?'

'Deakin, sir.'

'Are the visitors still here, Deakin?'

'I wouldn't know, sir.'

Mackay had switched off the engine by this time and after Deakin had left, we could hear him and Collinson talking above us.

'Where do you think they've got to, Mr Mackay?' asked Collinson.

'You mean, the fugitives? If they haven't been picked up yet they're probably in The Smoke by now.'

'Do you suppose the Met. will winkle them out?'

'In the end, certainly. Too late to do us any good.'

'How do you mean?'

'Oh come, come, Mr Collinson. You know the Governor likes to run a tight ship. It's going to be everything by the book from now on.'

'Surprised about Fletcher, sir.'

I again felt Len squeeze my arm but somehow this time I could tell it was playful.

'Really? Why?'

'Normally keeps his nose clean, doesn't he?'

'The eyes, Mr Collinson! You have to learn to read a man by his eyes. When they bring Fletcher back – as they will – take a good look at his eyes. Beneath that soft exterior lurks a hard, ruthless villain.'

Once more, Lennie squeezed my arm only this time I brushed his hand away irritably.

'No,' continued Mackay. 'Godber's the only one I'm surprised at.'

'Why's that, sir?'

'Good stuff in that boy. Fine athlete, basically decent.'

'He broke out,' Collinson reminded Mackay.

'Don't know the whole story yet, do we? Quite possibly he was forced along by the two evil older men. I'd stake a pound to a large Haig that the lad's clean.'

Lennie, no doubt carried away by this obtuse drivel, poked me slyly in the ribs. It was so unexpected that I let out a yelp.

'What was that?' asked Mackay.

'What, sir?'

'Thought I heard – the cry of some small animal. Get foxes in here sometimes. Did you know that, Mr Collinson?'

'Don't they bark, sir?'

'I didn't say it *was* a fox, did I?'

'No, sir.'

After this there was silence for a couple of minutes and then the voice that meant so much to us, the voice of the gatekeeper, Deakin, spoke again.

'The visitors have gone home, sir.'

'Oh? By train, I suppose?'

'Yes, sir.'

'And what about the coach driver?'

'He's our . . . guest for the night, sir.'

'Is he? Well, where shall I park this thing?'

However, the continuing conversation was then drowned out by the engine of the coach coming to life again with a roar. A moment later, Mackay had apparently reached a decision, because the vehicle started rolling again. It did not move far this time and then the engine was cut for the last time. We heard the two screws getting out and the door slam.

'Beautiful night, Mr Collinson.'

'It is indeed, sir. You can tell that the moon is just behind those clouds.'

Then there was the sound of retreating footsteps and all was still.

'Come on,' I whispered to Lennie.

'What's the point?' he asked. His voice sounded very sad.

'Can't stay here, can we?'

'Why not? Sooner or later someone's going to drive this out again. Worst thing that could happen to us would be to get nabbed here in the outer enclosure.'

'Which is just what will happen if we stay in here. You don't think they're going to pass this thing out again without searching it, do you?'

'Don't care,' said Len. 'Fed up, I am. Think I'll give myself up and say I was forced by you two evil, older men.'

'Godber—'

'We haven't got a chance, Fletch.'

'We're still free, ain't we?'

'No. We're trapped like rats.'

'We're not giving up, Godber.'

I leaned forwards and very slowly eased the luggage compartment door forwards. I let it fall again.

'Len, we is parked immediately outside the door to the dressing-rooms. It's possible they haven't bothered to lock it.'

'So what? Doesn't lead anywhere.'

'Be more comfortable than in here. We could even have a smoke and make plans.'

'I don't mind,' said Len wearily.

I took a deep breath and then eased myself out of the coach. On all fours, I scuttled across to the changing-room door, reached up, turned the handle and pushed. The door opened. I beckoned Len to follow and crawled into the cold, dark room. A moment later, he joined me.

'Hate this place,' he said dully. 'Where all our troubles began, this is.'

'Come on, Godber, get out the snout.'

We went behind a partition, which concealed us from the small barred window, and I very carefully lit a cigarette in my cupped hands the way we used to do in the jungle in Malaya when the terrorists was all around us. After that, we smoked for a while in silence. Finally, I said:

'Got any ideas?'

'We could fill them washbasins with water.'

I was puzzled by this suggestion.

'Then what?'

'We could drown ourselves.'

'Will you snap out of it, Godber?'

'This is the end of the line, Fletch. Can't take another three years in here. Either go bonkers or top myself.'

'It won't come to that, if you will only put your mind to it.'

'Put my mind to what? Our situation is obvious. In the morning, someone's going to find us and then it's all up.'

'Not if we can get into the inner yard.'

'Pity we haven't got one of them flying gorillas along. He could just float us over.'

'It's been done before, Godber.'

'It's been done after months of work and planning. We ain't got nothing – no tools, no ropes, no ladders.'

A light winked on in my mind.

'There's a step-ladder down in the barn. We might reach that.'

'Then what? Do a bit of whitewashing? Because we ain't going to get over that wall with no step-ladder.'

I sighed.

'You're not being very helpful.'

'Do you think there's a heaven, Fletch?'

'I think—' Then I stopped. Heaven? Maybe that's what the lad needed. But no! Naffing hell, even in this situation it was more than I could bring myself to do. In which case, our situation was just as desperate as Len was making it out to be. So. Crossing the fingers of my left hand firmly, and keeping them out of Len's sight, I said,

'Godber, if you snaps out of it and helps me to solve this problem, I'll let you date Ingrid when you gets out.'

He took a drag on his cigarette. I was beginning to think he was too far gone in despair for even that glowing promise to affect him. Then he dropped the fag end to the ground, stepped on it and said:

'You mean that?'

'Straight up.'

He squared his shoulders. He went to the window and looked out cautiously. He returned to where I was and sat down on a bench. He placed his elbows on his knees and his head in his hands. He said:

'Don't disturb me. May take some time. Just don't disturb me.'

I reckon it must have taken him very nearly fifteen minutes and, in our situation, it seemed more like fifteen hours. What's more, he'd sat down to do his genius act with the snout in his pocket so I couldn't even smoke to pass the time. But I did like he'd said. I sat down on a bench opposite him and kept shtum. Just as I was giving up hope, he got to his feet.

'Right. You say we can reach that barn?'

'Should be able to, crawling along the wall, like.'

'Then, let's go.'

This was a new, commanding Len and for the first time in our relationship I felt like his junior. I asked humbly:

'Want to let me in on the secret, Len?'

'We get the step-ladder.'

'But, Len, like you said, it wouldn't reach a third of the way up the wall.'

He smiled, the steely, confident smile of 007 about to swim through a swarm of sharks, scale a mile-high sheer precipice, parachute into Doctor Slime's HQ, blow up his whole army and steal his truss.

'How high is the coach, Fletch?'

'What?'

And then I caught on. Mackay had parked the big vehicle practically up against the main wall. With the ladder on top of it and perhaps a bale or something as well for extra height, it might just be possible—

I gulped in admiration.

'Think you've hit it, Len.'

'Let's move.'

We moved, but very, very slowly. We crawled a few paces and then paused. There would undoubtedly be screws surveying the enclosure, so we had to look like two stones, two shadows, two hardly visible shapes that just materialized now and then a bit further along the wall. Took us twenty minutes or so to reach the nearest point to the barn. Now the difficult part began.

'We wriggle,' hissed Lennie, 'on our bellies.'

And wriggle we did. Dunno how snakes get about as nippily as they do. Having sampled it, it seems to me the most tiring, painful, difficult form of locomotion there is. Took us at least another twenty minutes to get to the cover of the barn. And then at last we could stand up.

'Here, Fletch,' whispered Lennie anxiously, 'never thought. The door'll be locked, won't it?'

Proud to be of service to my gallant young commander, I reassured him.

'No problem. I know where there's some loose planks.'

Stooping, we circled the building until we came to the spot. Carefully, we levered out the planks and crawled through into the barn. Then I fetched the ladder from where it was stashed against a support post.

'Er, shall we have another snout, Len?' I asked hopefully. 'Could use a rest. My abdomen feels like a nude bareback rider's bum.'

'No time,' said the young officer sternly. 'Night's passing. Take us even longer to get back with the ladder.'

'Very good, Len. Do you think we ought to take something else – sack of pig-feed or something – for extra height?'

'Won't need it. I calculated exact. Besides, we'll have to take the ladder over with us. Who was it said: don't leave no trail, you won't need no bail?'

'That was me, Len.'

'I have an idea it was Churchill originally. Anyway, best get cracking.'

Wriggling is one thing. Wriggling with a ladder makes ordinary wriggling seem like a Sunday stroll through Muswell Hill with the trouble and strife. Far as I could see, the ground was smooth except for sharp flints left over from prehistoric times with which our free ancestors, before nicks was invented, cut up their mammoths. But the naffing ladder kept getting snagged as if we was trying to pull it through the teeth of a harrow. Took twice as long getting back to the wall as going the other direction. But finally we made it.

'Two minutes, Len,' I pleaded. 'Got to get my breath.'

'Very well, Fletch, you've earned it,' said the captain graciously.

I panted for the full two minutes and then Len whispered,

'Time to move.'

I nodded and off we set again. Wasn't quite as bad because we could part carry the ladder and part drag it in the shadow of the wall. But it took us another twenty minutes to get the thing back to the coach. We pushed it under the massive vehicle and retreated to the changing-rooms to tidy up a bit. Wouldn't do, when we appeared on exercise the next day, if we looked like we'd spent the night potholing. As we ran the water into the basins, I said to Len:

'Feel different now, don't you?'

'How do you mean?'

'Less than an hour ago, you was talking about drowning yourself.'

Len had the good grace to grin.

'Think I'll take Ingrid to the "Bon Goo", for our first date. That's French for good taste.'

'Ain't you had enough of goo, Godber? Anyhow, with the money you'll leave here with, you'll be lucky to take her to the bon fire: "Waiter, bring me some scraps from the dustbin and a bottle of vintage meths." '

Lennie ignored my sally.

'The "Bon Goo" specializes in creeps, which is a kind of thin pancake. I'll be very interested to see if they makes them the Paris way or the Nice way.'

'Don't want to shatter your fantasies, Len, but we has still to find the nice way back into the nick.'

'We're as good as there.'

'Oh, listen to him, all of a sudden? Not the moaning Minnie you was a little while ago. What makes you so confident?'

'Can't go wrong. The guards is not watching out for break-*ins*, is they?'

'But they is still watching.'

'We'll be over that wall in a jiffy, stash the ladder, behind the dustbins and a bit of a wait till morning.'

'Well, I just hope you is right. Ready to go?'

'Aye.'

We had a good look round, slowly opened the door and crawled quickly back to the coach. We extracted the ladder from under it. We looked at each other. This was going to be the tough bit. We was going to be upright, out in the open, standing on top of the coach. I never thought I'd have a good word to say for the Slade weather but I was grateful for it then. There might have been a full moon or there might have been a new moon but all of it that showed through the surly cloud bank was a faint gleam of silver now and then. Wasn't going to be easy to see us without searchlights and with a bit of luck no one was going to switch them on. Slade is not one of your new-fangled nicks with telly cameras on every ledge and even if it had been telly cameras can't see in the dark any more than screws can.

So we felt fairly confident as we carefully made our preparations. Len, being the more agile, got up on the roof of the coach and I passed the ladder up to him. He set it up sideways to the wall. Its top was about two foot lower than the top of the wall and about four feet away from it. But we was prepared for that. We also had brought along a plank from the changing-rooms. This was really the broken top of one of the benches but it would make a nice bridge from the ladder to the wall. Should be just a case of climbing the ladder, walking along the plank, tricky but quite possible, getting on the top of the wall and then, of course, the jump. Oh, the plank and the ladder? You is wondering how we planned to take them with us? We had a few bits of rope from the barn and we was going to tie them to our bridge and so pull it after us.

So Lennie set up the ladder, climbed it and put the plank in position. Then he climbed down the ladder again and hissed:

'Right, Fletch, up you comes.'

I mounted the fixed metal ladder in the side of the coach and joined Lennie on the roof.

'Who goes first?' I asked.

'I will. Younger. Better balance. Be able to give you a hand from the wall.'

'Just as you say, Len,' I murmured gratefully.

Len started to climb the ladder – and then there was a sudden clang. We both froze. We both knew what it was. It was the little door set in the massive main door of the nick opening. A minute later we heard voices.

'For Gawd's sake, Len,' I urged. 'Get down here quick.'

He swiftly descended the ladder again. By this time, we could hear footsteps approaching us.

'What about the ladder?' asked Len.

'No time. Down flat. And pray hard.'

We both of us flattened ourselves on the roof of the coach. From the voices, I could tell it was Mackay and Collinson again. They entered the coach. A moment later the engine started.

'Gawd!' I whispered to Len. 'When he starts this thing, the whole of our edifice is going to crash down.' But the coach did not start moving. I heard Mackay say:

'Where the hell's the switch? Is this it? Yes.'

And we knew the switch he'd been looking for because all the lights in the coach came on. Our situation was now very cosy. The ladder, the plank and us were all clearly visible in the light from the coach to any screw that happened to be glancing in our direction. In addition, the ladder was rattling from the throbbing of the coach in spite of Len's efforts to hold it firm from the base. Any moment, it might come down even if the coach never moved. It was time to come clean with the Almighty.

'If we gets out of this one, Gawd,' I said under my breath, 'Lennie really can have Ingrid's hand – all the rest of her too for that matter!'

At that point, the engine of the coach stopped although the lights stayed on. Now we could hear the voices of the screws beneath us again.

'I'm damned sure I had it during the drive,' said Mackay irritably.

We heard them ferreting about.

'What colour was it, Mr Mackay?'

'Solid gold, Mr Collinson. Present from my old regiment. I've never lit my cigarettes with anything else since it was given to me in a very touching ceremony. Quite apart from its sentimental value, it's worth a considerable sum of money.'

'Well, I don't— Hang on, sir. Yes, here it is.'

There was an appreciative gurgle from beneath us.

'Well, that proves one thing, Mr Collinson.'

'What's that, sir?'

'There are no cons out here. Otherwise they'd have found their way to it.'

Collinson chuckled dutifully at this feeble jest.

'Well, I'll be getting back to the club. Care to join me, Mr Collinson? Stand you a drink?'

'Er – that would be delightful, sir. But I'm afraid I have a few letters to write.'

'I see,' said Mackay, sounding none too chuffed. 'Well, suit yourself.'

Then, to our inexpressible relief, the lights went out again. We heard the two screws leave the coach. Its door slammed, causing our rickety assembly to give a heart-stopping lurch, and then the footsteps retreated. Finally, we heard the little door into the nick shut too.

We was both too shaken to move for some minutes.

'Talk about shaves,' muttered Lennie.

'Still – good omen, that.'

'How do you mean?'

'If our luck'll stand up to that it'll stand up to anything. Ready for lift-off?'

We both stood up. We made our improvised bridge steady again and then I held the ladder while Lennie mounted. He reached the top, stretched out his hands like a tightrope walker, and nimbly crossed to the wall. Then I heard his low voice:

'Right, Fletch, let's have you.'

There was no one to hold the ladder steady for me so I mounted with great care. To my relief it seemed stable. But when I got to the top, the plank looked very narrow. It was so dark that I could hardly see Len squatting on the wall.

'You there?' I whispered anxiously.

' 'Course! Get moving!'

Now you may have noticed that in this narrative I have used the word 'gulped' quite a lot. This is because in prison a good deal of gulping goes on. Situations are continually arising when the larynx tries to shoot out the mouth. But even if I has sometimes been a bit free with the old gulp, I tell you no lies when I says that I gulped before setting out on that plank. In the old pirate days there was nothing but a shark-infested sea beneath the carefree captive. What we had was a screw-infested nick and the likelihood of three long years of extra incarceration. So, as I set foot on the plank, I gulped. And then, as I put my other foot on it, I gulped again. And then I stopped gulping because it was making me unsteady and I concentrated on putting one foot in front of the other, across that terrible gulf, until Lennie came clearly into sight. When I was getting close he put out his hand encouragingly and just as he put out his hand the need for encouragement became pressing. The plank slipped a few inches. This caused me to – no, not gulp, but gasp – and hastily plonk my other foot down to try and recover my balance. But the sudden weight caused the plank to shift another little bit and then, heedless of screws or anything else, I shouted:

'Lennie! I'm going!'

'Give me your hand, Fletch! Your hand!' the lad shouted back.

I reached for it and, in the nick of time, grasped it. Only it would have been better if I hadn't because by then I was completely off balance. The plank tilted sideways, tipping me off and, pulling Lennie with me, I plunged to the ground. The lad came down on top of me and the ladder and plank on top of us both and the din it all made was enough to set dogs barking in Carlisle.

So then we just lay and waited for the searchlights and the handcuffs. We waited for a minute and then another minute and then we waited for another minute and then I remarked:

'Gawd, Len. They still hasn't heard us. Our stars must be in the right grouping for once. Come on, let's set it up again.'

'No good, Fletch.'

'How do you mean? It nearly worked. Perhaps I better go first this time and you can hold the plank steady.'

'No good. My ankle's gone.'

'What?'

'Twisted my ankle when I fell. Dunno if I can walk – never mind climb.'

I didn't even have the heart to gulp. But, as I took Len under the arms and began to drag him, as gently as I could, back to the naffing dressing-rooms, I sighed very deeply indeed. When I had him seated on a bench, I went behind the partition, lit a fag, and gave it to him. As he pulled, I could see that his face was wrinkled up in pain.

'We'll just have one last snout, old son, and then I'll go and get help.'

'Three years' worth of help,' muttered Len.

'Ain't got no more room to manoeuvre.'

'Naffing hell,' complained Len. 'It's so unfair.'

'But,' I finished for him, 'when was life ever fair?'

We smoked most of our snouts in silence. Then I stubbed mine out and, from habit, slipped the remains into my ankle pocket. Then I stood up.

'I'll bring the M.O. for you, Len,' I said.

'I'm not a wino, Fletch,' said Lennie wryly. 'But I'd give a lot for a drink right now.'

'And I would happily stand you one, my son, if—'

And then I stopped. It was so fierce that I shuddered. Must be how the helmsmen on the old schooners felt when a dirty great lump of ball lightning came slithering down the mast and dropped on their bonce.

'What did you say, Len?' I asked very quietly.

'Said I'd go a bundle on a drink.'

'A drink?' I said and my own voice sounded dreamy to me. 'That would give you pleasure, would it, my son?'

'Well, what do you think?'

'I think it's a good idea, Len. I think after the troubles and miseries and griefs and horrors of this day, we deserves one. We deserves a big drink. We deserves a whole bottle each!'

And then young Godber stared in amazement as I staggered about the miserable, cheerless changing-rooms doubled up with laughter.

About one hour later, in the select Slade Prison Officers' Club, Chalky the barman cast an anxious look upon the plainly inebriated figure of Mr Mackay who was blinking at him owlishly.

'Do you think you should, sir?'

'Should?' repeated Mackay stupidly. 'Should what?'

'Should have another, sir. You've had five large whiskies and five pints already.'

'What are you then, some kind of mathematical genius?' asked Mackay, surprising himself slightly by being able to pronounce the long words.

'It's just that—'

'It's just that you're exceeding your 'thority, Mr Chalky. You are the barman here, not the Governor of Slade Prison. Are you under the impression that you're the Governor of Slade Prison?'

'No, of course not, Mr Mackay, but you did tell me—'

'I did not tell you.'

'When you first came in, you said: "No more than five, Chalky." That's what you said.'

'Prove it.'

'I can't do that, sir.'

'Then it wouldn't stand up in a court of law.'

'Maybe not—'

'I know what you're implying. You are implying that I am intoxicated. And if I was intoxicated, it would be very understandable considering that I've stopped more flak from the Governor this evening than the whole flaming RAF did during the war. Prison officer with thirty years of unblemished service. Not my fault if the man insists on having stupid celebrity football match without celebrities, is it? Is it?'

'No, sir.'

'Obviously something dodgy about it from the start, as I told the bloody idiot fair and square. Madness to bring a coach into the grounds of this prison. Might as well issue holiday vouchers. Mr Treadaway wants his head examined. Most incompetent Governor this prison ever had! Large whisky.'

'But—'

Here, Mackay brought his fist down forcefully on the bar. Chalky turned to the other screw present.

'What am I to do, Mr Barrowclough?'

No sooner had he spoken than Mackay swung round eagerly which made him look like some demon of the glens.

'So you've graciously decided to grace us with your gracious presence, have you, Frank? We were beginning to think you were

200

too high 'n mighty for our little club. Weren't we, Mr Miller?'

Chalky coughed discreetly.

'Mr Miller left half an hour ago, sir.'

'Did he? Had to write letters, I suppose. When I first entered the prison service there was not this mania for penmanship. No good will come of it. What will you have, Frank?'

The bovine screw coughed nervously.

'Do you think, Mr Mackay, that it's wise?'

'What's that mean? Reminds me of a nursery rhyme. Does it remind you of a nursery rhyme, Frank?'

'Not that I can think of. I do feel I should point out, Mr Mackay, that we're all going to have a very difficult day to-morrow.'

'And the day after that, and the day after that. And what kind of blasted day do you think I've had today, Mr Barrowclough?'

'Well—'

'Father William. That's the nursery rhyme. *You are old, father William, do you think at your age that it's right?* Well, I am *not* old! Seasoned, that's what I am. Up to all their nasty little pranks! And I told the Governor that I had no intention of retiring before my time. Do you think I'm old, Frank?'

'Certainly not, Mr Mackay.'

'Then don't call me Father William. Two large whiskies, Chalky.'

Chalky looked helplessly at Mr Barrowclough.

'What do you think, sir?'

'Doesn't matter what he thinks!' roared Mackay. 'He is my subordinate. That means that I am the senior and he is the junior so he does not decide what I drink. Isn't that right, Frank?'

'Good heaven, yes, Mr Mackay. The only thing is—'

'Well?'

'Well . . .'

And in the brief pause that ensued, a new voice was heard. Only it did not belong to anyone in the room and it was very faint. It spoke one word only:

'Help!'

'What do you mean "help"?' asked Mackay turning his attention back to Chalky.

'Wasn't me, sir,' maintained Chalky.

'You said "help". I heard you. Didn't you hear him, Frank?'

Barrowclough glanced about uneasily.

'I certainly thought *someone* said "help".'

'Well, it wasn't me,' asserted Mr Mackay. 'Although God knows I could use a bit more help than I get from my staff.' His tone changed. 'Chalky, you're a good lad. Might be some promotion coming your way. Get me a double whisky.'

Chalky sighed and turned to draw it.

Again there was a silence and again the faint voice was heard: 'Help!'

Chalky turned immediately and looked hard at the door to the store room.

'It came from in there,' he said wonderingly.

'Well, who's in there?' asked Mackay thickly. 'Is that where Miller writes his blasted letters?'

'It's the store room, sir,' protested Chalky. 'You know that – and it's locked!'

'Well, unlock it. Could be an officer in trouble.'

Chalky hastened to comply. The door was thrown open and the light switched on. And what met the gaze of the three in the bar was not a prison officer in trouble but two prisoners in clover: Len and me, each with a half-empty bottle of the best, ten-year-old malt whisky in our hands.

'Thank Gawd!' I exclaimed pitiably. 'We is saved!'

12 No place like home

'You maintain,' said the Governor, 'that Oakes forced you down the delivery hatch?'

'That's right, sir,' I said earnestly. 'Aint it, Len? Oh, no I was forgetting, you was concussed, wasn't you?' I turned back to the Governor: 'Total milk of magnesia, sir. He don't remember nothing.'

Mr Treadaway sighed and turned his attention to young Godber who, with a bandage round his ankle and another round his head, looked like a young hero just back from the front.

'Is that true, Godber?'

'Remember scoring that goal, sir,' said Godber, apparently searching his memory, 'and then – then – the next thing Mr Mackay was handling me rough—'

'He's lying,' snapped Mackay. 'All I did—'

'Please, Mr Mackay,' urged the Governor. 'There were witnesses. You were certainly none too gentle with these men.'

'They were inebriated, sir, on our – that is the Prison Officers' – whisky.'

'Well, so were you, Mr Mackay, and I shan't forget it,' said the Governor primly. He looked in my direction again: 'It's a pity you and Godber had to drink so much to keep warm—'

'Never have survived in that freezing cellar if we hadn't, sir—' I took the liberty of interrupting.

'That may be so – but the result was that we were unable to get any sense out of you last night.'

Too true, I thought. In fact, after warding off Mackay's fury, with the help of Chalky and old Barra, Len and I had spent a very comfortable night in the infirmary.

'Let me question them, sir,' snarled Mackay, his plastic teeth bared unpleasantly, 'I'll get the truth out of them!'

'Are you disputing my competence, Mr Mackay?'

'Of course not, sir.'

'Then perhaps you'd keep quiet for a few minutes, and let me continue my interrogation.'

'Certainly, sir,' agreed the screw reluctantly.

'Fletcher,' asked the Governor earnestly, 'how did Oakes force you into that store room? Did he have a gun?'

'A gun? No, sir. At least not that I saw. But he had a dirty great iron bar. Len, being concussed, didn't give him no trouble and I knew I wasn't no match for him, armed and desperate as he was.'

'In your opinion, was this escape planned in advance?'

'Don't see how it could have been, sir. Unless you're suggesting it was me what planned it.'

The Governor looked surprised.

'You, Fletcher?'

'I think I'm right in saying, sir, that the celebrity football match was my idea in the first place. Just been reading about one in Carlisle and it seemed like a good idea. But I think Mr Mackay will confirm to you, sir, that I don't have the contacts or the clout to set up an operation like this. And if I had been the mastermind would Oakes have treated me like he did?'

The Governor nodded thoughtfully.

'Did you get any idea from Oakes where he might be heading?'

I shook my head positively.

'No, he never – hang about, there was something. When he forced us down that black hole, I pleaded with him and said we could die of starvation or thirst down there.'

'You seem to have warded off the latter danger quite successfully,' the Governor remarked drily.

'Yes, sir. Anyhow, Oakes just laughed and said: "If I make it I'll get someone to give the Governor a bell when I get to the jacket." '

'Jacket?' asked the Governor mystified.

'You see, sir,' I explained earnestly. 'Before he became the Al Capone of Manchester, Oakes was a London man, from the East End originally.'

'I still don't—'

'Rhyming slang, sir. Jacket and vest equals West. That's the West End of London, sir. Yes, I think we can assume that Oakes was headed for The Smoke.'

'If he had been,' growled Mackay, 'he'd have been stopped at one of the road blocks.'

'I think you're forgetting, Mr Mackay, how good he was at disguise. Made himself up exactly like the coach driver—'

'How do you know that?' snapped Mackay eagerly, thinking he'd trapped me.

I shook my head impatiently.

'Saw the driver when he brung in the coach, didn't I, sir? That's how we ran afoul Oakes. I asked a bloke what I thought was the driver for a light and then when I realized who it really was, I tried to talk him out of it. I said: "Don't be a mug, Oaksey, you won't get five miles." '

'Very public spirited, Fletcher. Except that you're lying!'

'We have no reason to suppose that, Mr Mackay,' said the Governor firmly. 'All right, Fletcher, you and Godber can return to your cell. I have no doubt the CID will wish to talk to you later.' Then he turned to Mackay. 'These men are excused duties today, Mr Mackay, and they are not to be harassed. Is that understood?'

I could practically see Mackay choking on his own venom but what could he do?

'It is, sir,' he muttered.

'Course, the title of this chapter, 'No place like home', doesn't refer to the nick. A place where six hundred men, some of them looney and others like wild beasts, are kept locked up in cages could never be called home. I read somewhere that some penal reformer said: if prisons didn't exist, it would be impossible to invent them in the twentieth century. Thought a lot about that. Must have meant the idea is too crude and brutal for our age. Bit hard to believe when you think of some of the things that's happened in my own lifetime. Then again, what is you to do with real hard cases? I mean, blokes like Len and me is no menace to society. We would be better punished doing useful work that no one else wants to do. But what is you to do with the real vicious nurks? Put them on an island, I suppose, where they can hack at each other if they wants. I don't pretend to have the answers but there's one thing I do know: there is nothing that keeps crime going so well as the nick. That's where your ordinary, slightly bent kid learns to become a professional. The nick is a crime polytechnic and as long as there is nicks there will be crime. So it can't be the answer, can it?

No, the title of this chapter is meant to be about real home, Muswell Hill, the old woman and the kids, your own little terraced house and bit of garden, the one place in the whole world where you can be sure you belongs. It was ironic really. By getting back into the nick, Len and I had managed to get much closer to home.

'I'm happy to say,' said Mr Barrowclough, stopping by the dell that afternoon, 'that you two seem to be in the clear.'

'How's that, sir?' I asked.

'I've just spoken to the CID Inspector that interrogated you this morning. He's convinced that Oakes acted on impulse. I must say, I was very relieved to hear it. Frankly, I'd have been disappointed if you two had been involved.'

'Would have been daft, wouldn't it, Mr Barrowclough? We is both due out in less than a year.'

'Exactly. That point weighed heavily with both the Governor and the CID.' He sighed, looking like a cow that's come to the end of the clover. 'Only Mr Mackay seems reluctant to accept your innocence.'

'Oh yeah?' I said negligently. 'Then he'll have to prove we was out of the nick, won't he?'

'That's just what he claims he's going to do. Seems determined to continue the investigation on his own.'

I shrugged.

'Keep him off the lads' backs, won't it? Don't you worry, Mr Barrowclough. He won't find nothing.'

But when the amiable screw had ambled away, Lennie said anxiously,

'Think he's a threat? Mackay?'

I shook my head.

'Mackay ain't. But we is not in the clear yet.'

'How do you mean, Fletch?'

'If Oaksey don't make it, Grouty is going to be short-changed and he ain't going to like that.'

'You mean, he'll blame us?'

'He'll have to punish someone to keep up his reputation.'

'But that's—'

'Unfair. 'Course it is, Godber. But it's high time you got past lesson one.'

'Don't think I ever will, Fletch. Got a built-in sense of justice, I have. When do you think we'll know?'

I shrugged.

'Oaksey's got two choices: go to ground somewhere until the heat's off or head straight for an airport and get on a plane, maybe in disguise.'

'Which do you think he'll do?'

'Well, if it was me, I'd lay low. But then with my figure disguise ain't too helpful. Just have to wait and see.'

That evening when I turned up in Funland with my half of the chessboard, I was gratified to notice that a stir went through the assembled cons. There was a good deal of nudging and muttering and glances were cast in my direction. 'Course, I've always had respect in the nick but the feeling now was as if I'd pulled some big stroke. It was, as I've said, rewarding but it made me feel a bit uneasy too.

'Few red faces in the Governor's office today,' remarked Old Hedley as I sat down opposite him.

Beneath the table, I put a black and a white pawn in each of my fists and held them out. Hedley picked the white one.

'How come you always pull white? You got x-ray eyes or something?' I asked irritably.

Hedley shook his head.

'Noticed years ago you always put the white one in your left hand.'

'That's cheating, that is!' I exclaimed outraged.

'It's not. Using my brains, which is what you need for chess.'

'Well, you is going to need them tonight. I'm going to try a new opening on you.'

Hedley shrugged.

'Know all the openings,' he said calmly.

As I set up my pieces, I asked,

'What's this about red faces then?'

'Well, last night they put it out on BBC: "Three men escaped from Slade Prison." Today they have to say: "Oh sorry, we only meant one." '

I smiled.

'Must look as if they can't count, mustn't it?'

Hedley gave me a shrewd look.

'I reckon.'

'Come on then,' I said. 'Let's see what you can do with this one.'

And I advanced my king's rook pawn two squares. Hedley frowned.

'That's a daft opening.'

'Is it?'

'Not in any of the books.'

'Maybe not in the ones you've read.'

Truth was, it wasn't in any of the books I'd read either, mainly because I'd never read no books about chess. I made the move simply because I was so sick of always being beaten when I made an ordinary opening move. I thought at least it might confuse Hedley. About twenty moves later I began to feel myself going tense. It had confused him and all. I studied the board. I had a good position, for the first time I could ever remember when playing the old scroat. Then suddenly my heart gave a jump. I had better than a good position. It was my move and if I made the right one, and I could see what that was, I'd got a won game. I reached forwards to check Hedley with my knight and just at the moment a hand touched me on the shoulder. Now a hand on the shoulder is always unnerving. In the nick, it usually spells trouble and the normal response to jump. I jumped.

'Right,' cried Hedley. 'You touched the rook. Rook moves!'

'What do you mean rook moves?' I exclaimed indignantly. 'Accident that was. I jumped.'

I turned quickly and saw that it was only Rudge behind me who'd touched me. I turned back to Hedley.

'Rules of chess,' said Hedley firmly. 'If you touch a piece you got to move it. Rook moves.'

'Yeah, you'd like that,' I said bitterly. 'Let you out, that would. But rook does not move because I just jogged the board by accident. Knight moves.' And I moved it. 'Check. Checkmate next move.'

'I ain't playing a man that don't abide by the rules,' said Hedley firmly and then, to my amazement, he swept all the pieces together in the middle of the board.

'What the hell is you doing?' I roared. 'I had a mate, I did. My game, that was.'

Hedley shrugged haughtily.

'You can think that if you want. Far as I'm concerned the game is cancelled through cheating.'

'Why you—'

'Could I have a word with you, Fletch?' said Rudge, behind me. I turned on him angrily.

'Don't you know better than to sneak up on someone and tap him? When is you going to learn the first thing about life inside? You've just ruined my game.'

The kid looked at me coolly.

'I heard you ruined your own game. Thought maybe you'd like to have a bit of a chat about it.'

I could tell he thought he was being clever and was not referring to chess. I sighed and stood up.

'All right, let's go to your cell.'

When we got there, it was empty. His cell-mate was out.

'So?' I asked.

'Disappointed in you.'

'Is that right?'

'Was beginning to think you was different from the others, that you used your head.'

'And may I ask what has disillusioned you, young Rudge?'

'It's not using your head to give up your freedom voluntary.'

'What freedom?'

'You was out and you came back in.'

I wasn't happy at this conversation but I tried to keep my voice level.

'Who told you that? Mackay?'

The boy smiled and I noticed that he'd already acquired the slightly twisted, sideways smile of a villain.

'Everyone knows it. But you needn't worry. Nobody's going to say anything.'

I shrugged, to give myself time to think. It was probably true that everyone *suspected* that Lennie and I had been out. There are no secrets in the nick. But no one could really know it.

'Don't want to believe all the daft rumours that circulate in this place,' I said severely.

It was his turn to shrug.

'Just wanted you to know. I'm disappointed in you.'

And he turned to leave.

'Hang about,' I said. 'As it happens I didn't bust out but in my long criminal career I've known lots that have. You think that's freedom, do you?'

'Being outside these walls – that's freedom.'

I shook my head.

'No, it ain't. It's just a different kind of imprisonment, in some ways worse. At least in here you knows when you is going to be really free and you knows that you can look people in the face without them frowning and maybe rushing off to the nearest cop shop to report you. It may be marking time doing time but when you is on the run it's living in limbo. Worst way there is for any man to live.'

Rudge shook his head slightly.

'I'd go – if I got the chance.'

'Well, you may and all. Because if word gets about that you're willing sooner or later some firm is going to approach you to do a little tunnelling. And then you is almost certainly going to get nabbed in the bowels of the earth and lose your remission and get another three years slammed on your sentence. There's only one way you'll ever be free and that is if you do your porridge and gets released. And then it's up to you to stay out.'

There was a silence. We looked at each other.

'Is that all?' he asked.

'That's all. I don't expect you'll take my advice. None ever does take advice. But if you start on the absconding lark at your age, your life is finished before it's properly started. How long has you got to do?'

'Fourteen months.'

I shook my head with a wry smile.

'Like a summer afternoon,' I said. 'I've done more *years* than that. You're a lovely striker, Rudgie, and one day you could be in the big league. But only if you're not a mug and keeps your nose clean.'

Again we looked at each other and this time I thought I saw perhaps a hint of doubt on the lad's face, as if maybe some of my words had got home. But just then, Warren appeared at the door to the cell.

'Grouty wants to see you, Fletch.'

This was not the most cheering news I could have had, but I wasn't too worried neither.

'All right, Bunny,' I replied. 'Tell him I'm on my way.'

I turned back to Rudge.

'Think it over,' I suggested.

He nodded. Then he actually smiled.

'Like working with you, Fletch.'

'Then stick around. By the time I leave, you'll be practically packing your things too.'

Then I turned and hastened down to my own dell. Lennie was there. As soon as I entered, he said:

'Bunny find you, did he?'

I nodded. 'Grouty want you and all?'

'Yes.'

'Then this is it.'

'You think he's heard? How could he?'

'Signal fires on the hills. I dunno how Grouty finds things out but he does. Let's just hope the message was the right one.'

We went slowly down to Grouty's superior quarters, slowly because Lennie, with his strapped ankle, could still only hobble. When we got there, Grouty was alone and doing nothing, both of which facts was somewhat surprising.

'Come in, lads,' he said cordially and so of course we did. 'Hear you've had a tiring day. Lot of questions asked.'

We both nodded and I felt that it was tactful to add,

'Pity we wasn't able to be of much help.'

Grouty nodded sympathetically.

'Have to feel sorry for the Governor under circumstances like these. Probably cost him promotion to the Home Office.'

Grouty seated himself on his little armchair, reached round and withdrew from a locker a large box of glittering liqueur chocolates. He opened the box, removed what looked like a cherry brandy, slowly peeled off the paper, popped the lovely thing in his mouth and munched thoughtfully. He then replaced the box, remarking:

'I'd offer you each one but it's my last box.'

'We didn't really want one, did we, Len?' I said wistfully.

The lad shook his head.

'No. Might get hooked.'

'However,' continued Grouty, 'I think I can do something for you.'

'Oh yes?' I asked, aware that my heart was doing a nimble somersault. I noticed that Lennie glanced quickly towards the door, doubtless to see if Samson had materialized there. But he hadn't.

'You've had, like I said, a very exhausting time. I thought you'd appreciate a little music.'

We both stared at him uncomprehendingly.

'Local Carlisle station – listeners' requests. Sit down, boys. It starts in –' Grouty consulted his massive wrist computer and continued '– exactly thirty-three seconds.'

'Very good of you, Grouty,' I said humbly. 'Ain't it, Len?'

'Oh yeah, just what the doctor ordered.'

We seated ourselves gingerly on Grouty's bunk. I realized it was the first time I'd ever been privileged to rest my bottom in the great man's cell. But would it prove to be a privilege or a hot seat? Grouty kept his eye fixed on the changing numerals on his watch face and then abruptly reached over and flicked a switch on his hi fi and a voice said:

'*And hello again. This is Don Wightman with your own programme, another hour of listeners' requests.*' After that another voice came on and strongly recommended a furniture shop. Then Don Wightman returned. '*And first of all this lovely Autumn evening we have a request from Mr Sydney Oakes of 12 Slade Street. Mr Oakes wants us to play the ever popular "Blue Skies". Here, it is, Sydney, and I hope you find them.*'

And, as the familiar strains poured out into Grouty's glamour pad, Lennie and I just gaped at the wizard. He chuckled:

'That's it then, lads. Seems he's away and you're in the clear.'

'Amazin', Grouty,' I exclaimed. 'How did you—?'

But he held up his hand.

'You know better than that, Fletch. Oh, now I remember, I *have* got a spare box.'

And the big-hearted baron opened his locker once more and withdrew a full box of liqueur chocolates.

'Split them between you, lads. 'Course, this is only a token. There'll be something in the way of cash in your Christmas stocking.'

I gulped – well, wouldn't you?

'Thanks, Grouty.'

'I'm always fair, Fletch. You know that.'

'Oh, I've observed it often, Grouty.'

'On your way then, lads, and I don't have to tell you to stay shtum.'

We made our way back to our cell with our treasure. We had just finished stashing it in Lenny's mattress when Bunny Warren came bounding in.

'Can I have one, Fletch?' he asked eagerly.

'Certainly, Warren,' I assured him, balling my fist, 'on the chin or the ear?'

'No, I meant one of them chocolates with booze in it.'

I sighed deeply.

'Naffing hell,' I said bitterly. 'If Marconi had been a prisoner he'd never have bothered to invent wireless. How does news travel so quickly in this place?'

'Timkins saw you leaving Grouty's cell—'

'Never mind, Bunny. If we give you one you is to keep it under your hat.'

'But I want to eat it, Fletch. Besides, I ain't got no hat.'

'You is to keep the glad tidings to yourself, see? We ain't got enough for the horde of scroungers that will descend.'

'Won't breathe a word, Fletch.'

I nodded at Len. He reached into our mattress-safe and withdrew the box. Inevitably, Black Jock slouched into the flowery.

'What's this?' he asked eagerly. 'Is PIST back in business?'

'No, it is not, McLaren. But I suppose, since you is here, you can have one too. One, mind.'

And I handed out one to him and one to Bunny. There was a disapproving cough from the doorway.

'I can't understand why you people are so determined to ruin your teeth.'

'Really, Banyard?' I asked, with a hint of irony. 'Well these chocolates was a little present from Grouty. They may ruin our teeth but at least they don't damage our nose. How is your trunk? Fully recovered.'

'No. I think the septum has been distorted. I've applied for remedial treatment at Carlisle General.'

'You is learning,' I nodded approvingly. 'Here, have some caries.'

And I extended the box to him. He inspected it.

'These are very superior chocolates. I suppose one wouldn't do any harm.'

'Just to set your mind at rest,' I assured him, 'we is all going to scrub our molars before kipping down.'

'Ah, but do you know *how* to clean your teeth? Very few people do.'

'That could be another attractive dodge,' Len piped up. 'Apply to the Governor to let you give a course in teeth care.'

'I'll get my guitar,' exclaimed Black Jock, 'and we'll have a bit of a sing-song to celebrate your return.'

'We ain't been nowhere,' I protested, but it was too late. Jock had hurried out.

A few minutes later, and the dell resounded to the discordant twangings of Jock's instrument.

'Where'd you nick that, Jock?' I asked wearily. 'From a reject warehouse?'

He didn't reply but launched into a jangling version of, as far as I could judge, 'Danny Boy'.

'I know that one,' said Banyard, and the next moment his flat baritone boomed out in a version of 'Home on the Range'.

Bunny smiled contentedly:

'I've always had a weakness for music,' he said.

Mercifully, the concert was short lived. After about ten minutes the warning bell rang and our house-guests reluctantly got to their feet and made off to their own charming homes.

'Put the rest of the chocolates away, Len,' I said, shaking my head to try and clear the last echo of the hideous din we had been enduring.

Lennie picked up the box.

'Here, Fletch, there's none left.'

'What?'

We both looked vengefully at the door and exclaimed, at the same moment,

'Bunny!'

But through the door, leering evilly, walked Mr Mackay.

'I won't buy it, Fletcher,' he announced without ceremony.

I held up the chocolate box and turned it upside down.

'Just as well, Mr Mackay. It's empty.'

'You know what I'm referring to. The Governor may believe your story but the Governor doesn't walk these floors.'

'Mr Mackay. Is there any point raking up the ashes?'

'There certainly is. If strokes are pulled and those who pull them are not punished, discipline suffers. I've been scouting about a bit today. There have been some peculiar sightings in the neighbourhood.'

I shrugged.

'What, UFOs or something?'

'Yes. Unidentified fleeing objects. Two men, one of them in football shorts, spotted at various points on the moors. Also, there's a step-ladder in the changing-rooms which comes from the barn.'

'Probably was took there for the whitewashing, Mr Mackay.'

'No, I've checked up on that. I just want you to know, Fletcher, that I intend to pursue my investigations until I have assembled a cast-iron case.'

'Well, I don't want to spoil your detective practice, Mr Mackay, especially since you is approaching retirement age and may soon need a new career but I think you is wasting your time.'

His neck jerked gleefully from side to side.

'We'll see about that, Fletcher.'

'I know you haven't got a very high opinion of me, Mr Mackay. You might even think that beneath my soft exterior there lurks a hard ruthless villain.'

Mackay's eyes widened and I saw Lennie stiffen. But I knew what I was about.

'How did you know—' began Mackay.

But I held up my hand firmly.

'However, I think you'll admit, sir, that Len is not like that. There's good stuff in that boy. Fine athlete, basically decent.'

'Those are my words!' exclaimed Mackay, highly excited. 'That proves it. You must have been—'

'Not your words, Mr Mackay. No one owns words. They just use them. For instance, the words you was using about the Governor when we was trying to attract your attention in the Prison Officers' Club. Anyone could use those words. And if the Governor started interrogating me again, I might feel that I had to use them and tell him who used them originally. Mr Barrow-clough and Chalky would never drop you in the clartes but they could hardly deny you said them if they was asked direct, could they?'

There was a brief pause. Mackay's neck jerked again, less gleefully this time.

'I don't know what you're talking about, Fletcher.'

'Oh, we heard very clear, sir. You said that Mr Treadaway was an old—'

'That's enough, Fletcher.'

'That's what I've been trying to tell you, sir. It's enough. We is all back in our appointed places and going about our appointed duties. Why don't we call it a day, Mr Mackay?'

There was another long look, more like a glare. Then the thwarted screw turned on his heels, and began to stride out of the cell. I knew we'd have no more trouble from him about this particular matter. With an audible chuckle, I called after him:

'Or, if you prefer, a day trip, sir?'

He swung round but he knew when he was beaten. He shook his head grimly, turned again and departed.

A few minutes later the cell door was slammed fast and locked. We was once again caged beasts. Another few minutes later and the lights went out. Time for the animals to rest. But in spite of everything I didn't feel too low.

'Made a break, Fletch,' said Len, from below me.

I chuckled.

'Did and all. Even if it wasn't our own.'

'I suppose Oaksey'll be in the Azores or somewhere by now.'

'Just don't envy him, my son.'

'Hard not to. Sun and sea, wine and women – he's clear.'

'No he's not. Worse off than what we is.'

'How d'you mean, Fletch?'

'Obvious, isn't it? At least our sentence is getting shorter. His is getting longer.'

'They may never catch him.'

'They almost always does, in the end. And even if they doesn't, it'll be hanging over him. Long as he lives. Better to do your porridge and get it over.'

'But you always does yours and then comes back for more, Fletch.'

I sighed deeply.

'I've always been a mug. But no more.'

'What'll you do?'

'Dunno. Work, I suppose, whatever that is.'

'Is that all?'

'Is there any other alternative?'

'Yes, there bleeding is!' snapped Lennie and I was taken aback by the fierceness in his voice.

'Don't tell me I've offended you in some way, Godber?'

'You always manages it.'

216

'How?'

'Didn't I tell you? In the coach? I'm going to take care of you.'

'Oh, I have to admit I'd forgot that. Head waiter is it, in your flaming French chip shop?'

'I meant it, Fletch.'

'I'm sure you did, Len. But do you know what it takes to start any kind of business? It takes capital which is just a fancy word for money and the only way the likes of us has of acquiring it is – what we has both of us sworn off.'

'Not the only way, Fletch. Can work for it.'

'I'm getting on a bit, Len. By the time you opens your fancy goo shop, I won't have the strength to lift a champagne bucket.'

'Not true. I've done some calculations. If I get a well paying job – storeman, say, or driving a lorry – could save enough for a modest start in a couple of years. You could help too.'

'Help you start a business?'

'*Our* business, Fletch. Family concern, like.'

'It seems you is forgetting something, Godber.'

'What?'

'We ain't a family. You is merely some young villain they bunged in a cell with me.'

There was a long silence. Finally, I could stand it no longer.

'Godber?'

'What?'

'Ain't you got nothing to say?'

'Nothing more to say, is there? Thought we was more than that.'

'Why?'

'Dunno.'

'Oh well, if you dunno, then—'

But here Lennie burst into one of his emotional torrents of words.

'All right, I *do* know! It's because you helped me through it, that's why. You do yourself down, Fletch. Maybe to some you just seem like an old lag but to me you've been a lot more than that. I never met anyone else – in the nick or out of it – I respect more. I know we ain't family – not blood family – but you mean a heck of a lot more to me than any of my real family ever done. But I suppose you've been through it all before. You're the only cellie I've ever had and the only one I ever intend to have. But you must have shared a dell with a lot of others. Obviously, they didn't mean nothing to you when you got out. So why should I expect it would be any different with me? Goodnight, Fletch.'

I didn't say anything for a while. I looked about the bare cell. No way to live. And it's the way I'd lived for half my life. I said:

'Len?'

'What?'

'Wrote to Ingrid this morning.'

'Did you?' he asked coldly.

'Long chatty letter about things in general. Sent her your love.'

'Did you?' he asked and now there was a little tremor in his voice. 'Straight up?'

'Straight up. And, Len, could be something in what you say. We pool our miserable earnings, plus whatever pittance Grouty's going to bung us, and work for a couple of years, might be possible?'

'The French restaurant?'

'Why not? I has to confess I've been very impressed by the way you has been studying cookery, all those recipes you've been learning and the lives of the great frog chefs and all. You certainly looks the part, even here in the kitchens of the nick, with your white hat. Might make a go of it.'

'I could do it, Fletch. I know I could.'

'Here,' I said, reaching over the edge of my bunk and handing something down to him.

'What is it?'

'Kept two for us – last of Grouty's chocolate liqueurs.'

'Beats Horlicks,' said Len gratefully, taking the sweet from me.

'So that's what we aims at is it – a high-class French restaurant for the top people?'

'That's it, Fletch.'

'On one condition.'

'What's that?'

'I do the cooking.'

Leslie Thomas
Bare Nell 90p

Little Nell Luscombe, paddling naked in her native Devon streams, was the delight of the local GIs. She grew up into BARE NELL, learning that there was a good living to be made from her substantial charms. From servicing the Weymouth fishermen, she progressed to the pinnacle of her profession . . . running a high class establishment — within earshot of the division bells at Westminster . . .

'A most disarming heroine, guileless and open-hearted, innocent and lascivious . . . it is all good fun. And Nelly's a love!'
DAILY TELEGRAPH

Victor Canning
The Doomsday Carrier 70p

'Charlie is loose — an amiable, omnivorous chimpanzee as innocent as the English summer countryside into which he has escaped. The trouble is that Charlie hasn't slipped out of some zoo or wildlife park, but from a top secret biological warfare research station . . . in 21 days he will become a devastating biological weapon, as the plague bacillus within him becomes active . . .
OXFORD MAIL

Shel Talmy
'Whadda we do now, Butch?' 70p

London in the 1900s. Hansom cabs on Sloane Street and every gentleman with his club in St James. If you thought that the legendary pair with the improbable names were filled with lead in darkest Bolivia, RIP, then you will be fascinated to learn how they stayed very much alive as the house-guests of Lord Reggie Ratlett in Mayfair . . . and very much afloat in the very-secret service of HMG . . .

Leslie Thomas
Dangerous Davies, The Last Detective 80p

When Dangerous gets a murder case, it's a twenty-five-year-old sex crime. His witnesses range from a veteran of the Zulu wars to a mad policeman who thinks he's Peter the Great . . . and the mightily endowed Ena Lind, catsuit-wearer and crème-de-menthe drinker.
Exhibit A is the pair of pale green knickers that the victim wasn't wearing
'Cheerfully vulgar . . . sharply observed' THE TIMES

Come to the War 70p

Christopher Hollings, a young British concert pianist and pop image idol, is caught up amid the blankets and bullets of the not-so-virgin soldiers of Israel during the Six Day War, and fixes his attention less on the battledress than on the bosom straining against it.

Orange Wednesday 70p

The interior-sprung mattress took the excitement out of sex for Prudence. Prudence took the excitement out of Lieutenant Brunel Hopkins. Then she told him of Orange Wednesday.

Tropic of Ruislip 90p

'A romp among the adulteries, daydreams and nasty woodsheds of an executive housing estate . . . there are Peeping Toms, clandestine couplings, miscegenation on the wrong side of the tracks, the spilling of gin and home truths on the G-plan furniture, and the steady susurrus of doffed knickers' GUARDIAN

George MacDonald Fraser
Flashman 80p

This fascinating first instalment of the Flashman Papers solves the mystery of what happened to Harry Flashman — that cad and bully from *Tom Brown's Schooldays* — after he was expelled from Rugby.

Self-confessed rotter, liar, womanizer and coward, he relates to us his early career in Lord Cardigan's exclusive 11th Light Dragoons, his scandalous conduct in bed and battle and how he quite undeservedly became a hero of the British Empire.

Royal Flash 80p

The second part of the now celebrated Flashman Papers — that saga of triumphant dishonour — reveals how Sir Harry Flashman VC, the arch-cad and lecher, confuses the Schleswig-Holstein question. Lured to Germany by an unscrupulous adventuress, Flash Harry is soon involved in a desperate succession of escapes, disguises and amours. His talents for dirty fighting and fast running have never been at tauter stretch.

Flash for Freedom 70p

The third outrageous instalment of the immortal Flashman Papers, 1848–9, plunges our hero, all unwillingly, into the West African slave trade. Soon he is fleeing from Dahomey Amazons, outwitting the American Navy, helping the abolitionists up the Mississippi and being rescued from slave catchers by Abraham Lincoln . . .

Both the fighting and the wenching are fast and furious as Flashy goes from bed to bed and from fix to tighter fix — saved only by the skin of his chattering teeth.

Tom Sharpe
Blott on the Landscape 80p

'Skulduggery at stately homes, dirty work at the planning inquiry, and the villains falling satisfactorily up to their ears in the minestrone . . . the heroine breakfasts on broken bottles, wears barbed wire next to her skin and stops at nothing to protect her ancestral seat from a motorway construction' THE TIMES
'Deliciously English comedy' GUARDIAN

Porterhouse Blue 70p

To Porterhouse College, Cambridge, famous for rowing, low academic standards and a proud cuisine, comes a new Master, an ex-grammar school boy, demanding Firsts, women students, a self-service canteen and a slot-machine for contraceptives, to challenge the established order — with catastrophic results . . .
'That rarest and most joyous of products — a highly intelligent funny book' SUNDAY TIMES

Riotous Assembly 70p

A crime of passion committed with a multi-barrelled elephant gun . . . A drunken bishop attacked by a pack of Alsatians in a swimming pool . . . Transvestite variations in a distinguished lady's rubber-furnished bedroom . . . Famous battles re-enacted by five hundred schizophrenic Zulus and an equal number of (equally mad) whites . . .

Tom Sharpe
The Great Pursuit 80p

The hilarious new bestseller from the author of *Wilt*.

'Frensic . . . a snuff taking, port-drinking literary agent . . .
receives a manuscript from an anonymous author's solicitor
– "an odyssey of lust . . . a filthy story with an even filthier style."
Foreseeing huge profits in the US, Frensic places the book with
'the Al Capone of American Publishing, Hutchmeyer, "the most
illiterate publisher in the world" . . .' LISTENER

'The funniest novelist writing today' THE TIMES

Wilt 80p

'Henry Wilt works humbly at his Polytechnic dinning Eng. Lit.
into the unreceptive skulls of rude mechanicals, his nights in
fantasies of murdering his gargantuan, feather-brained wife,
half-consummated when he dumps a life-sized inflatable doll
in a building site hole, and is grilled by the police, his wife being
missing, stranded on a mud bank with a gruesome American
dyke' GUARDIAN

'Superb farce' TRIBUNE

Blott on the Landscape 80p

'Skulduggery at stately homes, dirty work at the planning
inquiry, and the villains falling satisfactorily up to their ears in
the minestrone . . . the heroine breakfasts on broken bottles,
wears barbed wire next to her skin and stops at nothing to protect
her ancestral seat from a motorway construction' THE TIMES

'Deliciously English comedy' GUARDIAN

George MacDonald Fraser
Flashman in the Great Game 90p

The most decorated coward in Her Majesty's service – ever
ready to cock an elegant leg over Princess or get-away horse as
opportunity or self-preservation dictates – plumbs new depths of
knavery in the Indian Mutiny . . . In and out of disguise, in and out
of beds and battles, Flashy remains a fellow of infinite cunning
and resource.

Flash for Freedom 75p

The third outrageous instalment of the immortal Flashman Papers,
1848–9, plunges our hero, all unwillingly, into the West African
slave trade. Soon he is fleeing from Dahomey Amazons, outwitting
the American Navy, helping abolitionists up the Mississippi
and being rescued from slave catchers by Abraham Lincoln . . .
Both the fighting and the wenching are fast and furious as
Flashy goes from bed to bed and from fix to tighter fix . . .

Flashman's Lady 90p

'The sixth adventure of the inimitable Victorian cad lands him
up the creek with Borneo headhunters and sweating with
terror in the arms of a black female Caligula, as he rogers, blusters
and cowers his way to fresh laurels' OBSERVER

You can buy these and other Pan Books from booksellers and
newsagents; or direct from the following address:
Pan Books, Sales Office, Cavaye Place, London SW10 9PG
Send purchase price plus 20p for the first book and 10p for
each additional book; to allow for postage and packing
Prices quoted are applicable in the UK

While every effort is made to keep prices low, it is sometimes
necessary to increase prices at short notice. Pan Books reserve
the right to show on covers and charge new retail prices which
may differ from those advertised in the text or elsewhere